Pride Publishing books by Evelyn Mahony

Single Books
The Billionaire and the Escort

THE BILLIONAIRE AND THE ESCORT

EVELYN MAHONY

The Billionaire and the Escort
ISBN # 978-1-83943-723-6
©Copyright Evelyn Mahony 2021
Cover Art by Erin Dameron-Hill ©Copyright August 2021
Interior text design by Claire Siemaszkiewicz
Pride Publishing

Published in 2021 by Pride Publishing, United Kingdom.

Pride Publishing is an imprint of Totally Entwined Group Limited.

THE BILLIONAIRE AND THE ESCORT

Dedication

To my husband, thank you for your unwavering
support.
To Glory, I don't know where I'd be without you.

Chapter One

The bar wasn't too busy for a Friday night. Soulful jazz filled the air of the midtown Manhattan hot spot that attracted wealthy businessmen and young, single, gold-digging women. Not many people came here unless they were looking to settle a big business deal or celebrate one — or, of course, if they were looking for one of those drunk, happy, successful men to take them home.

Which was why Josh Roberts was here tonight. He didn't necessarily belong there. He wasn't on Wall Street, wasn't a millionaire, wasn't a CEO or even someone who worked for a CEO. No, he was a college graduate with an art degree…and a booming business as an escort.

He hadn't always been an escort. It was a fairly new profession he'd taken up by accident. It was a strange story to tell someone he didn't know, and honestly, the industry was so hush hush that not many asked. But he didn't mind getting paid for taking people out and sleeping with them. It had been odd at first, but it paid the bills—and beyond—and he was good at it now. He had a pretty full calendar, already booked a month out with regulars who took very good care of him financially. At twenty-four years old, he was well on his way to paying off his school loans and saving for the art gallery he hoped to open one day. And he was able to help pay his mother's mortgage on the Brooklyn townhouse he'd grown up in. That alone made it worth it.

His mother didn't know what he did—of course she didn't. She couldn't. He wouldn't allow her to refuse his money. He didn't live at home anymore, but she was his only family. He couldn't risk losing or disappointing her. She was beyond supportive and would give him the benefit of any doubt...unless she knew he was being paid for sex. She wouldn't be able to understand that. And honestly...sometimes he wasn't sure he did. But it was satisfying his bank account, keeping food on the table, a roof over his head and more—so he kept it up. His art couldn't pay him the way this could.

As he leaned against the end of the long mahogany bar, he surveyed the men in attendance, sipping his Old Fashioned. He wasn't too much of a drinker and he needed to keep his wits about him when he was working—especially in a place like this. Class meant everything.

There weren't many options this particular evening. Josh had a way of seeking out the ones who might be susceptible to his services. He worked with a lot of referrals, but tonight he'd been open and available, so he'd decided to head out and offer his services to someone in need of a good time. So far, that hadn't been playing out too well for him. Most of the men were older, wearing rings or a little too drunk for Josh's liking.

His gaze settled on a handsome guy in the middle of the bar who was sitting with a pretty blonde woman to his right. When Josh had first watched them, the man had been engaged as the woman had approached. He'd offered her a smile and invited her to join him.

That had been about an hour ago, however, and now the man looked somewhat tortured. He'd downed three Scotches in that time frame and was asking the bartender for another. A man in a suit stood a few feet behind him, but Josh suspected he was security of some sort, as that man had an earpiece and hadn't had a drink all night. It made Josh curious as he watched, wondering who the guy was and why he'd need security in a bar like this. And if the man standing behind him *was* security, how come he wasn't saving him from the ditz currently droning on and on about some nail polish line?

Josh finished his drink and was about to pay his tab and try his luck elsewhere when the blonde excused herself. He couldn't hear if she would be gone for a minute or for the night, but he watched the guy's shoulders sag slightly in what looked like relief as soon as she was a few feet away. Josh had a moment to make up his mind. Give it a shot or head out...?

The man was beautiful, about six feet tall with thick, dark hair that matched his beard. Even in the dim light, Josh could tell his temples were graying. It was a good look on the guy...fitting. Josh could see laugh lines around his eyes, no ring, a royal blue suit with a white shirt underneath and no tie. He was well dressed but not stuffy.

Josh glanced down at his own chocolate-brown three-piece suit. Being so young, he had to overcompensate to fit in. But for the man across the bar, the unbuttoned collar of his white shirt and the playful mid-range blue of his suit gave off the opposite feel, and it worked well for him. *Is he into men?* Josh couldn't tell from where he stood. But he was visibly bored of his female companion, so Josh took a chance and headed his way.

"That looked brutal," he remarked as he stood a barstool's distance away from the man. The guy peered up at Josh with a raised eyebrow, taking Josh by surprise.

"Was I fakin' it poorly?" The attractive man — even more attractive up close than he had been from across the bar — winced with a half-smile. Josh glanced up at the woman over his head, watching her gait slow as she returned from the direction of the restroom and saw Josh standing in her place.

"Well, she's coming back, if that helps you feel any better about your acting skills." His new companion cursed under his breath and took a long swig from the rocks' glass.

"Maybe she'll think we're talkin' business and find someone else to talk to?" He looked up at Josh, questioning, and he raked his gaze subtly over Josh's suit. He wasn't sizing Josh up. He was actually *looking* him over. Josh felt a little proud as he pretended not to notice. "Need a drink?"

"Sure." Josh took the invitation coolly to avoid seeming eager and settled into the seat the woman had occupied before him. Her expression was clearly one of annoyance, but he watched her turn to find another rich man to fawn over. *Phew.* "Old Fashioned. Rocks. Thanks."

The man nodded and quickly grabbed the bartender's attention. Drink ordered, he turned back to Josh, seemingly still curious. "Nice suit."

"Thank you." Josh couldn't stop the flush that heated his cheeks. Compliments always did him in, especially when the man was looking at him with those haunting steel eyes in a way that Josh hardly ever noticed his own clients looking at him.

"I appreciate you saving me," he began, settling his gaze on Josh's face. Josh held his look with the smallest of smiles. "Not many men would do that. They'd probably just enjoy watching me be miserable." He huffed a laugh, and raised one side of his lips in a true half smile. "It's not that she was a terrible gal or anything. She just…isn't my type." The way he said it gave Josh everything he needed to know to push on with his own agenda.

"I couldn't bear to watch you sit through another monologue about wearing blue nail polish in the fall." Josh mimicked her slightly, and he was pleased when the attractive man chuckled. He sipped his beverage, thoughtful. "Don't like small blondes?" Josh then asked, licking his lips and savoring the taste of his new drink. He said it a little teasingly but was surprised when the guy just looked toward him and eyed him up and down slowly.

"I think I prefer them…bigger." He didn't sound so sure as he responded, and Josh had to wonder what that meant. Josh was, of course, blond, but he couldn't be referring to him… Could he?

"You think?" Josh pressed, tilting his head as he regarded the man.

"Well, they're usually her size, but I'm thinking of trying something new these days..."

Oh. Well, that was an interesting development. Josh hadn't expected this to go so well.

The guy toyed with his rocks' glass, spinning it in his fingers before turning completely to look at Josh, his body now sideways. Josh leaned against the bar, facing the man the same way. "Josh Roberts." He extended his hand with a slight smile, roaming his eyes around the man's gorgeous face.

The guy took Josh's hand in a firm shake with zero hesitation. "James Barnwell... A pleasure to meet you, Josh." He gave Josh a half smile of his own, and Josh couldn't get past how beautiful the man was — one of his more handsome endeavors, for sure.

"So you're looking to try something new?" Josh decided not to beat around the bush now. He'd go right in for the kill. James nodded with a lick to his sinful bottom lip. Josh wouldn't mind kissing it. He *definitely* wouldn't mind.

"I've uh... I don't have any experience, but it's been on my mind for a while." James seemed slightly nervous now, but Josh wanted to reassure him there was no need. He gave Josh a look that was almost adorably unsure. Josh couldn't help his own confident grin.

"Well, as it happens, I'm very well versed in such activities." He nibbled on his bottom lip, tilting his chin down and looking up at Barnwell through his lashes. He wanted this sale, wanted to show this man a good time — especially now, knowing he'd never been with another man before. It became a challenge that spoke to Josh's competitive soul.

James' eyes widened a fraction and he seemed to consider the statement. Then he laughed, throwing Josh off a little. "You must think I'm some fuckin'... I've gotta be at least ten years older than you, and I've never experimented like that. I mean I have...with my — you know — but I've never actually *been* with a man. You've gotta be getting a kick out of this."

Josh didn't know which part he should be getting a kick out of — the fact he'd never been with a man, the age difference or the fact that James was insinuating that he'd played with himself. Josh was eating it all up, if he were to be honest. He'd never taken a man's virginity, but he was up for the adventure and knew he was a safe bet as the man's first. He knew just how to do it right and gentle, make it worth James' time. "Well, if you think I'm judging you, you're wrong. I'm in the wrong business to judge anyone." Josh kept his voice low so he didn't make a spectacle of their conversation. "It doesn't matter how old you are or what you've done or not done. If you want an experience, you wanna try a taste, I can give you one. I'm happy to do it."

Josh wasn't one to play games. He was straightforward and as honest as they came. He pulled one of his sleek matte cards from his pocket and slipped it across the bar to James, who picked it up and looked it over, a look of surprise and a flush covering his high cheekbones as he seemed to read the word printed under Josh's name on the card — *Escort*.

James cleared his throat, biting his bottom lip as he set the card back down. Josh noticed that he kept it close and he took that as a good sign. "And here I thought you were just picking me up." James laughed a little and Josh liked the sound.

"In a way I was. You're a handsome man. I couldn't tell from afar whether you'd be interested in men or not, but I took my chance anyway." Josh offered him a gentle grin.

"Do I look like I need to pay someone for sex?" James cocked his head to the side and regarded Josh through squinted, guarded eyes. He might have even been slightly offended. Josh held his ground, undeterred.

"You look like you wanna sleep with a man—but you haven't yet and don't know how. I'm sure you have women dying to sit on your cock. But that's not what I'm here for."

"And if I wanna sit on *your* cock, is *that* what you're here for?" Hearing the word fall from James' lips made Josh want to squirm a little. He *definitely* wanted that. It was always a bonus when he was physically attracted to his clients and that they had chemistry. It was often not the case.

"You can sit on anything you want, Mr. Barnwell. That is, in fact, what I'm here for."

James grew silent at that, dropping his gaze to his glass. Apprehension bloomed in Josh's chest, but he sipped his drink and watched the man mentally battle over whatever waged inside his mind. He took the moment to let his eyes roam the broad shoulders, the peek of chest hair, the gray on his temples. This man had to look exquisite naked, judging by the way that suit jacket pulled in all the right places.

James lifted his gaze back to Josh's, and Josh could feel the heat and question that lingered in those blue-grays. "I'm not familiar with…your business. What's it you want? How much do you get paid? Do you do weekends in exchange for money, gifts?"

Josh couldn't help but chuckle…amused. "I mean, I don't have an ad saying 'sugar daddy wanted' on my back, but if you're offering…" Confusion then amusement dawned on James' features. "Money is how I'm usually paid. I can be booked for any length of time. I can be a date to an event, a party or a companion on a trip. It's really whatever the client wants. *Whatever* they want." He stressed the word because he catered to any and all whims. He had a few hard limits but had experienced a *lot*. And at this point, he'd say yes to anything with James out of pure curiosity.

"Whatever they want? Give me an example, please." He spoke quietly as he asked, as if unsure if he should. Josh was an open book. He never gave names, but he'd absolutely give examples.

"Sure. Most women want to be dominated in some way, but most men want to dominate me. I've gone to Hawaii on a business trip with a woman who only needed me to pretend I was her fiancé. I've been collared and expected to crawl on my knees like a dog. I had a woman who would pay me for one weekend a month of as much sex as she could handle. I have another woman who just wants me to sit in my briefs and rub her feet. I've had a few men who prefer roleplay, and I'm decent at it." He shrugged lightly. "The 'usual' is I show up to the client's place and we have sex, I fulfill whatever their fantasy or need is and I'm out of the door afterward. But like I said, it's the dealer's choice. Whatever the client feels like, needs or *wants* from me, I give. I haven't had a single complaint." Josh felt more than confident in his track record and his services. Sure, when he'd started, he'd had some catching up to do, had to learn his ways around certain kinks and scenes, but now he had zero issues. He felt at ease behind closed doors.

James was intrigued, if nothing else. It was written all over his suddenly expressive face. "So...kinks? Toys? Trips? Everything is on the table?"

Josh nodded. "I draw the line at violence, degrading play and extreme, potentially harmful things. Marks are fine, spanking is fine, but you can't hit me — and I won't hit you. You can call me names, but you can't shove my face in a carpet or make me lick your shoes. Luckily, no one I've been with has tried to punch me or worse." Josh smiled ruefully. James looked a little disturbed by that.

"Well, at least you're taking care of yourself," he replied with a concern that surprised Josh.

"I get tested monthly. I'm careful. It's my job to deliver a safe and fun experience." He wanted to make sure James knew all the details and his intentions. This business relationship had to be based on trust.

"What do you cost? Is it by the service or...?"

Josh pulled out his phone, opening the app he used to take payment. He set it down on the bar for James to see. He had no secrets. "I don't do it by the service. I do by the hour. You can have whatever you want in the time frame you pay me for — and there's fifty percent off your first experience, no matter the length. If a person comes back, which I can usually guarantee they will, it's full price after that."

James whistled low at what he saw on the screen. "You certainly are looking for that sugar daddy, aren't ya, pal?"

Josh blushed at the term but laughed too. "I think it's a fair trade. Good money for great sex." He shrugged. James eyed him.

"You think you're that good, huh?"

Josh simply smiled, nodding once. "Yes, sir. I'm *that* good."

James glanced back at the security guard a few feet away then to the bartender. Josh, for a brief moment, wondered if he was about to be physically removed from James Barnwell's presence. Then James was laying down crisp cash from his wallet on the bar and standing.

Josh followed his every move, his hopes deflating. He'd really enjoyed their banter. It had been a long time since he'd been shot down—and by someone like Mr. Barnwell...

"I've got a car out front. We'll go back to my place. That's how it works, right? My call? My place?" Josh stood before James could finish his questions.

"Absolutely, sir. Your call. Everything is your call."

"Good. We'll go back to my place, I'll pour us a drink then I want you to take over. Understood?"

Josh was surprised by the expectation, but it was nothing he couldn't handle. In fact, he looked forward to blowing this man's mind...and hopefully more. "Yes, sir."

* * * *

When James said he had a car, he wasn't kidding. It was a Mercedes town car—luxury, with a driver. Heated seats were welcome as autumn started to settle into New York. Josh made himself comfortable and reminded himself of all the things they still needed to go over.

He pulled out his phone again, opening a document he used for new clients. "While we drive, maybe it's a good time for you to fill this out. As I mentioned before, this is my business and I run it like one. I don't get too personal besides name and phone number, but there's a list of options and services I offer—kinks, whatever you might be into. If you wouldn't mind filling it out..." He handed his phone to James, watching the man eye the device with slight disdain.

"I'd rather talk it out over a drink," he suggested, handing the phone back. Josh hadn't been prepared for that.

"I…at least need a contact number," he tried, preparing himself to type it in. James didn't seem all that willing to give up such a personal detail already. "I promise it's confidential. Would you like to see my terms and conditions?" He offered the phone back, ready to produce anything the man needed to make him comfortable.

"If I'm satisfied when you leave, you'll get my number. I have yours from your card. And I promise I'm good for the money."

Josh pulled his phone back and clicked it off. *Well then…* "What do you do for work, Mr. Barnwell?" Josh asked cautiously, wondering if the man would tell him anything. James shifted, staring out of the car window. Josh registered his body language. He was very tense.

"I design luxury resorts," James began, his tone turning up affectionately. Josh tilted his head with interest. "I have a line of resorts. Each one is put together and laid out by me. I love it. It allows me to mingle my affinity for architecture with my love of design and art." He looked quickly at Josh with a smile.

Josh was surprised. Now *that* was a job. "Oh, wow. That sounds like the kind of job that makes you want to go to work every day." Josh almost opened his mouth to mention his art, but he was careful to never talk too much about himself. Clients didn't pay him for that.

James' smile was sincere now and he looked slightly less rigid. "It is."

Josh settled back into his seat with a flirtatious smile returning. "I had a hunch you had a *very* successful job."

James turned a little toward Josh with a look of confidence and what Josh would describe as arrogance. "I own luxury resorts from here to Bora Bora and back," he told Josh. "I've worked *very* hard to be this successful."

"Sounds like Mr. Millionaire to me," Josh bantered back. James just smirked.

"Think a little higher…"

Billionaire. Fuck. This was Josh's biggest client yet.

Before Josh could ask any further questions, the car turned and rolled up to a row of well-lit brownstones. They looked homey and inviting against the trees that lined the wide sidewalk. Josh recognized where they were. He'd driven down this street but had never been inside one of the townhomes. For all the money he was making, this was far out of his range. He was sure these were million-dollar residences.

The car parked against the curb and the driver came around to open the door for them. They slid out and James thanked the man — the security guard from earlier — explaining quietly that he'd be fine alone with Josh. Josh rocked on his heels and assessed his surroundings. He had some high-end clients, but this? This was another level entirely.

"This way," James called to him as he headed toward the front door. Josh's long strides caught him up quickly, and he marveled as he stepped down from street level to the front door and entered the foyer of the brownstone. It was wide open, with wood floors and beautiful art along the walls. It smelled of vanilla and sandalwood, and Josh took a deep breath. This was a *home*—nothing like the small three-bedroom apartment he shared with two of his friends. That apartment seemed to fit in one room of this place.

James guided him silently through to the kitchen then to the wet bar. "Same drink?" James asked as he extended his arms for Josh's suit coat. He slid it off and handed it to James with a gracious thanks. *So, the man has entertaining skills.*

"Yes, please," Josh replied, slipping his hands into his pockets. He looked around the kitchen, which was pristine and clean, and wondered silently what it would be like to live like this. "Beautiful home."

"Thank you." James looked over his shoulder at him with a genuine smile. "Bought it a few years ago. Did some upgrades. This is my main home," he explained as he handed Josh his drink and held one for himself. He kept his own coat on as he guided them through the vast first floor to the stairs, right to the bedroom. Josh was once again surprised. James wasn't wasting any time.

The hall was dark, and they passed several closed doors before they reached the bedroom at the end. It was lit by the moon through open curtains, and Josh could tell that the room was impeccably styled and looked as though it could be featured in a magazine spread.

Jams flipped on a lamp and drew Josh's attention to him. Josh sipped the fresh drink, savoring in the burn at the back of his throat as he mentally prepared himself for what was to come. "You mentioned you wanted me to take over? What exactly did you have in mind?" Josh asked, slipping into the confident demeanor of a professional, someone who was experienced.

James took a long drink and seemed to ponder what he'd meant. "I, uh...want you to take over. You're in charge."

Josh blinked then narrowed his eyes slightly in question. "Okay. Usually it's the other way around. You're sure?"

James rolled his eyes, but Josh could see the heat in his cheeks. "I haven't done this before. Aren't you supposed to seduce me? Walk me through this?"

Josh couldn't help but laugh a little. "If that's what you want, I'm happy to do it. I can seduce you. Let's be clear on a few things first, though." Josh set his drink on the table by the door and walked slowly toward James. "You want to do it *all* tonight? Or do you just want a taste? You want me to tell you what to do, correct? And you've never been touched by a man, but you've played with yourself?" Josh tilted his head down, looking up at James in an unmistakably seductive gaze. James swallowed and his Adam's apple bobbed with hesitation.

He cleared his throat, not moving as Josh stepped closer. "Yes to all of the above. I want everything. I've...touched myself, used toys. I've never been with another man, ever, but I've...wanted to for a while." His voice grew softer with every step Josh took until they were inches apart. James' breath hitched audibly. Josh smiled.

"I like the sound of all this," Josh replied, his voice husky. He was attracted to the man, there no denying that. His cock was already rousing in his dress pants. This wouldn't be hard, other than the important need to go slow. He honestly wanted to show James just what this could be like in every way. But he had to take his time. Rushing James would do no good.

Josh ran a hand along James' graying temple then down over the man's shoulder. James shuddered ever so slightly. Josh kept his grin in check. "Why don't you take a minute to get yourself into something more comfortable. I'm going to set up your room." He glanced around, deciding on mood lighting and where he'd lay his items for use. "How's that sound?"

James merely nodded, but Josh could tell he was sold. Normally he'd ask for payment up front, but in this case, it seemed like he needed to show he was worth it first. He was confident that wouldn't be a problem.

James shut the door that led to his large master bath and walk-in closet, taking a slow, deep breath. He took a few steps, caught sight of himself in the mirror over the sinks and stopped short. What was he even *doing*? He'd taken a male escort, a *male* escort, home to fuck him. *Am I out of my mind?*

Clearly not enough to send the guy home.

James slipped off his suit coat but left his slacks and simple white T-shirt on. Honestly, he wasn't sure changing was going to make him more comfortable. He really needed this Josh guy to be a professional. Because if he wasn't, this was going to end in disaster.

James let his thoughts trail to the man currently moving around his bedroom. Josh was tall, maybe an inch or two taller than he was. He was handsome — and *young*. Too young for a guy like him. Though, if this were a young woman of the same age, he probably wouldn't have thought twice. Somehow he was allowing Josh's sex to make this difficult for him. He shook his head as he washed his hands and splashed water over his flushed face. *Stop it, Barnwell. You're overthinking. You've wanted this for a long time.*

A long time, indeed. He'd been fantasizing about being with a man for as long as he could remember, but he'd never been able to make the move. No one knew how he felt, what he wanted. He'd always had a different woman on his arm every month.

One relationship had lasted longer than the rest. Connie was the manager of his biggest resort in Jamaica. They'd met after she had been hired for the position and had been set to open the resort. The months of planning had also been spent in bed with her. She was sweet and young but fiery. She was the only woman to pull him away from his playboy ways for a little over a year. It'd ended shortly after the resort had opened and James had set off back to New York to work on his next project. It had been amicable, and they remained very close friends. It was far better that way. They'd fought as well as they'd fucked.

But men...? He'd never allowed himself to taste, to dabble, for fear of attachments, his career and worse. But *this*, paying someone... Maybe this was the way to keep it confidential and attachment-free, as well as allow him to get exactly what he needed. Money wasn't an issue. Sure, he'd been surprised by the hefty price tag on the pretty man, but if he fucked half as good as he looked, James was pretty sure it would be worth every penny.

He'd showered before going out and he was always clean—one of the perks of playing with oneself often.

So, with one final deep breath, he headed for the door. *I can do this.*

Josh had turned on two lamps, a tall one in the far corner and one beside the bed. James could see a few foil packets and slender tubes in the light from the bedside table. Josh had slipped out of his vest, his white shirt unbuttoned to reveal his bare chest. James had to swallow hard. He was as defined as James had hoped he'd be. His skin pulled across his pectoral muscles and stretched perfectly over his rippled abs. That hard-to-attain V-cut was exposed as the slacks hung low on his slim hips. The man was broad at the top but tapered at the middle. It was hard to believe he was actually real. James' cock was swelling with anticipation already. The desire to touch that skin pulled at him.

Josh grinned as he obviously waited for James to acknowledge him other than the blatant staring. "Like what you see, Mr. Barnwell?" He was clearly amused as he faced him fully. James flushed hard.

"It's James." His thick voice cracked, and he cleared it abruptly. "Call me James, please."

Josh's eyes widened just slightly but he nodded. "James it is. Come 'ere, handsome."

Josh wasn't wasting any time, James quickly realized. He was honestly thankful for it. He gravitated to Josh on command, standing before him.

"Just relax," Josh soothed in a low tone. He ran a hand up James' right arm, dancing his fingers across the skin. "Let's set some lines first. Saying 'red' means stop, in case you don't like what we're doing. I'm guessing you're probably pretty vocal, so I'm sure I'll know when you *like* what we're doing." Josh smirked a little and stepped a couple of inches closer.

"All right," James acknowledged, wondering if Josh could hear his heart pounding out of his chest.

"We're gonna let things flow tonight. Next time we can work on specific things you want. Tonight, I just wanna get to know your body, get to know *you*." Josh let his fingers travel up James' left arm now, the sensation making goosebumps cover James' skin.

"I-I like that plan," he agreed softly. Josh's smile widened.

"Good." He took another step closer until he had one foot in between James' and their bodies were almost touching. "I'm going to kiss you now. But after this, I'm not going to warn you anymore. Just *trust* me," he urged in a whisper, and before James could reply that he wasn't sure he could, Josh pressed their lips together in a tentative kiss.

Josh's lips were soft. That bottom lip was plump and felt like it simply *fit* against James' own. Josh was guiding and slow, no tongue, and only offered gentle and encouraging strokes of his mouth against James'. James followed gladly. He could kiss. He had no problems there. But his brain was short circuiting at the simple fact that he was kissing a beautiful man and it was *scorching*.

And they'd only just begun.

Josh moved his hands to James' hips, and he urged their bodies together with a squeeze. James couldn't stop the groan that slipped out, and it seemed to only encourage Josh further. He let one hand move up into James' thick hair and he tilted their heads, building the kiss into deeper territory. James went with it and finally let his hands settle on Josh's hips, his grip tight and unyielding. *Oh yes.* He didn't want this to end. His heart was racing and his brain going blank as he gave in to the experienced guidance of the man in front of him. Josh sure didn't kiss like a man who was being paid. He kissed with desire, and he reacted to James' every tell. It only made James want more.

Josh was shocked by the way James kissed. He shouldn't have been. He should have known, but something in the way it had felt as soon as their lips had touched had surprised him. James tasted of whiskey and sugar—but also something he was sure was just distinctly James Barnwell. He smelled even better up close, and his hair was so damn soft under Josh's fingers. He lost himself in the kiss, let it take him and, in turn, trusted himself to guide James.

And guide him he did, until they were kissing and panting, their tongues dueling in the most heated of ways. When their bodies were pressed together, Josh could *feel* James' erection and he knew there was no hiding his own—and he didn't want to. This was all part of what he offered—the attraction, the clear evidence that Josh wanted to fuck him. It wasn't always this simple, but tonight it was *very* easy.

Josh pulled at James' T-shirt, yanking it over his head. He marveled at the shape of the man's body as he roamed his bare skin. In the dim light he could tell James took care of himself. Time in the gym had made those abs, his chest. Josh had hit the jackpot.

Dark hair was sprinkled across his broad, chiseled chest. It was nice to be with a man the same height as Josh. There was an even playing field in that. And knowing he was topping James for the first time made it all-the-more satisfying.

James sucked in shallow breaths as Josh touched his bare skin. His fingers were soft and reassuring. He seemed to be taking the time to memorize what he saw, and for a moment, James got lost in it. He had this beautiful man catering to his every desire. He wanted to forget he was paying him, but that wouldn't leave his mind. And that was all right. Maybe it would always be better this way.

Josh slid his hand low to James' belt, and James held still as Josh unfastened it. He caught his blue eyes through those sinful lashes and had to fight the urge to moan. He bit his lip instead, worrying the plump flesh as the clink of the belt filled the room. A button then a zipper and the material of his pants was pooling at his feet. His white cotton boxers did nothing to hide his length, hard and aching beneath the fabric.

"Mm-m." Josh groaned in appreciation, gazing down between them. "I'm pleased to see you're enjoying yourself. I bet you taste fucking brilliant." Josh rasped the words and dropped to his knees before James. James' eyes widened in a hint of panic, but Josh soothed him with a gentle smile. "Shh-h," he started before James could. "Be a good boy and let me suck you. I'm dying to feel you in my mouth."

James' throat went dry, watching the man pull the fabric down his thighs. He stepped out as instructed and let his arms hang as Josh nuzzled his nose to the soft underbelly of James' length. He gasped lightly, his balls tightening and skin aflame as he stared in wonderment.

Josh's moans sounded genuine as he grinned and took the heavy cock in his grasp. He shook and sighed, unable to look away as Josh stroked him. A steadying hand landed on the back of his thigh, encouraging him to stay upright. "There you go," Josh encouraged as he snaked his tongue out to suck the bead of pre-cum off the tip. James shook again, and this time he placed his hands on Josh's shoulders, which were still covered by the white shirt. "Hold on, handsome." Josh glanced up with a smirk as he encouraged him before rolling his tongue around the notched tip.

When James had imagined a man sucking him, he hadn't had anyone to fantasize about. He knew what type of man he liked, but he'd never had a face to dream about. Well, *now* he did.

Josh stretched his mouth beautifully around him as he sucked just the tip at first. He was no stranger to blow jobs and being on the receiving end, but *this* felt like the *first* time. Watching that pink mouth and blond head sink lower onto him, sucking in his sensitive length, was almost too much. He was shuddering and pulling Josh off after two sucks, shaking his head and gasping. "I'm— I'm—"

"Shh-h," Josh comforted, seeming to know just what was happening. Josh held the base of his cock, and the tip turned almost purple and angry. "Take a breath."

The heat rushed into James' cheeks and he nibbled his lip. "It's just that…you…you look so beautiful doing that." It was meek and nervous, but he said his thoughts anyway. Josh blushed and glanced away briefly.

"Thank you," he replied, low and sincerely, moving to stand. He let go of James' cock and slipped off his shirt. "Go lie down, James. Let me show you just how *beautiful* I can make *you*."

It felt like an out-of-body experience, walking to his bed and lying down in the center of it as Josh shed his clothes. He was all lean muscle, toned everywhere in the way men dreamed of. Josh stepped out of his boxer briefs and into the dim light, and James saw the dusting of freckles across his shoulders. That made his heart and stomach clench in ways he wasn't prepared for. This man was the man someone fantasized about being with. James would sure be dreaming about him for nights to come.

His focus slipped farther down to catch his first look at Josh's length as he kneeled on the bed and grabbed the lube off the side table. Josh was long, thick and curved just slightly to the right in a way that made James' body tense. It was going to feel so good inside him — but could he take that size? Nothing he owned was quite that thick and he —

"Stop thinking," Josh commanded, calling the attention back to him. "You're fucking adorable in your panic, but I promise I'll make this good. It's what I *do*." Josh lathered his fingers, slinking between his legs. James was still gaping a little at Josh and his perceptiveness, but he closed his mouth as Josh descended on him like a Greek god. He leaned in to kiss him again and James all but burst off the bed to meet him halfway. Josh groaned into the kiss, biting at James' lip and keeping him occupied while he slipped his hand south.

Josh bypassed his cock and slipped his hand down between his smooth cheeks, unable to hold back his own groans as Josh rubbed the untouched hole firmly. James inhaled sharply and bucked his hips, but Josh was quick to shush him, repeating the touch over and over as he continued to kiss him.

James' gasp broke as he pushed himself back into the sea of pillows. Josh went deeper with every move of his finger and the breath rushed out of James' lungs each and every time. It was entirely different than playing with himself, being at the mercy of this man above him, who was seemingly enthralled in watching James grapple with the feeling of someone else penetrating him for the first time.

"Feel good, handsome?" Josh asked with a lazy grin, pulling his finger away every so often to slowly rub at the hole before pushing back in. James didn't keep himself quiet, and judging by the way the thick cock against his thigh jumped every time he groaned loudly, he made a show of it.

"God, Josh…" James whined, writhing as he started to rock down on the finger. Josh leaned up slightly to watch, apparently interested to see how James' ass looked wrapped around his finger.

"Oh baby," Josh sighed with audible need, licking his lips. "You should see yourself, taking my finger so beautifully. This ass is fucking perfect, baby. So tight and fresh. You want two fingers? You can take them, can't you?"

James hadn't ever had someone talk dirty to him, wouldn't have known he'd like it as much as he did right this second. But if Josh stopped talking like that… He just couldn't. The praise was making him flush bright into his chest, and the way Josh was gazing at him made him feel so exposed and yet so pretty and… "Yes, Yes, more, please," he begged, and the words sounded foreign to his own ears. Josh beamed darkly, obviously pleased.

"That's a good boy. There we go. I knew you'd be needy," Josh murmured as he stretched him with a second finger. James sucked in a ragged breath and stopped moving to adjust as Josh stayed still, kissing along the lines of his chest as he whispered sweet words of encouragement. He didn't want to think about how he treated all his clients like this. Just for a little while, he wanted this to be all for him. "Good job, James. Opening wide for me, gonna take my cock so good."

It was the oddest of feelings, being stretched open. The pain gave way to a heat and a pleasure that James couldn't describe. While he'd toyed with himself, the thrust of Josh's fingers felt like nothing like he'd ever had before. They were wet, sliding in and out with ease, despite the drag, and the more he moved them, the more James accepted them. The pain disappeared in a cloud of pleasure and he was soon hungrily driving himself down on Josh again, sucking his fingers in as deep as they could go. He was shameless in his noises, and every bit of praise Josh lavished on him only made him louder.

"One more finger and you can take my cock." Josh pressed a third past the rim, and James bit out a cry and braced himself, throwing an arm over his face as he breathed through the sudden pain. Josh wasn't having that, though. He clearly needed to see James' face as it eased in pleasure. "Look at me, handsome," Josh commanded, forcing James to glance down at him. James let his arm fall and he took long, deep breaths as he locked eyes with Josh.

The air was charged and electric as they stared at one another. Josh watched James' chest rise and fall, seemingly with intense sensations, and he couldn't help the way his own breathing matched. Knowing someone had never done this to James before was wreaking havoc on his own arousal, and if he didn't get inside James soon, he was going to combust right there, untouched on the sheets. "Good boy." James started to relax and let out a shuddering moan as he rocked tentatively to the thrust of Josh's fingers, three buried deep and spreading him wide. "Your ass is gonna look so pretty on my cock," he murmured as he started to truly fuck James' ass slow and hard with his fingers.

James squirmed and rode them just as he had been, and it wasn't long before he was whining and gripping the sheets like he'd explode any moment. Josh pulled away when he was *sure* James could take his cock, making him moan wantonly at the loss.

"Gonna fuck me now?" James rasped the obvious, his voice haggard and worn from making so much noise. Josh was loving every sound, and this new voice in particular sent chills down his spine.

He slid a condom over himself, lathering his length in a generous amount of lubricant as he grinned up at James through his lashes. "Oh yes, James. I'm gonna fuck you so hard you'll be begging me to fuck you again tomorrow."

James let his legs be spread obscenely wide without complaint. He was heated, slick and hot with arousal as Josh moved between his legs again. Josh pushed one of them up high, then let it come rest in the crook of his elbow. "Go slow?" James asked quietly, anxiety in his voice. Josh took himself in hand but stopped at the request, trailing his fingers over the neglected cock that lay weeping against his stomach.

"Don't worry, Jamie." He rasped the shortened name. "You'll take it inch by inch, slow and steady, until I'm *buried*, and when you're ready, I'll go nice and slow until you're *begging* me to pound this tight ass." Josh spoke the filthy words so sweetly that arousal pooled in his stomach.

James gasped and was visibly trying to relax as Josh pressed into him, and it took a moment and a fair amount of effort until the head finally notched inside him. James cursed and closed his eyes at the intrusion.

Knowing he was the first cock in this perfect ass almost made him come on the spot. He was a professional at holding back and had the stamina to go for hours, but something about watching James grapple with his first penetration was making him want to shoot off far too soon. He breathed deeply and pinched his eyes closed, unable to look at that handsome face any longer until James started to let go.

When he opened his eyes again a moment later, James was watching him with an intrigued, almost-soft expression. They locked gazes as Josh started to move. It was shallow at first, just the tip and a slow thrust and pull, though he never slipped out completely. James groaned deeply as Josh sank lower and farther into his body, the sound lighting him on fire.

James was overwhelmed. He was stretched so far, and the heat from Josh's entire body was intense. It was addictive — every slide and every touch — and soon Josh was kissing him again, rough and sloppy as he started to really *move*, driving his hips into him with practiced precision.

He wasn't quiet, and Josh had told him that he didn't want him to be. There was a banter back and forth, praise slipping from Josh's lips and whines from his own as they worked their way up and up, higher and higher. When he finally felt Josh's balls against his ass, he knew he was bound to be done for soon, his cock untouched and throbbing against his belly.

Josh seemed to read his mind, balancing himself on one arm as he grasped his cock in the other. James cried out and his hips jumped. He squeezed around Josh's cock and it became very evident very quickly that this was all coming to a head.

He hadn't ever felt anything like this. It was like free-falling as the pain and pleasure melted together into something he couldn't describe. It was too much all at once. It was so surreal, and his body felt so punished in the best way that when Josh started to really jerk him off, he thought for a moment that this was how he would die. And he also then became infinitely sure he would *need* this again more than he needed air.

Josh was perfect, his cock hitting deep and hard, and his own groans seemed sincere. He watched himself slide into James occasionally, stared at his face then his cock, and James felt worshiped. Everything was about his own pleasure, and it was an entirely new experience — one he'd be touching himself to for *days*.

"I'm — Oh, God — I'm —" He started to babble, but Josh was right there to guide him, squeezing his cock and fucking him hard now, driving those perfect hips up with a snap as his tip rubbed against James' sweet spot and made him howl.

"Now, James! Now, baby, come for me. Come all over my hand and milk my cock!"

James cried out and did just that, coming with a sharp shake and a cry as he spilled all over Josh's fist. Josh went off like a shot after him, spilling hot and hard into the condom as he pumped him through his release. Josh closed his eyes and groaned low as he rocked until he was empty and spent, dropping James' cock on top of the mess he'd made.

Josh let him relax a moment but stayed buried there as he obviously waited for any sign from him as to what he needed. James shuddered and moaned quietly every so often until he finally opened his eyes, catching Josh's intrigued ones. He flushed hotly, grinning slowly. "That was…deeply satisfying," he complimented in a whisper.

Josh flushed brightly, sliding his eyes down as he grinned. Honestly, words hardly described it.

"That's what I like to hear," he whispered in reply, caching James' lips in a kiss. "Let me get you a towel and clean you up." Josh slid out of James' relaxed body and James whined at the loss.

Josh was careful as he used a warm cloth to soothe and clean James. He filled a glass full of water and gave it to him, making sure he was comfortable as he went about picking up. James lay on the bed with hooded eyes, unable to find the ability to get up after such an experience.

Josh was reaching for his boxer briefs to get dressed when James finally moved on the bed, sitting up.

"You leaving?" he asked abruptly. Josh stopped and shifted so he could see him.

"That's how it usually goes," Josh explained, his tone unsure. "But it's your call. I can do whatever you want—"

"Stay…please." Josh nodded, settling his briefs into place as he padded back to the bed. He switched off lights on the way. "I'll make you coffee in the morning and pay you for your services," James added with a small grin. Josh nodded and slid in next to him, and he opened his arms for Josh. "Thank you."

James didn't know *what* he was doing, but he absolutely couldn't let Josh walk out of that door—not after what he'd just done, what Josh had just made him feel. He needed to hold him, needed to feel that skin-to-skin connection. He soothed his already-churning mind with *You are paying for this, Barnwell* and left it at that. Because he was. This wasn't a date. This was an agreement. A purchase.

Chapter Two

The sun was warm on Josh's face as he sat on the cushioned window seat of his Brooklyn apartment. It was a bright day, but the sun was deceiving. Autumn had arrived and the temperatures outside had dropped into the fifties. Josh didn't mind, though. This particular window wasn't drafty, and the sun was still beaming.

His gaze flickered from the park across the small street to the sketchpad against his thigh, but the image on the paper couldn't be found outside. It could only be found miles from there and on the other side of Josh's phone — that had yet to ring.

But Josh couldn't get James' eyes out of his head, couldn't get the man's face to leave him be. The way he'd looked in the throes of bliss, the way their gazes had held as James had driven him home and the expression he'd had as Josh had opened his eyes after coming harder than he could remember in so, so long. Josh kept drawing James' face, trying to get every damn detail right. He wanted to see him again to compare…and for other reasons.

"You're thinking about him again," his roommate Andrew Wilson said from the kitchen, interrupting his thoughts. Josh turned his way and schooled his features, scoffing as he flipped the page so he wouldn't be caught.

"Nah. Just enjoying the sun."

"Shut up. You're not a cat and you can't lie like one either. You're still thinking about the resort guy." Andrew's smile was all-knowing, and Josh regretted telling him and his other roommate, Nadia Riley, anything. He'd come home with such a high, though, that he couldn't stop himself as he'd divulged his evening to his two closest friends.

Josh had gone home with a lot of people, but no one had been quite like James Barnwell.

The following morning, Josh had woken up alone on his stomach in the very big bed. The room had looked bright and cheery against the morning light and it had taken him a minute to remember where he was. Slipping from the bed, he'd realized it was nine in the morning and James hadn't woken him. He hardly ever stayed the night for this exact reason. *The awkward escape.*

Josh had been able to hear James talking and had chosen to take a minute to splash water on his face and run some through his short hair. He'd swiped some toothpaste along his tongue and slipped back into his slacks and dress shirt, not bothering with the rest.

As he'd reached the bottom of the stairs, he'd followed the voice into the kitchen. James had been in the middle of an important-sounding conversation, but he'd still taken a moment to notice Josh's presence and had poured him a cup of coffee. It had been a Styrofoam travel mug, but Josh had appreciated the gesture.

James had given him the universal 'one minute' motion with his finger before stepping out onto the back patio. As he'd paced, Josh had read the paper that had been sprawled along the counter, mindlessly going through the articles before he realized it wasn't the Times. It was one from Miami. *Huh.*

"Sorry about that, Josh," James had interrupted his reading, and Josh had raised his head to truly take a moment to appreciate James Barnwell in the morning. He'd showered and dressed in jeans and a gray button-down, which was rolled up to the elbows. His hair had been just slightly damp and his beard so perfect in the brightness of the morning that Josh had wanted to look away. It had been like looking into the sun.

"No problem at all. Thank you for the coffee. I'm sorry I slept in. Usually my clients are eager to throw me out." Josh had said the words with a chuckle — but they had been true. "Your bed is very comfortable." Josh wasn't sure when he'd last slept so well.

James' smile had been sincere as he'd picked up his own coffee mug — a matte-black one. *"You looked very comfortable when I got up at seven to hit the gym. I couldn't bear to wake you. It was the least I could do in return after the night you gave me."* James had slid an envelope across the counter. *"I hope cash is okay. I'd prefer to keep this off my statements for now. My assistant would have a field day with it. No offense."*

Josh had blushed a little and laughed, still surprised by James' honesty. "None taken. I understand completely. And cash is totally fine." He'd slid the envelope into the pocket of his jacket and picked his coffee back up. *"So, you enjoyed your night then? Any complaints?"* Josh had pressed, curious. James had shaken his head almost immediately, that damn grin seemingly permanent.

"Not one. You're just as good as you say. I'm impressed, to say the least. And you're professional, which I appreciate."

"Would you like to book another session? I have some dates available..."

"I'm actually headed out of town for a few weeks. But when I get back, I'll definitely call you."

Josh had suddenly been unable to tell if James was being genuine or not. He'd been rounding the counter toward Josh and while Josh had wanted to press, he'd known better. *"No problem,"* he'd repeated. *"You have my card. Call me whenever the mood strikes."* He'd flashed James a grin and blushed when it had been returned.

And that was the last he had heard from James. It had only been three days, but he'd hoped to see James again sooner. He'd also paid him an extra thousand dollars. Josh tried to tell himself that was the reason why he wanted to see him again. He was obviously good for the money.

"Earth to Josh," Andrew called, rattling Josh from his memory. "God, what is with you?"

"Nothin'," Josh quickly defended himself. "I'm just trying to get this tree right." He focused on the large oak tree across the street, beginning to sketch. Andrew looked at him, seeming less than convinced.

"Sure, whatever. Just don't forget it's your night to cook. Nadia will be home by seven. I'm going for a run. He'll call. *Relax."*

Andrew shut the door behind him, leaving Josh alone with his thoughts. *He'll call in a few weeks. It's just good money. That's all.*

* * * *

It was a week later, while Josh was cooking on his night, when the phone rang. Distracted by the boiling water and the chicken in the pan, he probably shouldn't have answered. Nadia and Andrew were going back and forth about painting the small living room, and the television was blaring over their argument. It was a normal night in for the three roommates but definitely made a less-than-professional moment for him to answer such a call.

Not recognizing the number, Josh slid the bar across the screen and put the phone to his ear, stirring the pasta as he answered, "Hello?"

There was a short pause, one that almost made him pull the phone away from his face to see if the person had hung up, when Josh immediately recognized the voice. "Josh? Is this...Josh Roberts?"

Josh dropped the wooden spoon with a clatter and grabbed the television remote off the kitchen island, muting the TV frantically. Nadia and Andrew both turned to look at him like he'd lost his mind, but he was far too distracted to care. "Yes, hi, hello... It is." He was suddenly out of breath for no damn reason and his cheeks were heating up instantly.

"Hi, Josh. It's James Barnwell from a couple Saturdays ago when we—"

"Yeah," Josh interrupted quickly with a chuckle then immediately regretted it, "I remember." He was smiling as he stood in the kitchen, ignoring his roommates' curious glances.

"Oh." James cleared his throat before continuing, "Good. I, um... Is this a good time?"

Josh spun to look at the overflowing pot and the sizzling chicken then spun back with a look of desperation at Nadia and Andrew. "Yeah! Yeah, absolutely!" He tried to sound smooth and relaxed, but judging by the giggles Nadia was holding back, he knew he was failing. She stepped in to man the stove as he moved away and down into the short hall.

"Oh, good."

James sounded great, Josh decided. He liked the sound of him over the phone. But as soon as the thought crossed his mind, he cursed himself and pushed it away.

"I've been thinking about our time together and I had an offer for you, if you're available."

An offer? "I can check. What are you thinking?" He chewed his lip and paced a little. He'd been *waiting* for this call like some silly girl. Whatever the offer was, he was determined to take it.

"I'm in Jamaica on Saturday. If you're available, I'd like to fly you down and pay for you to stay the week I'm there." James sounded so confident and at ease as he spoke. Josh's heart thumped away.

"Let me check my calendar. Just give me a second here." As Josh pulled the phone away, he made a conscious decision that regardless of who he had scheduled, he'd move them for this opportunity.

And sure enough, he had three appointments that week. Taking a moment to gather himself, he reinforced his decision. "I can do it, definitely," he replied, trying to sound just as confident.

"Great."

Was that *relief* in James' voice?

"That's great, Josh. Text me your email and I'm going to have my assistant get in touch with you. She'll book your flight and give you all the information. Everything is on me. You won't need to pay for anything, okay?"

Josh didn't know what to say, so he simply replied, "Okay... Wow, that sounds great. I've never been to Jamaica." He wanted to smack his head against the wall as he mentally replayed the words. James chuckled, and it was a lovely sound.

"I think you'll love it. Stephanie will be in touch. If you need anything or have any questions, don't hesitate to call me."

"Okay, I look forward to it," Josh replied with a small smile before they exchanged goodbyes. He ended the call and stared at the phone.

"So, you're going to Jamaica? With James Barnwell, CEO of Winter Luxury Resorts?" Nadia asked expectantly, holding the bowl of salad Josh had made earlier. He snapped out of his trance to find both of them smirking at him.

He glowered.

"Yeah? So what?" He tried to act like he didn't care, feigning nonchalance as he went back to the stove to find that Nadia had already handled the pasta and tossed it in the lemon sauce with the chicken. He shot her a look of apology.

"You've been thinking about this guy nonstop since you slept with him," she began as Andrew sipped his beer and looked on. "Is this a good idea? You know we're not supposed to get attached to clients. You had this guy one time, and he has messed with your head already."

Josh and Nadia had met one night, trying to pick up the same man in a high-end club downtown. They'd each ended up determining that the other was also an escort and had taken the man back to his room, showing him a good time—and also getting to know each other. And while sexual chemistry was there—and it was *very* good chemistry—they only saw each other as a best friend. They'd met Andrew, a firefighter and paramedic, through their mutual friend Clint when Andrew had been looking for roommates. While Andrew wasn't sure what he'd gotten himself into by sharing his Brooklyn apartment with two escorts, the rent was always on time and they both knew how to cook—so it worked out for all parties.

"He hasn't messed with anything," Josh argued, setting the table. "And besides, who turns down an all-expenses-paid trip to Jamaica?"

Andrew and Nadia exchanged silent looks that Josh ignored, and they all seemingly decided to put the subject to bed. Andrew turned the Yankees playoff game back on and Nadia brought the food over. They picked up baseball talk throughout dinner, but her words didn't leave easily. He had to get his head on straight or this would go downhill—fast.

* * * *

"Ladies and gentlemen, we have begun our descent into Montego Bay."

Josh buckled his seat belt and powered off his phone, knowing he'd have to go through customs before he could power it back on. James' assistant Stephanie had assured him that she'd be waiting with a driver for his arrival. Staring out at the ocean from his window seat, he pondered how this trip would go. What did James expect from him? Sex, surely, but what else?

He was also secretly excited for a week of vacation. Maybe he could get some sun, work on his art. He'd been on business trips with clients, but it had always been to someplace less exciting. He'd never been to the Caribbean before. A trip to Ireland in his senior year had ensured that he had his passport, but he hadn't used it since. He was eager to see what Jamaica was like, to experience things he'd only seen in pictures, like sunsets against palm trees and clear blue ocean.

The plane landed smoothly, and customs was easy. Josh had packed a reasonably sized suitcase with various outfits and plenty of bathing suits, just in case. He'd also packed two suits — expensive ones, because James was a CEO, and the last thing he ever wanted to do was embarrass the man. His suits were nowhere near the caliber James wore. Josh was certain James wore Armani and Hugo Boss, but his would be fine in a pinch.

Walking down the long corridor, he spotted a pretty, curvy brunette and an older man holding a sign that read in big block letters 'Roberts'. Josh wondered for a brief moment if this was what it felt like to be James Barnwell. *Probably not*, he quickly corrected himself. James flew on private planes that he owned. But for a moment in time, Josh felt important. He relished it and put it away deep inside, in case it never happened again.

"Mr. Roberts?" she asked, smiling brightly as he got closer. Josh wondered if it was the eye contact that had given him away. He grinned.

"Yes, but please, it's Josh. You must be Stephanie." He shifted his garment bag into his left hand and shook her right hand firmly.

"Yes, Stephanie Markus. It's wonderful to finally meet you." She had a sparkle to her eyes that caught Josh by surprise, but he just gave her a friendly smile in return. "Mr. Barnwell is waiting for you back at the resort. He tried to come but he unfortunately got caught up in meetings. He sends his apologies."

Josh shrugged a little as he followed the older gentleman, who was obviously the driver and very familiar with the airport, to the baggage carousel. "It's not a problem. I was figuring you'd be here to make sure I didn't get lost." He laughed a little and she blushed as they stopped by the claim area.

"Oh, he wanted to surprise you," she explained — and Josh couldn't help but raise an eyebrow in question. She didn't seem to notice. "He's been very excited for your arrival."

She glanced up at him with what Josh perceived as a knowing smile, making him shift a little awkwardly under his backpack and garment bag. Had James told them that he was an...?

"Wait until you see the view from the room. It's *incredible.*"

Well, at least *that* sounded promising. Having James' staff knowing he had hired an escort for the week sounded a little less so. There was sure to be judgment, right? Why would he tell everyone? Josh blinked and shook his head a little, coming back to the conversation to hear Stephanie going on about some kind of event at the end of the week. By then they were moving too, out into the small and crowded lobby toward the exit.

"Mr. Barnwell has been working so hard on this remodel," she explained, thinking he'd been listening this entire time. Josh nodded as if he had, pushing the rest of his thoughts away. "I'm sure he's told you, but this is going to change the resort—the common area, the stage, the shows and shops, not to mention the chefs he's hired for the Italian and Asian restaurants. I don't know how he does what he does and manages to find time in between all that for you. I admire him. I haven't been on a date in two years."

She rambled on as she opened the door to the Mercedes sedan waiting for them. "Which is fine," she added, as Josh had yet to reply—because what exactly was he supposed to say?—"because I truly am married to my work at this point. I couldn't ask for a better boss. Mr. Barnwell is wonderful to me, to everyone."

Josh slid into the car and wondered for a moment what exactly was going on and who exactly Stephanie was. He also wondered what on earth he was in for this week, because he usually operated under complete cover. No one ever knew he was an escort. A bubble of anxiety started to grow in his stomach, but he slid on his sunglasses and managed a smile, turning his phone back on as the car started. It was warm out, but in the most inviting way. Josh wasn't going to argue, though, when the driver turned on the air conditioning.

"So, Josh," she began again once she seemed to realize he wasn't exactly sure how to reply to her previous conversation, "Mr. Barnwell tells me you're from Brooklyn. I grew up in Queens."

Josh had to admit that her bubbly attitude did make her endearing, and she obviously had enough energy to keep up with whatever James seemed to put on her plate.

"Where do you live now? Do you miss it?" She cocked her head and waited wide-eyed and curious for an answer, and Josh wondered what kind of twilight zone he'd just stepped into. *What the actual....?*

"I live about three blocks from where I grew up. My mom still lives in the same house," he replied with a friendly smile. Stephanie seemed delighted with that answer.

"Oh, wow! That must be so nice, to be able to go home. I visit as often as I can, but Mr. Barnwell has me based in Miami, working out of the office I have there, so I don't get home much more than during the holidays. He gives *great* time off."

"How's Miami?" Josh decided that if he could keep the conversation steered away from him, maybe this would be easier and less awkward — and maybe the anxiety causing his blood pressure to rise would ease.

Luckily Stephanie had a *lot* to say about Miami, and it took up the entire fifteen-minute ride until they were pulling through the security gate at the resort. At that point, she grew much quieter, seemingly wanting to let Josh take in the sights of the resort James had designed and built.

Winter Montego Bay stood out in a rich cursive font on either side of the large wall into the grounds. Stephanie explained briefly that there was an adult side and a family side, but people could intermingle if they wished. The car steered toward the family side, to which Stephanie said, "Mr. Barnwell resides on the seventh floor on the family side. He likes the view, and he has a soft spot for families. His sister is actually visiting this week, too, as part of the big grand-reopening."

Josh absorbed all that information, but he was far too busy staring out of the window as they came to a stop at the front doors of the open-air lobby. The driver opened the doors and Stephanie explained that he would get Josh's luggage. She'd see him up to the room first. Hefting his carry-on only, Josh followed her through the lobby and questioned if *everything* was made of white marble. It was gorgeous. The view out of the main windows overlooked the pools and the ocean, a gazebo standing out among two coves. Every staff member acknowledged him with a smile and a hand over their heart as she guided him through the hotel, giving a mini tour. She assured him that Mr. Barnwell would give him the full one later. If he didn't, Josh was sure he could explore on his own—and planned on it. He had to see every inch of this place and send pictures back to Nadia and Andrew, who had sworn they'd evict him if he didn't buy them Jamaican coffee and rum and give them a full report, including pictures.

A special key unlocked the elevator to rise to the higher floor, and Stephanie went on to tell him about the owner's lounge he'd have access to during his stay. All his drinks and food were included, anything he wished. It was also an all-inclusive resort, but Stephanie made sure to repeat that "*anything you wish*" was his, at no expense. Josh thanked her graciously, but she just smiled and told him to thank Mr. Barnwell. Josh would surely do that—as best he could, anyway.

"If you need anything at all, dial twenty-two for the concierge on this level. If you need me"—she handed him a business card—"my cell is at the bottom, and it works over here on and off Wi-Fi, day or night. While you're here, I'm happy to help with anything you need. I'm sure I'll be seeing you around quite a bit anyway, but just in case…" Stephanie offered him a very sincere smile as he handed him the key to the room. "It was wonderful to meet you, Josh. We're very happy to have you."

As he thanked her again, genuinely, because she had in fact been a wonderful hostess thus far, she headed back toward the elevator and Josh flashed the keycard over the round door lock. The light turned green, and he pushed open the heavy door, taking a moment to marvel at the details as he stepped inside.

He forgot all about his sudden curiosity with James as he looked around the room. It was bigger than his entire apartment, with a balcony extending along the entire front of the room displaying an ocean view he didn't even know could really exist. There was a dining area all the way to his left and a king-size four-poster bed to his right—in its own bedroom. In front of him was a desk area and a living room, with far more furniture than he could ever need. The room was immaculate. The sliding doors to the balcony in the bedroom were open, the sea breeze enticing him. After going into the bedroom and dropping his backpack on the bed, he looked around, still in complete awe. *This* was far beyond a first for him. This was a *dream*. Josh almost pinched himself, just to make sure this was real life.

He heard the shower running and wondered if they'd turned *that* on for him too. Laughing to himself, practically giddy and beyond ready to clean away the germs of traveling, he began pulling his clothes off—beginning with his shirt and shoes, leaving them neatly on the bed and by the bed—he wasn't about to mess up the state of the room—before heading for the giant marble bathroom.

He stopped short and the wind rushed out of his lungs at what he saw on the other side of the only slightly fogged-up glass. James stood with his back to the door, hands on the wall as the water ran down his completely naked body. For a moment Josh didn't breathe as he simply took in the view. James' round ass was on complete display for him. This had to be his welcome, the immediate change and call to work for him. James had been waiting for him in his room, looking for what Josh was sure to be the first of many sexual services he would provide. He was still put off by the fact that it seemed people *knew* why he was there, but after being treated like a king and apparently being put up like one, he'd do *anything* James asked him to.

Josh slipped out of his jeans and boxers, settling them quietly on the counter to avoid disturbing James from the seeming trance he was in. He licked his lips as he gazed at the body before him, and his cock was already roaring to life. This would be an easy week for what he needed to provide James. He refused to acknowledge aloud or to himself how many times he'd gotten off on his own to thoughts of their time together. Pleasing James would *not* be an issue.

He pulled open the full glass door slowly and James popped his head up instantly. Josh grinned, feeling himself flushing a deep crimson as James' eyes widened and roamed Josh's body, not once but *twice* before he caught Josh's eyes. Josh kept his grin, albeit he was slightly nervous, and forced himself into *work* mode as he took a step toward James and the hot water.

"Hey, handsome," he greeted in his signature low tone, running a few fingers up James' wet left arm, which was still placed on the wall in front of them. James shivered under the touch, but it seemed to finally knock him out of his head as he found a small smile.

"Josh," he replied, and Josh didn't miss the way his name sounded rolling off James' tongue in a pleased and surprised tone, "you're here."

"Stephanie just showed me up. She didn't tell me you'd be waiting, though she seemed very aware of what I'm here for." Josh stepped closer, his cock hard and brushing against James' thick, warm thigh. Josh fought his own shudder at the temperature change and brushed his lips against James' triceps.

James opened and closed his mouth a few times and his cock started to swell and hang heavy between his legs. It was an impressive thing, but the darkness of the bedroom had nothing on the brightness of the bathroom lights, and Josh was getting his real first taste of naked James. And he liked it…very much.

Josh dragged his lips over James' arm then ducked beneath it, falling to his knees between James and the wall. He'd sucked him very briefly that first night and decided that *this* was how he wanted to say hello to James for the first time in Jamaica. And while he didn't necessarily know what *James* wanted at this very moment, James had asked him to call the shots in the bedroom, so that was what he was doing. And what man had ever complained about an epic blow job in the shower? Not any Josh was aware of.

"She's, um… She's… Sorry she didn't tell you," James stuttered as Josh took his cock in hand. His groan was obscene, and Josh wondered if anyone ever touched this man or if this was just how he sounded. It didn't matter, Josh decided for the moment. He chose to think that maybe it was only him who could pull these noises from James. It helped with his confidence, regardless, as he licked a bead of pre-cum off the tip of the now very hard, very thick cock in his hands.

"I don't mind at all," Josh murmured, glancing up at him through his lashes as he licked the underside of James' length. "Truth be told, I've been looking forward to this all day." He smirked up at James before sucking the tip into his mouth just for a moment, then pulling back. "You got so hard for me, so fast. Such a good boy. You've been thinking about this week? Thinking about all the things I'm gonna do to you?" James' cock jerked in his hand and Josh received his answer loud and clear. James stared down at him with wordless lips, open and slack, and Josh memorized the look of pleasure as he sucked all of him into his mouth and swallowed.

He relished in James' taste, the weight of him on his tongue. Closing his eyes, he listened to the sounds James made, the hums and grunts, as he worshiped his cock. He made a show of it, hollowing his cheeks and sucking hard as he drew his lips up and down the man's length, thoroughly enjoying his first meal on the island. James slipped a hand into his short hair and tugged, and Josh found himself gripping his own cock and stroking a few times, just enough to ease the need. He pulled his hand away, but James managed to say, "No, don't." He panted, gripping Josh's hair harder. "Please…keep going… Wanna see you come with me."

Josh was never one to deny his clients, but they rarely asked for the show or granted him his own pleasure. Josh didn't hesitate to give in, though, wrapping his right hand back around his cock as his left hand on James' thigh steadied him. He then gave James everything he had, sucking and swallowing him down into his throat and lapping at him with his tongue when he pulled off, putting pressure just where James needed it as he slid back down to the base. He buried his nose in the short hair there, inhaling, swallowing and slowly impaling his throat with the thick tip in a practiced manner, and it only took a few moments before James was bursting in Josh's throat, pouring himself into Josh with an unashamed string of curses and groans that Josh wished he could memorize for the next time he was alone. All Josh needed was to pull on himself a few more times before he made a mess of the shower floor, quietly coming as he lapped up everything James had to give.

When he was sure James was clean and he was empty, he leaned his head against James' hip to recover for a few moments. A tug at his hair had his head rising, then he was being pulled up and pressed to the wall in a kiss he hadn't anticipated. It was slow and lingering, and he kissed back immediately, sliding his hands up to grip James' shoulders as he tried not to let himself get lost in it.

James pulled away, breathless after several long moments, then abruptly stepped back, separating their naked bodies by at least a foot. They stared at each other, both gasping and coming back to themselves, when James spoke, his voice raspy.

"I should have told you this on the phone before…you got here, but I wasn't sure you'd come and I wanted to fully explain. I'm about to ask a lot and I don't know what you usually do, but I *really* needed you here for this since I sort of backed myself into a corner."

That bubble of anxiety Josh had managed to pop by sucking the hell out of James' cock was suddenly tenfold and threatening to drown him. "Okay…"

"I need you to be my boyfriend…for the week. And not just like any boyfriend… A pretty intense relationship one. I sorta lied to my sister. She called me out, she's expecting to meet you and I *really* need this to be very convincing. So Stephanie thinks that is what you are, my boyfriend who I somehow kept secret from everyone and everything the last six months. I'm sorry I didn't tell you. I just…didn't know how to say all of that over the phone and not to your face. You'll be fully compensated, I promise." James' sheepish grin and wildly apologetic eyes made him so damn adorable that Josh didn't know what to do with himself.

So he laughed. He leaned against the wall and chuckled in relief at the fact he'd been so worried and so weirded out, and when James joined him, albeit looking at him like he was crazy, Josh reveled in the sound. "I'm sorry. I'm sorry." He pulled himself back under control, wondering what this moment must look like — the two of them hysterical under the hot water in the shower. "I thought you'd told Stephanie, and everyone, that I was an escort and that's why I was here. She was acting so…strangely. I understand now, but at the time…" He shook his head, looking down at the marble under his bare feet. James was now red and giggling wholeheartedly.

"Oh man, I'm sorry." He was sincere. "That's not what I intended at all. She's…very good at her job but also very easy to read and has a knack for talking a lot. She's very sweet, but I'm sure she made it very clear that I was looking forward to my *boyfriend* arriving. Though after that blow job, she wasn't wrong."

They shared a glance and continued to laugh for a minute before James grabbed the shampoo. "I'll finish up, then you can shower. I'm sure you want to after your trip. We will be rooming together," he went on as Josh shifted to the back of the shower, the cool wall feeling good against his back as he watched James wash his hair and body, "since everyone thinks you're here for me. I do hope that's okay. I can sleep on the couch if you'd feel more comfortable."

"Absolutely not. We can share a bed. I'm fine with that. And besides, I still have a lot to show you," Josh replied suggestively before looking down. James glanced back at him over his shoulder and Josh flushed down into his chest.

"I have to say," James began, turning slowly and letting his eyes roam Josh's body, "that I am *definitely* looking forward to that. But we'll have to get started after dinner." He frowned, his tone carrying regret. "I've gotta meet my sister for coffee. You can get settled, though. We'll do introductions tomorrow. It'll just be you and me for dinner. I made us a reservation at our Brazilian steakhouse…if that's okay with you."

It was all for show and Josh shouldn't care, but something about what James said made his head spin a little. His stomach flipped and he had to fight the urge to step forward and kiss the man. And that was *unusual*.

"Of course. I could probably use a rest anyway, if that's okay. And I'd like to explore this beautiful place. It's honestly incredible, Jamie."

James stilled briefly and blushed. "Thank you. I love this resort a lot. I really hope you enjoy it here. And again, thank you for coming. We can talk backstory later — "

"What if we just embellish the truth? We can say I picked you up in a bar in midtown, and it was just…on from there?" Josh suggested offhandedly then widened his eyes. "I mean, if that's not too personal…"

James shook his head with the hint of a smile. "No, I think that's good. I like it. Easy to remember too." He flushed a little deeper and ran a hand through his wet hair. Josh would not admit that he could get used to seeing the man like this.

"Great. That way, if I run into anyone on my travels around this place, I'll know what to say."

James eventually left Josh to shower alone, dressing and heading out to find his sister. Josh finished up, ignoring the urge to get off one more time to the memories, and quickly slipped on some track pants and a T-shirt, the afternoon sun still being hot. Right now, he wanted to work out, to see this amazing place and to try *not* to think about how much fun it was going to be to pretend to be James Barnwell's boyfriend.

* * * *

"So when do I get to meet this mystery man?" James' sister Rebecca asked as they strolled around the brand-new common area James had just designed. They were sipping their coffee and catching up. She'd just arrived the day before. James' parents were back home in Florida, waiting for the opening of his newest resort in the Bahamas. Rebecca, on the other hand, loved this one. She and her family visited once a year.

"Tomorrow." James grinned, feigning the joy of keeping Josh, his *boyfriend*, a secret a little longer. "Let me have one night to show him around, will ya?"

"Where is he now?" Becca continued with her tactic, looking around as if she'd recognize him if she saw him, excitement on her pretty face. "Is he upstairs? Did you already wear him out?"

James made a face. "Bec! Seriously?"

"What? I didn't even know you were into men until you fessed up about your *dreamy* attitude last week at Mom and Dad's. Now I'm just trying to figure it all out. Do you...top? Is that the way you say it? Or does he? God, I can't wait to put a face to the name—"

"Will you stop? He tops, and no, I'm not telling you why."

The sibling banter carried on as James showed off the area, the beautiful fountain pools and marble architecture. Becca was obviously more enamored with the prospect of meeting her brother's boyfriend than anything else.

James couldn't blame her. He hadn't been able to get Josh out of his mind since that first night. He'd left to visit his parents for their anniversary and had unfortunately been in a 'best sex *ever*' haze the entire time. When Becca had called him out for being aloof and awfully smiley, he'd spat out the lie about seeing someone—a man—and Becca had eaten it up.

All his family wanted was for him—the thirty-eight-year-old—to settle down. He was beyond successful, he didn't need to build another resort and he was *that* financially secure. But James had dreams and goals and wanted to provide the best vacations possible. Settling with someone would slow him down...and he wasn't ready for that.

Not to mention he'd never found someone to *slow down* with.

James had immediately seen Josh as soon as he'd said what he had to Becca. He'd practically burned the view of Josh above him, rocking into him, into his mind, so it wasn't hard to recall. But something about Josh's demeanor had said he'd be good at this lie. And their conversation after the shower had only cemented that thought—not to mention he was incredibly handsome, seemingly built by the gods. If Becca wasn't taken with his personality, at least he wasn't hard to look at, and she could tell their mother that.

"James, as beautiful as this resort is—and it is, it's my favorite—stop showing me around and go cuddle your boyfriend. It's his first time here, isn't it? Show *him* around. Dan has the kids around here somewhere. I'll just go hang out with them—"

"Hey, Jamie!"

James' throat tightened at how unprepared he was for this. He'd orchestrated for Becca and Josh to meet in the morning after breakfast at the pool, *not* now.

Josh was walking toward them, wearing a fitted gray Under Armour shirt and navy track pants that left little to James' imagination. The man was ridiculously fit, and the outfit put that on display gloriously for James' sister...and him.

"I thought the map I had was going to get me to the gym, but this place is *huge*." He was obviously apologetic as he approached and held up the map as proof. "I was gonna ask someone, then I saw you, so..." He trailed off as Becca looked from James to Josh as if expecting some kind of explanation of the nickname or maybe the fact that he had left out that Josh, his *boyfriend*, was significantly younger than he was.

Josh, maybe more practiced than James thought, seemed to know just what to do. He jogged toward them the rest of the way and placed a quick but sweet kiss to James' unsuspecting lips, carrying on the boyfriend act for Becca. He brushed James' hand that held the coffee with his, careful not to jar it but also as a sweet gesture. Becca's eyes and smile grew with every passing second Josh was in front of them.

"Oh, yeah," James managed to get out dumbly, his lips tasting of some kind of fruity substance — pre-workout, maybe? "I thought you were going to rest?"

"I decided I'd rather squeeze in a quick workout before dinner." He shrugged a little with that smile, and unfortunately for James, he found it adorable. Becca seemed to as well, as she cleared her throat expectantly.

"Good. Yeah, the gym is just straight down this path, back by the lobby, second floor." He flashed Josh a smile as he recited the words, glad his sunglasses hid his eyes and the surely panicked look in them. "Josh, this is my sister Rebecca. Becca, this is Josh."

Becca extended her hand and Josh gave her the warmest of smiles. "Rebecca, it's so nice to finally meet you." He made eye contact with her, zeroing in on her in the way he had James that first night, and Becca melted under his gaze.

"Josh! It's so nice to finally meet *you* and put a face to the name I've heard so very little of." She glanced at James, not bothering to hide her surprise and obviously impressed expression.

"Well, it's been a whirlwind. I don't blame Jamie for not talking about it yet." He threw James a secretive grin and James blushed, while also wishing the ground would swallow him whole. He was far too unprepared for this week. *Maybe this is a bad idea...*

"He's always been pretty quiet, even as a kid." Becca nodded, seemingly considering his silence as she glanced at him. "But I've been really looking forward to meeting you. James said we'll see you in the morning after breakfast. You can meet my husband and the kids."

James opened his mouth to intervene — he hadn't yet told Josh the whole plan — but Josh was already graciously smiling and replying before James could stop him. "I'm really looking forward to meeting the kids. I love kids — no offense to your husband, of course," he replied with obvious humor, and Becca ate it up, laughing along with him. "Well, I really need to get a move on to the gym if I wanna get my workout in and get back and showered before dinner. I'm sorry to interrupt your walk." Josh bowed at the waist a little as he skirted by then said, "It was wonderful meeting you, Rebecca. I can't wait to talk more tomorrow and meet the rest of the family. James" — he stopped at James' shoulder, running his fingers over his bare forearm and giving him a soft smile — "see you back at the room before dinner?" Before James could nod, Josh was pressing his lips to his again, in a slightly longer show of affection. Becca stared almost aghast as James kissed him back then waved him off.

When he was out of earshot and they'd watched him jog away in silence, James staring at his ass and Becca simply in shock, she turned to him. "You didn't tell me he was a *baby*! And a freaking fitness model!"

James pulled his eyes away from Josh's retreating figure and some feeling returned to his fingers. "He's not a model, and he's not a baby," James argued as heat rushed to his cheeks. "He's intelligent and kind, and it doesn't matter how old he is. His physique is just a bonus."

"Bonus? I can't even believe you left him in the room. I'd consider cheating on Dan with *that*." She glanced back, probably just for pure emphasis of her words.

"You would not. And I had to come meet you and work. We can't just fuck all day."

"Um, *yes*, you can."

"Shut up." James pushed her shoulder, annoyed but also thoroughly entertained by her reaction and Josh's performance. James would obviously have to step up his game if he hoped to have any match to that. They needed to be believable, and James hardly thought that his was. Lucky for him, Becca had been smitten with Josh's appearance and age before anything else. He might not get so lucky next time.

* * * *

Walking through the resort hand in hand with the CEO was an experience Josh wouldn't soon forget. Sitting down at dinner across from the man, eating the most incredible food, drinking a bottle of wine Josh couldn't dream of affording and pretending to be lovers was also unforgettable. The table sat outside in the warm air and Josh was glad to find his linen button-down and slacks were acceptable attire for the Brazilian steakhouse.

He let James take care of the ordering. The wine was white, aged and absolutely the best Josh had ever tasted. Every meat James got them was mouthwatering and to die for. Even the dessert was beyond satisfying. When the chef came out to ask James how his meal had been, he graciously introduced Josh as his partner, and judging by all the looks of surrounding wait staff and patrons, they all knew from the way James said it that he didn't mean business partner. Josh blushed to high heaven but stood and shook hands. It was the most important he'd ever felt his entire life. Really, this entire trip was making him feel that way, even though he kept every bit of conversation centered on James.

It was his job to shower affection and attention on his clients. And honestly, he enjoyed it. Learning about James was quite interesting, and listening to James talk about his life was eye-opening. From Brooklyn as well, he'd been raised in Miami after the age of fifteen, hence how they'd never met. He'd had an eye for art and architecture and had excelled in school. A company he'd interned with had given him a loan to create his first model resort, and with excellent credit and a fierce drive, he'd started Winter Luxury Resorts. He'd bought a plot of land in Exuma, Bahamas, and had begun work on his first property.

He'd never married and had no children, worked long hours, every single day with the exception of Christmas and Thanksgiving, and was extremely passionate. Josh found himself in awe as James talked, needing to know more and more as dinner wore on. By the time their food was done and they were carrying their glasses and their second bottle of wine back to the room, Josh knew more about James than he could find on Google if he tried — and yet also he felt like he'd only tapped the surface. He yearned to know more and hoped during the week he'd get to.

The room was oddly welcoming as they settled down onto the two large couches, their laughter over a story James had told carrying through the open balcony doors and mixing with the sound of the ocean waves. Josh sobered a little. He had a good buzz as he watched James top off their glasses and lean back on the white couch, his cobalt shirt and dark hair standing out. Josh could only see him and found James a little intimidating, since he usually had his emotions and desires under control.

"James, I have a question, if that's okay," Josh began when their previous conversation had lulled. James chuckled and settled his gaze on Josh's.

"You've been asking questions all night," he jested, his grin easy as he sipped his wine. "What's one more?"

Josh's cheeks heated and he peered down to straighten his shirt as he swallowed hard. "Well, this one is a bit different, so I hope it's okay I'm asking."

James nodded and used his glass in a 'go on'-type motion, encouraging Josh to continue. Josh briefly wondered why this question was so hard for him today.

"So...*sexually*, what would you like from me this trip? While some clients do take me away just to play pretend, we're here, sharing a suite and a bed, and I just...want to make sure I understand *exactly* what you want." Josh managed to somehow get the words out while maintaining constant eye contact with him across the living room. James held his gaze evenly.

"Well, if I can be candid, I haven't been able to stop thinking about our night together. It was an...eye-opening experience. You'll be fully compensated for your services, but I'm hoping you wouldn't mind indulging me in as much of it as we both...can take." James' cheeks were pink, and if Josh wasn't mistaken, that flush ran down his neck and under the blue shirt. That was a large request he'd made, but nothing Josh couldn't handle.

Josh pulled his bottom lip into his mouth then ran his tongue over it. "I'm sure that won't be a problem," Josh replied with a crooked smile. James matched it with one of his own then slowly stood.

"Good. Same dynamic as before? I need you to call the shots, if you don't mind," James prompted, setting his glass down. Josh did the same, following James' lead.

"Whatever you want, sir. I'm here to please you."

"And yourself," James was quick to add as he walked toward the bedroom. "Make sure you enjoy what you're doing as much as I am."

Josh sucked in a breath at the request. His clients never cared about his wants, and this was the second time today that James had. He followed James eagerly, unbuttoning his linen shirt as he went. He caught up to James beside the bed, where the man was working on his own shirt. "Only if you're sure. I mean, I enjoyed our last time together and earlier in the shower. I just—"

"I'm sure. Make sure you enjoy it just as much, Josh. That's part of it for me, I realized. Watching you come was…fuckin' beautiful." James' voice dropped into a rasp and Josh fumbled over the buttons on his shirt. He blushed hard and dropped his gaze. "And you're so fuckin' pretty when you do that."

"What?" Josh managed to ask, despite the sudden lump in his throat.

"Blush like no one has ever complimented you before."

Josh didn't know what was happening, and he couldn't articulate to James how those words made him feel. Instead, he simply reached for the man and kissed him the way he wanted to every time the man did something nice for him. He didn't have to, after all. Josh was there to serve. And somehow James always managed to make his knees a little weak and also took a minute to ensure his comfort. It was more consideration than anyone had ever shown him before.

And while he couldn't find the words to say it, he could show James just how much that meant.

The kiss was deep, and Josh wasted no time slipping his tongue past James' lips. He was rewarded with a sweet noise that made him shudder as he pushed James' button-down off his shoulders. His bare chest was soft, save for the short hairs there, and Josh suddenly had the urge to kiss and touch every inch of this man. He wanted to *show* him how much he wanted this.

Urging James silently onto the bed, Josh found himself slipping out of his own clothes as James pushed off his khakis. As soon as they were both naked, Josh was kissing up James' body, climbing onto the bed. Josh dragged his lips over James' hip, up his strong abdomen and between his chest muscles. He bit at each nipple, making James writhe and moan, and Josh suddenly wanted to know just how vocal he could make the man.

Josh pulled away briefly to find the lube and condoms he'd stashed in the side table drawer, but James didn't let him stay away for long. He was pulling at Josh, wrapping his arms around him as Josh dropped the items unceremoniously next to them, their kisses deep and almost sloppy as they writhed against each other with nothing separating them. The slide and friction of their cocks made Josh hum and James' groan vibrated through his chest. He kissed along James' jaw, feeling the way the man touched him and grabbed for him, the desperation in his touch.

"You been thinking about this? Getting me back between these legs, huh?" Josh began against James' ear, fanning the sensitive skin with his heavy breathing. "You been playing with yourself? Thinking of me?"

It was personal, asking such questions, but somehow, they just slipped out of Josh. James keened into them, mewling under Josh's mouth as he whispered, "I've been wearing a plug just for you tonight." Josh's lips stilled and his heart jumped. *A plug? Already? My my, James has been looking forward to this.*

"You wore a plug to dinner so you'd be nice and open for me to fuck?" Josh nipped at James' neck and sucked hard on one particular spot that made James squirm and groan deeply.

"Yes, Sir" — he gripped Josh's back hard and thrust up to meet him, making Josh give a few hard rocks of his length — "been wanting your cock so badly."

Josh's skin was on fire, his mind a jumbled mess as he considered just how much this man wanted him — and just how much those words were affecting him. He'd had sex since James — multiple times with multiple clients — but nothing made him feel the way those words did, nothing caused him to want to come that quickly like hearing how much James Barnwell wanted his cock — apparently so much that he'd worn a *plug* to their fancy high-end dinner. Josh kissed James with every ounce of heat inside him, thrusting harder against him. "Such a good boy, getting that ass all ready for me. You just wanna be fucked, huh? Want me to wreck you?"

"God, yes," James panted, and Josh marveled at how well the change in dynamic worked.

"On your knees," Josh murmured, shifting back to his own as James moved around, positioning himself on his hands and knees for his lover. Josh took a moment to appreciate the power this strong man had given up to him and placed a single kiss on his lower back, as if he could symbolize the appreciation in just that small motion. He couldn't — but he took a moment to gaze at the sight James made and remember it for later.

The black plug stood out against James' skin as Josh pulled his cheeks apart. It was silicone, with a long handle to keep it from slipping too far in and to make it easy to pull out. Josh took hold of the end and moved it, pressing it into James and pulling it halfway out of him. James mewled into the sheets, gripping then and thrusting back against Josh.

"Look at you," Josh murmured with sweet affection, "you're stretched just perfectly for me. You've been training yourself, haven't you?"

Josh could tell, and James didn't deny it. "I h-have," he confessed. "Sometimes when I think of you I...do things like this...or..." He drifted off and Josh was too shocked over the fact that James was admitting to thinking and possibly fantasizing about him to reply coherently. His cock was already hard, but all his blood flow ran south, making it actually hurt. *How did I get so lucky to find this man in the bar that night?*

Josh pulled the plug from James' body, watching the way the stretched rim fluttered with the loss of the toy. He had the urge to kiss and lick the abused hole, but he wasn't sure they were there yet. The last thing he wanted was to scare James away. He'd only had one encounter with a man, and he was now training himself to take Josh more easily. It was one thing at a time with James. Josh would never push or take advantage of that.

After opening the lube, he dribbled some along James' crease, rubbing it around slowly with his fingers. James was huffing and squirming, pressing back into him beautifully. He rewarded him with two fingers, stroking deeply and grazing his sweet spot. James cried out, jerking, and a flush ran down his back. "Feels good, huh? I'm gonna make you feel *real* good for being such a good boy." Josh slid the condom on and lathered himself in lube as he finger-fucked James slowly, watching how James' body took the fingers, the way James moved against them. "Tomorrow I'm gonna make you ride me, but tonight I'm gonna fuck you hard. I missed this sweet ass. It's gonna feel so good around my cock." Josh pulled his fingers away and James moaned at the promises.

Josh didn't hesitate to push inside, and his cock slid home slowly but fully in one push. James stretched around him, and Josh tenderly rubbed his thumb along his rim as James gasped and panted, adjusting to the intrusion. Josh was still for several moments, simply rubbing James' back and whispering sweet words of praise and encouragement as he waited for James to adjust. He knew the feeling, knew what it took to be ready, and he wanted to make sure James was well stretched and prepared for the fuck Josh had so badly wanted to give him ever since he'd seen this ass in the shower that morning.

James reached back and gripped his thigh, and Josh knew he was ready. "Fuck me," James whispered, turning his head to glance over his shoulder. "Give me everything. I can take it."

Goosebumps rose all over his body as he stared down at the man under him. *How can I deny him?*

He couldn't.

It was punishing. It was rough. Skin against skin, he buried his cock deep over and over. He gripped James' hips as he rocked him forward and back, then held him still and rutted into him hard. James took every bit of it beautifully, and the sounds James made would be burned into his memory forever. He pulled James against his chest when he was close, holding their bodies together, sucking at James' shoulder and neck. He wrapped an arm around his chest, keeping James against him.

"Do you know how good you feel? Wrapped around my cock, squeezing me? You need to come, don't you, sweet boy?" James' incoherent noises let Josh know how far gone he was. He reached down with his free hand, stroking James hard as he chased his own orgasm. "Your ass is incredible, Jamie," he rasped against James' ear. "Your entire body is. I want to fuck you every minute of this trip, make you come over and over until you're spent. You want that, don't you? Want my cock buried inside you, hungry man that you are? Never knew how good you could feel, huh? Come on, Jamie. Come for me. Come for me while I come so fuckin' hard for you…"

James shouted and held on to Josh's arm for dear life. Josh wanted to watch so badly, but his own orgasm took over and it was far too strong for him to keep his eyes open. They shook and gasped against one another as James made a mess of the bed and Josh's hand, Josh buried himself to the hilt inside of him until he was entirely empty.

"Shh-h," he whispered sweetly against James' trembling body. "I've got you." Josh held James tightly as he came down from his high. Josh was beginning to realize how much James turned control over to him in these moments. He gave Josh all the trust, all the decisions. Josh needed to ease him down gently.

The pull-out was slow, as easy as Josh could go. He settled James on the comforter away from the mess and was pulling the condom off when James reached for him. "Josh?" His voice was raspy and he was still short of breath, but Josh was at his side as soon as the condom was disposed of.

"Yeah, Jamie?" Josh asked as he kneeled next to James on the high four-poster bed. James' grin was sated, his eyes hooded and his body shiny with sweat and exertion. *He's gorgeous.* Josh was having a hard time reeling in his wide-eyed wonder at the man before him.

"Thank you," he whispered, running his hand along Josh's cheek. Josh flushed hard once more and hoped the dim lighting hid it. Judging by James' grin and how it grew, it didn't. "You always know just…what I need. Lemme hold you?"

Another request, another thing Josh couldn't deny him.

"'Course, Jamie. Let me get us cleaned up and I'd love it if you'd hold me."

Their roles were unconventional, but Josh was rapidly adjusting. He was happy to give James anything he wanted, but he was also well aware of how dangerous this already was for him. He'd never had a problem keeping a client at arm's length. But with every word he rushed out during sex, every touch, every time James said something kind, Josh was turning into a jumbled mess of emotions.

It was hard to pull away, but Josh did, then they were back under the covers, the top duvet discarded, thanks to James' mess. It would serve as another piece providing evidence for their pretend affair. The only problem was…it just *sometimes* felt pretend.

James pulled Josh to his chest, the large blond man folding into him as though it were the most natural thing for them to do. James' brain felt hazy. He hadn't felt this at ease since the last time Josh had fucked the life out of him. It was becoming a problem — a good kind of problem.

He let his fingers roam over Josh's strong back, his hand covering Josh's on his chest. This young man had found the quickest way to all of James' fantasies, had somehow gotten through the bullshit and right to the heart of what James had needed. There was no fakeness, no fraud. Other than their fake relationship, everything here in the bedroom was real. Well...as real as Josh's entire escort act could be.

It was real for *him*, at least. Everything James felt, every piece of pleasure Josh pulled out of him was *real*.

He had allowed himself to bring Josh into his life in a way he hadn't allowed anyone in before. He wanted to question why, wanted to ask himself what the *fuck* he was thinking, doing this. A week with this man? He'd be finished. He'd be attached... He'd be...

James had to be in Italy in two weeks. He could bring Josh along then for the same reasons. In the morning he'd ask. He'd give the man more time than a week to prepare. James chose not to think about the rescheduling of Josh's clients and the adjustment of his life. James needed him in Italy. His mind felt clear, and his body felt fucking fantastic. He couldn't bear not having that for the opening of his resort in Capri.

He pushed any other emotional thought from his mind. This was good for him. And he'd be good to Josh, keep it well worth his time. They could do this. Maybe it was genius. Maybe this was what everyone should be doing.

And if James felt at peace falling asleep with Josh against him, he didn't have to tell anyone about that part either. Like everything else, he'd keep the truth to himself.

And if watching Josh stretch shirtless on the balcony in those low-slung sweatpants as their morning coffee brewed was the prettiest sight James had ever seen as he lay watching from the bed, no one had to know the truth about that either.

Some things are just better kept to myself.

Chapter Three

"Fuck, Josh…Christ," James moaned heavily into the sheets as Josh assaulted him with his tongue. James had never felt anything like Josh's velvety tongue licking at a place he'd never thought anyone ever would. Josh was taking his time for reasons unknown to James. He guessed Josh thought this was a way to open him up. But he was *open*, as Josh had kept up his end of the deal and fucked James every moment they were alone. The man was ready to go seemingly at the drop of a hat, and he appeared to enjoy the acts as much as James did.

Josh hadn't warned James as he'd flipped him over after sucking him long and slow. It seemed he was determined to give James the most pleasurable experience of his life *without* letting him come, every so often gripping the base of his cock to ensure that James didn't go off early. James was losing his mind, pushing himself shamelessly back into Josh's tongue. The tip penetrated him every couple of strokes and it felt like *heaven*.

Josh gripped James' ass then, spreading him wide as he licked with more intent. James whimpered and cursed, gripping the sheets so tightly that his knuckles turned white. He was on his chest and knees, his legs and cheeks spread wide, his cock hanging heavily between his thighs. It was a vulnerable position that James had never imagined himself in, but somehow, at the hands and mouth of Josh, it felt natural. He had to give the guy credit. He knew what he was doing.

This action went on for what felt like an eternity, James' control slipping and entirely in Josh's hands before Josh pulled back, groaning and caressing James' wrecked ass. James buried his face in the bed for a reprieve.

"You're doing so good, Jamie. I need to fuck you so badly."

"Please," James rasped urgently as he lifted his head and glanced back at the man behind him. Josh was looking down at him with unmistakable hunger. It made goosebumps rise all over his body and his stomach tightened in anticipation. "Fucking hell, Josh. Please...fuck me so fucking hard... *Please*."

Josh grinned down at him and stroked up his back. "I fucking love it when you beg. You're so pretty when you do. You want my cock bad, don't you?"

James groaned desperately. "So bad. Come on, Josh," he panted, pushing his ass back toward Josh helplessly. "I need it."

"So fuckin' needy." Josh grinned, spanking James so hard that it made him shiver. James wasn't quiet in his moaning reply.

"Goddammit," he spat out. Josh did it again.

"You're so fuckin' fun, Jamie."

There was the sound of the tear of the condom pack and James found himself dangerously wanting to feel

Josh's bare cock inside him. He almost moaned it but bit his tongue so hard that it almost bled. At least he still had *some* wits about him. Asking his escort to fuck him without protection would certainly make this awkward — and at only three days into the trip, James couldn't afford that.

James came back to the moment as Josh bit his ass. "I want you to ride me."

His heart tripped over itself and he glanced back, eyes wide. "You want me to —"

"I do. I want you to sit on my cock and ride me until you come all over my chest. I won't last long. Playing with you has worked me up."

Josh's grin told James he had nothing to worry about, but somehow, he couldn't help but feel unsure. It seemed so —

"Stop thinking about it, Jamie." Josh's soft voice brought him back again as he lay down beside James. Their faces were close for a moment before Josh shifted forward and kissed him sweetly. They teased their tongues, rubbing against each other. With every caress, James' nerves relaxed, and he found the heat igniting in his belly once more. Climbing up, he kept their lips together as he straddled Josh's hips, his cock teasingly hard between them and already sheathed and lubricated. James grabbed the small bottle of expensive lube anyway and slicked himself up as Josh moaned into his mouth, making the need to be filled all the more pronounced. "I've been inside you seven times in the last three days. Got you good and open to slide right down over me," Josh mumbled into James' mouth, and for the *eighth* time in three days, James questioned if *that* was how Josh spoke to all his clients.

Josh gripped his hip with one hand and held his heavy cock up with the other. There was anticipation on Josh's face, in his blue eyes, and for one small moment James felt like maybe he held the control. Josh was obviously ready, and James wanted to believe it was *him* who Josh wanted to be buried inside—and only him.

James lowered himself slowly, feeling the blunt tip of Josh's cock begging for entrance. He sucked in a ragged breath and kept his eyes on Josh's face. He gasped and steadied himself with one hand on Josh's chest and the other on Josh's thigh as he let Josh fill him at a languid pace. Somehow this never lost its spark. It seemed that no matter how many times Josh was inside him, it only made him want it more.

"Good boy...that's *it*... God...this ass..." Josh's words sounded measured and raspy as his face contorted in true pleasure, and James watched in awe as Josh's eyes roamed him. Josh seemed to not be able to decide where to look when his focus darted to where they were joined, to James' chest, to James' face and back down. James would be lying to say he hadn't been working extra hard in the gym since he'd taken Josh on. Something about being with this specimen of a man, spending so much time naked with him, was keeping him in peak condition. They seemed to only be dressed together when they were in the company of others. When it was just them, they were naked within minutes.

Josh ran his hands up and down James' chest as he settled in his lap. James had him buried to the hilt, his body on fire from the thick intrusion, but it was all he wanted. He tentatively rocked and relished in the way Josh worked his jaw and groaned, slipping his hands down to latch on to his ass with an iron grip. "God, Josh," James breathed, starting to move. Josh groaned in reply, helping him move back and forth on him as James really began to ride.

This was how the sex was—never rushed, unless it had to be. Always experimental, as Josh taught James things about being with a man. James had no idea how he'd go back to women—if he ever did. And the thought of being with another man besides Josh? Well, he didn't want to go there.

The harder James moved, the more praise Josh showered on him. Josh had gotten quite the tan over the last few days, and James was thoroughly enjoying the look of his sun-kissed skin. His freckles stood out beautifully, his cheeks pink with just the right amount of sun. He was a stunning individual. James couldn't stop staring.

Josh surged up from the bed as they both grew closer to the edge, slipping a hand around James' cock to stroke him. "You've got me so close, Jamie. You feel so good. You gonna come with me? Ridin' me so good...*fuck*." He spat out the last word as James squeezed him, having learned just how Josh reacted to certain things. He grinned through the sweat and passion as Josh lost his mind for a brief moment before regaining his composure and coming back tenfold. "Yes, yes, yes," he chanted at James, leaning forward to lick along James' collarbone.

James jumped and hissed, then it was truly just a frantic and slightly sloppy rush to the finish as their rhythm started to falter and both men neared their edge. James lived to watch Josh in these moments when his jaw grew tight and his lips parted as his climax ran up on him. He almost wished he could hold off on his own just to watch Josh, but Josh was too good with his hands. As he pressed two fingers against his straining rim and squeezed just right around his cock, James closed his eyes and lost track of space and time for several moments as he went off like a shot between them.

He didn't even hear Josh's praise as Josh followed him to his end, their hips stuttering and slowing as they sagged against each other. They were sweaty and sticky but didn't care. The embrace had become something of a constant for them.

Somewhere in James' mind, he screamed that this was bad news, the need for all this affection and wanting it from Josh, but James ignored it like a professional.

When James finally raised his head, he found Josh smiling up at him sweetly, almost tenderly. He blushed then proceeded to flush hotter than ever when he realized that his cum had reached Josh's chin. *Holy shit…* Why did that make his exhausted cock jolt with such need for possession of this man? He was *marked*. James swallowed hard. "I, um… Y-you…" he stuttered. Josh's grin turned cheeky as he wiped it with his thumb and licked it off. *This man is trying to kill me*, James was sure.

"I actually don't mind when people come on me. You should try it later. If you *like* it," Josh encouraged with a far-too-innocent shrug. James wanted to push him down and fuck him again. Too bad he was too tired for that…for now.

"I would like that, I think," James put his arms around Josh's shoulders, leaning in to kiss him slowly. He tasted himself on Josh's tongue and that made his heart pound. It didn't slow as Josh hugged him and kissed back with equal eagerness. It was easy to get lost in those sweet lips, and it wasn't for several long moments that they pulled away.

"Let me get you cleaned up, handsome," Josh murmured against James' lips, chasing them for two or three more kisses before finally separating.

Josh always took care of them, cleaned them up, grabbed James some water and covered them both as he settled back into bed. But it was always him who snuggled up to James now, his head settling right against James' heart. James would hold him tight and that was how they'd fall asleep, sometimes recapping their day, sometimes simply enjoying the companionable silence.

James wasn't sure how he would go back to New York or Miami without Josh in bed with him every night. It had only been a few nights and he was already dreading the separation. This was not good, but there was no way James was stopping it. He'd keep ignoring that until he was forced to confront it. And lucky for him, he knew that wouldn't be any time soon. Stephanie was organizing a trip to Italy in three weeks. James couldn't help but fall asleep to thoughts of wining and dining Josh on the island of Capri. The man would look so damn handsome against the Italian backdrop.

* * * *

Four days into the trip in Jamaica, James realized he hadn't truly thought through pretending to be Josh's significant other. Well, he'd known it on the first day but then decided denial was a better idea...until now. He watched from a hundred yards away as Josh played with his niece and nephews like he'd been part of the family longer than those three days. The kids were laughing and splashing, and Josh was genuinely having a great time. He kept Quinn close, as she was only two and still wearing her water wings, while Jack and Jimmy climbed all over him. He made sure to pay attention to each of them, James had noticed over the last twenty minutes as he'd been standing by the bar, sipping on his own Red Stripe. He'd wanted to watch, to see how Josh did with his family without him. And to James' delight, or dismay maybe, Josh had slipped right into a role James hadn't even known existed before now.

"So, when is Mom gonna meet him?" Rebecca made him jump slightly as she spoke from beside him, a signature pina colada in her hand. She was a beautiful brunette, fit, wearing a blue one-piece that James teased her was mom-ish. She brushed him off, though, embracing her mom curves from bearing three children.

Her question caught him off guard, a lie rolling off his tongue before he could stop it. "Maybe Christmas? I've gotta tell them about him first."

"Oh, I already did that. I sent her some pictures." James widened his eyes as he turned to her, pulling off his sunglasses.

"Rebecca! I hadn't even—"

"He's playing with my *kids*, James. There was no way I couldn't send her those pictures. Look at them." She gestured across the pool. "She's dying to know when you two are gonna adopt." Rebecca was grinning like she was quite pleased with herself. James was trying to swallow down the urge to panic.

"I wish you'd kept it between us for a while."

"Don't be shy about him, James. Look at him. He's a good dude."

James *was* looking at him, and he knew firsthand how good Josh was. Too bad it was all a charade. James just didn't want to hurt his mother in the lie.

Or at least that was what he would keep telling himself.

* * * *

Days five and six were a whirlwind for Josh. The whole trip had been, if he were honest. The resort was incredible. He had gotten more sun in six days than he'd had in the last six years and drunk more rum in the last six days than he ever had. Rebecca and her family were a joy. They'd taken him in like he was truly dating James. James' staff had done nothing but make Josh feel at home. He'd slept so well, eaten like a king and sketched so much his hand actually hurt. It was a dream come true.

Then there was James.

James was even more charming the longer Josh spent time with him. He was kind, generous, had a sense of humor and was handsome as hell. He was beyond complimentary of Josh in ways Josh had never experienced from a client. It felt far more personal than a client-to-escort relationship. Josh was doing his best to keep the lines from blurring. But every time he had to pretend, it was getting less difficult. *Who am I kidding? It isn't difficult at all.* Other than feeling out of place in James' high-end world, Josh felt at home at the man's side.

It was jarring. But he was doing his best to ignore it.

The sex? That was proving difficult to ignore. They had a compatibility in the bedroom that Josh wouldn't have predicted. The sex was some of the best Josh had ever had. And the fact he got to indulge in it at his every whim? *How did I get this lucky?*

Nadia and Andrew had their reservations. They were in awe of the resort from the pictures Josh send them and of his general vacation, but they had their concerns about the fake boyfriend schtick and Josh's emotions. This wasn't some woman at a high school reunion using Josh to appear young to her friends. This guy was blurring the lines, and his friends warned him to keep himself guarded. *"Remember the money, Josh,"* Nadia had warned him via text on the sixth day. *"Thinking about the money will remind you to be careful."*

Truth be told, the *only* reason Josh had thought about money the whole week was because his mother's mortgage payment was due the week he got back. And this would allow him to pay two months ahead. Otherwise, the ability to be in Jamaica on this trip was enough payment for him.

That hadn't made Nadia feel any better.

Josh slipped his phone back into his shorts pocket as the door to the suite opened to reveal a smiling James. Josh headed in from the balcony to greet him, making sure his sketchbook was closed where it lay on the coffee table.

"Josh! Come with me," James greeted and waved him toward the door. Josh shut the sliding door and made his way toward him, raising an eyebrow.

"Where are we going?"

"You'll see," James replied as he opened the door and held it for Josh. Josh graciously slipped out, murmuring his thanks as he waited for James to lead the way. "I know you brought a suit for the gala tonight, but you've been so amazing in coming here that I really wanted to do something for you to show my appreciation."

Josh glanced toward James, frowning. "I know it's not as nice as yours, but really I don't need—"

"I insist, Josh. The suit *is* nice, but I want to do something for *you* – and I have the means to. Again, you've been so fantastic. I want to show you just how much I've appreciated *everything*." There was suggestion and kindness in James' tone, and Josh flushed so hard that he felt it up into his ears. He didn't receive gifts well. It was one thing to be invited on a trip, something completely different to be showered with presents that cost more than Josh could afford, even with his high-paying escort clients.

They slipped into the waiting elevator and James took them to the third floor and down a long hallway. At the end was the resort shop, which Josh had become familiar with, but James slipped them through a back door and into a much larger portion, full of evening gowns and suits, all set up for trying on. Josh's stomach dropped a little as he looked around at the displays. "We have had several celebrities come in for the event, so I called in a favor to a few designers I've worked with. They're going to set you up for tonight, sparing no expense. They'll take your measurements and find the perfect thing. Shoes, watch, cufflinks, you name it. Whatever you want, it's yours." James raised his hands in a gesture of giving then clasped them in front of him as Josh stood in a stupor.

"James," he stammered, eyes wide, "I can't accept this. You've already been so generous. I'm —"

James shushed him gently with a hand motion, stepping closer and taking Josh's hand in what Josh's rational mind told him was for display only.

"Let me do this for you. *Please*." He was so quiet, so gentle and genuine as he spoke that Josh didn't know how to deny him.

"I-I guess," he managed to get out. "As long as you're sure."

"I'm beyond sure. It's all I want." James grinned, leaning forward to place a chaste but slow kiss to Josh's lips before pulling back. "I'll come check on you in a little while. This is Cherie." He gestured to a beautiful European woman as she joined them. "She'll be assisting you. There is Stella Artois on ice for you over there and some hors d'oeuvres as well. Please enjoy the experience. I promise you're in great hands." He gave Josh one last kiss, smiling still at Josh's stammering thank you before he headed out to do some last-minute things. Josh had been looking forward to tonight for the sake of fun, but *now* he was much more invested. He'd never been fitted before.

"Mr. Roberts, follow me right this way." Cherie smiled and directed him back toward the suits. Josh couldn't help but plan his next text to Nadia and Andrew as he followed. *You will not believe this, guys…*

* * * *

Josh would be lying if he said he didn't feel a little like Cinderella in this moment. Hours after James had left him at the hands of his stylists, he stood showered and dressed in front of the suite's mirror, shamelessly snapping a full-length picture for his friends. The suit was navy blue with a light blue checkered shirt underneath, fitted with a tie, a vest and a pocket square. He was used to looking dapper. That was how he'd picked up James. But this particular suit cost more than Josh had made in the previous year in total. And the new watch on his wrist was so beautiful and so expensive that it hurt.

He grabbed his sunglasses and made his way to the door, knowing he needed to meet James down in the holding area in ten minutes. There was a ribbon-cutting ceremony, a toast, a live band, dancing and dinner. The new common area was being unveiled and opened for the first time and James had spared no expense in preparing for it. Josh had to admire his dedication to his job and his resorts. The man took serious pride in what he did—and it obviously paid off.

Josh felt out of place as he walked up the stairs to the private bar area above the new commons. The sun was beginning to set, and while it was quite warm for the few layers he was wearing, he knew he'd be able to shed his jacket for dancing as soon as the band started. Fans blew a light breeze from all directions as Josh reached the top of the marble staircase, three flights up with an incredible view of the mountains of Jamaica. He was busy looking around when a waiter handed him a glass of champagne. He took it graciously and caught sight of James a few feet away, chatting animatedly with whom Josh figured were celebrities or investors. He was dressed slightly more casually, but he was handsome as ever. Josh caught himself staring, ripping his gaze away as Rebecca and her husband came up the same set of stairs he just had.

"Hey, guys," he greeted, thankful for people he knew. Rebecca kissed his cheek and Dan shook his hand with a friendly grin. "Rebecca, you look gorgeous. Dan, I really like that suit."

"It's nice to get all dressed up." Rebecca blushed, slipping her arm around her husband's waist as another waiter brought them each a glass of champagne.

"It is," Josh agreed. "James is over there schmoozing." Josh gestured with a fond grin. He could watch James in his element all day.

"He's always been good at that," Rebecca agreed, "ever since college. He's always been able to sway people his way."

"He's very good at what he does…" Josh complimented, his voice drifting off as he watched James laugh.

Soon James was heading their way, stealing a glass of champagne off a tray as he went.

Josh blushed a little under James' direct gaze as he neared, as it was apparent that James was looking over the suit. As he reached them, James ran a hand over the lapel of the jacket, fingering the expensive material. For the first time, Josh noticed a designer platinum ring on James' middle finger. For whatever reason, it made his stomach clench in the best ways.

"They did a number on you," James replied without taking his eyes off Josh—and his cheeks heated.

"They sure went to town. I don't think I've ever worn shoes or a watch as nice as this. Any of it, to be honest," he replied bashfully. James just smiled wider.

"You're so fuckin' handsome when you blush like that, dammit," James murmured, sliding his hand up to caress Josh's cheek. Sometimes, Josh realized as he swallowed hard, it was difficult to tell when and *if* James were acting. "You look absolutely gorgeous." He'd said it loud enough for anyone near to hear. Josh wanted to melt. He was so flushed from James' attention.

"So do you, Jamie," he replied, hoping his voice wasn't too husky from his apparent heavy attraction to the man in front of him. James blushed just slightly and nodded. "I mean…thank you," he amended.

"Thank *you*." Before they could go on, James leaned forward and pressed a sweet, closed-lip kiss to Josh's mouth, surprising him a little and making the world fade away. Josh found James' arm and squeezed. It was all far more affectionate than Josh had ever played on these types of trips—all of it had been—but Josh was relishing it. Was this what it was like to have a *real* relationship with someone? God, it had been so, so long, and had he missed it? *Maybe I have...*

He yanked those thoughts from his mind as James leaned back, reaching down to tangle their fingers. Rebecca intruded playfully then, displaying her beautiful sequin gown for her brother, and the night wore on like that — fun and easy.

Josh minded his surroundings, staying close to James, playing it well and effortlessly. The part of the sweet, adoring boyfriend wasn't difficult at all. It was still shocking to Josh, after six days, how well they'd settled in together. Josh never let his mind wander back to those relationship thoughts, however. That wasn't anything he needed to think about now. Getting attached, forming bonds, getting in over his head...*not a good idea*. Especially when James Barnwell was the man he was getting attached to.

The ribbon cutting was a success and a great photo-op. Josh snagged a few photos as he stood by, beaming for James and his latest creation. That wasn't hard, either. James smiled like this was the best feeling in the world. And as his guests toured the new common area, white marble with beautiful fountain pools and lights strung all around, Josh could tell he was marveling in it himself. This was James and his vision, and Josh felt honored to see it.

They chatted along the way together, hand in hand, sipping champagne at first then gin for Josh, whiskey for James. James graciously introduced Josh to each and every person they met as his 'significant other' and Josh wasn't sure he'd ever felt so high on playing pretend.

Dinner was delicious, a plated array of steak, seafood and the island's delicious jerk chicken. James had taken Josh off the resort one day, down the road to a real jerk chicken stand, and ever since, Josh had been obsessed with the food from the island. He'd taken recipe notes with every intention of attempting to recreate it for his roommates.

Josh tried not to think about how the next day the trip would all come to an end.

He didn't drink too much, just enough to loosen his tie, literally, and relax into James' welcoming arm at the table. They sat with Rebecca and Dan, Stephanie and a few other close employees of James'. That helped Josh feel even more at ease.

Stephanie has been a godsend the entire trip, as well. She'd been there for Josh at each and every turn, sweet as could be and just as helpful. She was always in the background, only stepping in when needed, but he'd grown to like her very much. James surrounded himself with a great group of people. Josh, in many ways, felt lucky to be there.

After dinner, a Jamaican band started on the stage, and the large grounds opened for dancing. Josh couldn't resist the urge, and as James excused himself to chat with a few tables, he encouraged Josh to take Rebecca to the floor when she'd asked. With a quick kiss, they parted for the time being as Dan sat back and visibly marveled at his wife, Josh and their antics.

Josh wasn't a professionally trained dancer, despite Nadia's tries, but he had rhythm and wasn't bad on the dance floor. Maybe all that stuff about 'if men were good in bed, they were good on the dance floor' had some truth to it. He didn't know and didn't care. He just followed along with his partners and moved how he felt comfortable. And with Rebecca, it was easy. She was a blast.

They danced until Josh had to shed his jacket, then they danced some more. If this was his last night in paradise and his 'boyfriend' was busy working, Josh was going to live it up alongside James' sister. What better way to keep up the charade?

James had been doing very well. He'd managed to say hello and thank you to everyone who'd attended, eaten dinner then found himself another drink. Not all events went that smoothly. He was trying to figure out how this one had when his eyes landed on Josh and Rebecca dancing hand in hand on the expansive dance floor, laughing and enjoying themselves.

Josh had put him at ease. He saw that now. Normally, he was a reckless, nervous mess leading up to these events, overstressing every detail. Josh had been a pleasant distraction—a *beyond* pleasant distraction to James' normally addled mind. He had given James joy and focus. Honestly, that alone was priceless. James would pay him any amount for such a service.

Service. Something about that word put a sour taste in James' mouth. He tipped his whiskey back to wash it down as Stephanie slipped up beside him, her eyes fixed on the same view.

"It's so nice to see you happy, James." Stephanie pulled James' attention away for a minute, only to make him flush as he turned back toward Josh and Rebecca. "You've been so...relaxed this trip. You should bring him along more often."

Josh spun Rebecca quickly and dipped her, and James had to wonder if there was anything Josh wasn't good at. He contemplated Stephanie's words for a moment as she voiced his personal thoughts. "It's been nice having him here," James finally said. "Thank you for helping him this week."

"That's my job," she replied easily, sipping her champagne. "I'm here to help you, and by extension, that means him. He's so nice too. I like seeing you happy. You deserve someone like him."

James chewed his lip, trying to determine how to reply. While he had absolutely intended for this charade to work, he hadn't intended for his family and employees to create such a bond with the man. Obviously, he hadn't thought that through. That seemed to be a recurring theme, he realized.

As the song ended, Rebecca and Josh laughed their way toward James. Josh caught James' eyes and he'd be lying to say he didn't enjoy the flush that rose in Josh's cheeks every time that happened.

"Did you know your man had such moves?" Rebecca exclaimed through her laughter as they reached Stephanie and James.

"I didn't." James rocked on his heels, grinning. "Seems he's just full of surprises." He said it sweetly, because all the surprises were very, very good ones. Except...

"Come dance with me." Josh took James' free hand, pulling him slightly. James balked immediately.

"Oh no. That's one thing I don't do. I don't dance."

Stephanie, Josh and Rebecca all badgered him, begging him as the band picked up another song. He dug his heels in, shaking his head avidly. "Absolutely not," he pressed. "I don't dance."

"Everyone dances," Josh argued, laughing. James was really beginning to enjoy the sound — not that he'd admit it, though. "Come on. I can carry you through it."

"No way." James stood fast, holding Josh's hand but unrelenting. "You go on. Keep on dancing. I'll just keep watching from over here."

Josh stepped forward, and James wasn't sure if it was the drinks or him truly just playing pretend as Josh settled his hand on James' chest, toying with the open section of his white shirt. Suddenly James wanted to get him back to the room sooner rather than later. "Come on, Jamie. It's only me," Josh encouraged, dropping his voice a little and making James' heart rate spike. James licked his lips, his focus flickering from those icy blue eyes to Josh's plump bottom lip. Sucking on it had become one of James' favorite things to do in the throes...

While Josh's sultry words pulled at him, he wasn't about to get out there and make a fool of himself. "As much as I want to"—he stepped closer and slipped his arm around Josh's waist—"and I do, I don't dance. No good at it and not ready to make a fool of myself," he admitted quietly to Josh. Josh's grin was wide and sweet, his cheeks once again a little flushed.

"Fine. Maybe later then," Josh negotiated, and James couldn't help but chuckle.

"Doubtful. But you're cute when you beg, so we'll see."

Stephanie and Rebecca both raised their eyebrows while Josh stepped closer, their chests pressed together as he murmured for only James to hear, "We'll see who's begging later, won't we?" He leaned in and stole a kiss that stopped James from breathing before the world continued to spin on. Josh took Stephanie's hand and led her out to the floor. James laughed to cover his falter as he and Rebecca watched them go.

"So, when's the wedding?" Rebecca asked coyly. James shot her a glare, and she raised her hands in surrender. "What? That's the man you should be marrying. Just wait until Mom meets him. She'll propose for you."

* * * *

"James, I haven't had that much fun at a party in *years* — maybe ever. That was a blast!"

Josh laid his expensive suit coat over the back of the couch, still smiling from exhilaration. They'd slipped away as the party had dwindled a little after midnight, hand in hand down the lighted walkway. It felt like a dream — a dream Josh didn't want to wake up from the next morning, when he had to pack up and fly home, going back to his regular life.

James sipped his cocktail and grinned, taking a seat on the couch and propping his feet up on the coffee table. "I'm very glad you enjoyed yourself," he replied sincerely, enjoying Josh's high mood. "You were the life of the party. My sister adores you."

Josh threw a smile over his shoulder as he fussed with the stereo. "Rebecca is fantastic. Her whole family is. You're lucky to have such a cool sister." Josh clicked along on his phone until a song began to play that James recognized. Josh set his phone down and turned, undoing his tie as his hips began to sway. "Up."

James cocked his head curiously and narrowed his eyes. "Why?"

"You said you don't dance. I don't believe you. So I picked a song from your era, old man. Get up. We're dancing."

"I was born in the seventies. This song is older than me." James flushed a little and played offended as he watched the way Josh moved to the sensual beat. He clearly *felt* the music and was very sure of himself, which was no surprise to James, knowing how Josh was behind closed doors.

"Whatever… Come." Josh extended his hand, using those mesmerizing blues to pull at James' resolve. He swayed in front of him, singing the words softly until James couldn't stand it anymore. He stood, his mouth in a thin line as Josh pushed the table out of the way. He stepped closer, appraising Josh as he continued to try to appear unimpressed. It was difficult when Josh moved like that.

"You're drunk," James teased with a straight face. Josh laughed, rolling his eyes.

"A little. I prefer to call it 'feeling good'." Josh took James' free hand and pulled him closer, pressing their hips together.

"You youngsters," James rasped, trying desperately to keep his stoic appearance. It was now even harder. Being this close to Josh did more to him than he wanted to admit.

"If you want me to call you *daddy*, all you have to do is ask," Josh replied slowly, wrapping his other hand around James and moving them in sync. James didn't fight him. He couldn't. But he did groan deep in his throat at Josh's words.

"You're playing with fire, pretty *boy*," he taunted, watching the way Josh's eyes darkened, the ice blue turning to something of a midnight color. He tightened his hands and arousal pooled in James' belly. How had it become this natural between them? He didn't bother to think about it as Josh brushed his nose with his own.

"You think I'm pretty?" Josh asked quietly, seemingly staring into James' soul. He held the eye contact as he replied easily.

"Oh, Josh," James whispered, forgetting about the song and the dancing, solely focused on Josh now, "I couldn't take my eyes off you tonight—on the dance floor, at dinner, the entire night. You are far more than pretty." He was completely sure and sincere in his words. And the way Josh blushed was entirely worth it.

"Jamie," Josh whispered, as he ghosted a kiss over James' lips. James chased it, addicted and *needing* it. They played the game for a very short moment before Josh indulged him, all dancing forgotten as their lips and tongues meshed together perfectly.

James pulled at Josh's collar as Josh pushed James' jacket off his shoulders. It was quick, messy and the definition of rushed as their passion ignited a fire between them that could only be tamed with their naked bodies touching. James had no recollection of setting his glass down or where the condom and lube had come from. Josh had him naked expertly fast, Josh's mouth on his cock before James could comprehend how quickly the dynamic had changed. It was a flurry, heated and rushed. *How lovers behave*, James' wrecked mind told him as he fucked his cock up into Josh's hungry mouth. Josh swallowed him down as slick fingers teased his hole, and God, he didn't want this trip to end. Parting ways the next day was going to be painful.

And as Josh slid his cock into James slowly, praising him just like he had all week, James wondered how long he could possibly go without feeling Josh's hard length inside him, without tasting those lips, sucking on that plump bottom one he'd unknowingly gotten attached to? He gripped Josh's ass as he thrust into him over and over, not caring who heard their moans or James' submissive cries. He only cared that Josh heard them and that they spurred on the rapid thrusts, driving him closer toward his explosive end.

And as Josh groaned those sweet words about how *good* James felt, about how *tight* he was and about how *hard* Josh was going to come…well, no one needed to know James was burning every bit of that into his memory. He'd play the charade he'd created outside the bedroom, but inside was another story—one he wasn't ready to write just yet.

Chapter Four

"James, I just can't believe you let me find out from your sister. It wasn't like he's *new*. Six months is so good for you, honey."

The Miami sun beat down on him, despite it being the beginning of November, and James wished he'd declined her lunch invitation. The intercoastal restaurant was the perfect place for Saturday lunch. The view was phenomenal and the food casual. But it was far too early for how much this conversation made him want to drink.

Mostly because if he didn't subdue himself, his smile would be far too wide and maybe he'd let himself forget how he was lying to his mother and he'd focus on how actually fantastic Josh was. And selling his mother on his fake beau was not hard. Rebecca had already done all the work anyway. Maggie Barnwell was now just demanding more pictures and details — specifically the ones about major lifelong commitments.

"Mom," James whined to his mother the way children did, no matter their age. "We're not there yet. When I'm ready, I'll bring him here. I'm not ready." He sighed, sipping his unsweetened tea and offering his mother a smile that hopefully she'd interpret as secretive.

She sighed as well, though in a much more frustrated fashion. "Honey, I'm just so ready for you to settle down. Look at your sister. I just want you to have that too."

James stared out over the water for a moment, contemplating his mother's words and his life — and this lie. And he wondered briefly, for the fortieth time since nine that morning... *What is Josh doing right now?* It had been almost a week since they'd returned from Jamaica, Josh flying home to NYC out of Sangster International as James'd had his private jet take him to Miami for work. He entertained the question for a moment then shoved the thought away once more, determined not to think about how — and maybe with whom — Josh was spending his time.

* * * *

"Thanks for helping me, Josh," Nadia called over her shoulder across her bedroom as she turned on her Bluetooth speaker. Josh nodded, tapping his thigh with his fingers as he chewed his lip.

"No problem. Which client is this again?"

"That older guy from Queens. The burly one. I *think* I mentioned him? Anyway, he's super into my dancing and basically all but begged for this, so I had to come up with something. You're the perfect guinea pig. Andrew would just get weird."

Nadia stepped away from the speaker as a familiar, older song began to play, and suddenly her attire made sense. Black top hat, high heels, little black dress, his own sport coat that he wasn't even sure how she'd acquired prior to the performance she was beginning. A dancer at heart, she had the movement of someone who had spent years in the studio. Watching her wasn't a chore.

Watching her hips swaying, her movements suggestive, Josh wasn't immune to her beauty. He'd be lying if he said it didn't make him think of James and their last night together in Jamaica. Something about feeling James against him, the way they moved and remembering it, licked heat up Josh's spine. It didn't help as Nadia grew closer, her dance moves practiced as she shed layer after layer, keeping the hat and shoes on.

He'd agreed to help her in hopes it would get his mind off the lack of James in his life right now. A week home from Jamaica and regular life had continued. He'd had four clients that week, three of whom he'd canceled to travel, and now Nadia and her ridiculous lap dance. Still, James fluttered to the forefront of his thoughts. His jaw tight, fingers flexing on his thighs, he refrained from touching her as he imagined the roles being reversed with him and James for a brief moment. He mentally berated his cock for rising to the occasion and wished his thoughts and the dancing would cease and give him a reprieve.

Instead, Nadia drew his focus back solely to her as she sat down on his lap, rolling her hips forward and making him gasp at the friction. He grabbed her ass, gripping hard as he all but growled, "I'm not supposed to be the one seduced by this."

"Don't fight it." Her voice always got a little deeper, a little raspier when she was turned on, and Josh couldn't deny that he liked it. The feel of her in his arms reminded him that it had been a while since they'd messed around between clients, and if he allowed himself to even think about it, it had been Jamaica since he'd last had a truly *satisfying* orgasm. Maybe she could help him with that, since he'd helped her with her practicing. "You're always good at getting me off."

He gave in to her at that, finding her neck as he cradled her head with one hand and wrapped the other around her back. Her breathy moans were just the evidence he needed to know she was enjoying it, and he didn't stop, simply indulging her as she rotated her hips increasingly faster on his lap.

Josh couldn't deny his erection. While he could get hard for his clients, getting hard for someone he was comfortable with — Nadia, or James apparently — was infinitely more satisfying. He didn't allow his mind to ever entertain the idea of having James whenever he wanted, because it was far from realistic. But Nadia was here, and she knew what he liked because they'd practiced on one another more than was probably normal for platonic friends.

He also chose to ignore how much James had been entering his thoughts recently, blaming their week-long proximity for that issue and nothing more.

"Come on, Josh," Nadia coaxed, nipping at a particularly sensitive spot on his neck, making him groan, "That's all you've got? You've gone soft."

He was suddenly aware of his phone vibrating behind them on the dresser by the door and *what if it's...* He raised his head awkwardly and it almost made their faces collide. "I gotta get that. It's probably a client." He suddenly realized the situation he'd gotten himself into with her. His face flushed as he looked at her, frowning.

Nadia rolled her head back like she knew exactly what he was thinking. "You're distracted. Look at you," she fussed. "You *have* gone soft."

"I am not distracted. I am *busy*, and I need to get that."

"Mmm-hmm, sure," she replied coolly, sliding off his lap. "Keep telling yourself that."

"I don't need to tell myself anything," he snapped at her, standing. He grabbed his phone as he looked at her expectantly. "I know exactly what I'm doing, and I'm sorry you seem to think you need to question me about it."

"Maybe I do." She shrugged. "Someone needs to make sure your head is still in the game."

"Are you fuckin' serious?" He grumbled, unlocking his phone as he opened her bedroom door. Andrew was passing by just then, with his own unamused look.

"Guess James Barnwell didn't make too big an impression, huh?" he quipped as he continued down the hall. Josh let out a loud sound of frustration, looking up at the ceiling and praying for strength.

"What the fuck? You too?" It was rhetorical as he all but stomped off to his room like a petulant child, annoyed at the fact that his friends seemed to think he was falling for James. The fact that Nadia had tried to seduce him to prove he wasn't falling for James had him feeling used, and that was saying something, considering his job *was* to be used.

Slamming his door, he focused on that fact as he turned on his shower and his television to distract himself. He was undressed by the time he realized he'd never checked his phone. Josh grabbed it and unlocked it again.

He would *never* tell Andrew or Nadia the way his stomach swirled and tightened at the name on the screen above the word 'iMessage'.

He clicked the message, holding his breath because he was sure James had said he'd been in Miami until he went to Italy.

Hi, Josh. I hope it's okay I'm texting you. I wanted to see if you'd be available on Wednesday night. I'm flying up for a few meetings and would like to get an appointment with you if you have anything open.

Then, moments later…

Thursday would even work if you're not available Wednesday.

Josh stared at the messages, chewing his lip and slightly aware he was blushing hard for no reason. The angst over Nadia dissipated for a moment as he typed and re-typed at least five responses.

Hi, James. You can text anytime. Sorry for the delayed reply. I'll check my calendar and get right back to you.

He sent the text and clicked away to check his iPhone calendar. He cursed as he was free Thursday and not Wednesday. He would rather see James earlier, he thought, ignoring how unprofessional that thought was.

I can make either day work. Whatever is best for you!

The man had paid his way to Jamaica then paid him an exorbitant amount of money just to be there. No one paid him like that. He could call the shots. Josh didn't mind moving things around.

He got a text right away, as he stood naked and waiting to hear. His cock twitched as he read the reply.

Wednesday would be perfect. I'll send my driver to pick you up at six p.m. Make sure you're hungry for dinner. I've got a craving for DeGrezia's and I'm making you eat it with me. He ended with a wink emoji.

Dinner would be a good thing—and not out of the ordinary for his clients. DeGrezia's was really nice. His phone buzzed in his hands with another message.

We're eating in, though, so don't worry about dressing up.

Josh grinned as he typed back.

Not gonna give me an excuse to wear that suit again?

It was teasing and slightly flirtatious. As he hit send, he immediately wanted the message back for rewording. Swallowing hard, he followed it up.

Anything in particular you want to explore? Any kinks I should come prepared for?

Ugh. Awkward at best, but also a professional question for his job. Immediately, the typing bubble appeared, and Josh waited anxiously for the reply.

By all means, wear the suit. You know you look damn good in it. Sure wouldn't bother me any — another wink emoji. *Surprise me with something you think I'd like. I'm starting to feel adventurous.*

Adventurous, huh? Josh knew just the thing. His cock twitched again as he replied.

I've got an idea already. I think you'll like it. I look forward to Wednesday. Maybe I'll wear the suit. He ended with his own winking emoji.

These fucking emojis made him blush harder. James wrote right back.

I'm looking forward to it too. Glad you were available. One more emoji.

Josh wanted to type back 'Me, too', but it didn't feel right. So he left it at that, wishing his cock wasn't thinking about all the things he could do to James in three short days. He also had to move that one client, but that wasn't a big deal. He ignored the irrational guilt and irritation over Nadia as he showered and played with himself slowly, purifying his issues with thoughts of Wednesday.

As if *that* wasn't an oxymoron — and also completely inappropriate.

No one had to know. Even Josh wasn't sure how much he was allowing himself to know. He was a mess.

He chose to ignore that too.

* * * *

Nice jeans and a navy sweater — not too formal but not too casual. Brown cognac dress shoes gave the outfit a little something. Josh studied himself in the mirror and wasn't even sure why he cared so much, but alas, he did. It was Wednesday and the car would be downstairs in ten minutes. He needed to gather his things and slip his coat on. This late autumn cold was getting to be a bit much. They were forecasting snow on Friday. Maybe James would be forced to stay a few more days and need Josh's services.

He was putting the cart before the horse and he knew it as he dismissed those thoughts. Slipping on the warm jacket, he grabbed the duffel bag he'd packed for this particular evening. Nadia was already out on a job and Andrew was preoccupied reading a book, so he and Josh only exchanged a wave, which was a relief to Josh. He hadn't told them James was back in town and that he'd made another appointment. He didn't need them giving him any more of a hard time.

When he got downstairs, the Mercedes town car from the last time was waiting out front. An older man stood next to it, patiently waiting. This was his ride.

"Mr. Roberts?" the man questioned. Josh nodded as he approached. "Paul. I'll be your driver this evening." He shook Josh's hand and pulled open the door to the running car. Josh thanked him kindly and slid inside, noticing once again how warm the seats were. James had literally spared no expense. It was still impressive to Josh.

Josh fiddled with his phone as they weaved through the streets to James' home. Nerves filled his belly. It hadn't been long at all since they'd last seen one another, and yet it felt like a month. As the car pulled to a stop, Josh glanced up at the warmly lit townhouse.

It was the kind of place someone like him only dreamed of owning. He felt pretty lucky to get to spend a little time there, no matter the reason.

Paul pulled open his door and Josh thanked him again. He stepped down to knock on the familiar entrance. It swung open almost immediately, revealing a bearded, tanned James Barnwell. Miami had done James good, Josh immediately realized.

James' gaze roamed him quickly as a smile broke across his face. "Josh! It's good to see you. Come in!"

Josh tore himself away from staring at the man. He floundered for a moment then a smile stretched across his own face. "Hey, Jamie," he replied easily, not even aware as the nickname slid off his lips. It had become natural in Jamaica. He stepped inside with his bag, turning toward James as he closed the door. "It's good to see you too. I—"

He was cut off as James turned and pressed his lips to his. It was shocking at first. Josh was completely unprepared as his back hit the wall behind the door. But he was quickly kissing back, having missed the taste of James, the feel of his body. His own body roared to life, heat rapidly filling his veins as he dropped his bag and held on to James, wrapping his arms around him.

James gripped Josh's shirt under his coat and held him against the wall. Josh couldn't help himself as he groaned into James' mouth, his brain clouded by the overwhelming need for this kiss that he'd had since he'd left Jamaica. No one needed to know that, but he felt it to his very core.

Gathering back some semblance of control, he slid his knee up between James' thighs, rubbing him just the way Josh knew James liked. And as Josh knew he would, James moaned into the pressure. He settled into the fact that this was James and not Nadia or any other client. This almost didn't have to be a game for him. It came naturally. It scared the shit out of him, too, but he refused to acknowledge it.

It also helped soothe the wound Nadia had left — no matter how right she apparently was. Nope. He wasn't acknowledging that, either.

James rocked into his thigh, and Josh let out a shuddering gasp. He could feel how hard James was already and it drove him wild to know it was all for him. He'd caused this reaction, to some degree. While Josh was practiced in getting an erection for someone he wasn't attracted to, James was not. This hardness was his tonight and his own cock throbbed with need.

Pulling back after furiously kissing and rocking together for several moments, Josh marveled at James' wrecked look already. His eyes took a minute to open, their pupils blown. His lips were red and swollen as they parted to his breaths, and Josh's face burned from James' beard — but he didn't care. He'd take that burn anywhere on his body, had yet to feel it anywhere. Not that he minded, but a guy could dream…

He reached for James' belt, anxious to drop to his knees. He locked eyes with James as he began to undo it, but as he moved to slip down, his jacket even still on, James stopped him with a gentle touch to his arm. His face was still flushed but his expression was softer.

"Let's eat first…then play," James suggested quietly, a slight rasp to his voice. Josh blushed hard, having been so forward, and he fixed James' belt.

"Dinner. Right." He nodded with a shy smile. "Y'sure know how to distract a guy," he let out before he could stop it. He didn't miss the blush that rose in James' cheeks—a new hint of pink.

"It wasn't my intention, but then you walked in and I—" James stopped himself, drifting off as he rubbed the back of his neck. "Anyway, let me take your coat. I had take-out delivered and set up in the sitting room," he explained as Josh slipped his coat off his shoulders and handed it to him. James took the bag too, setting it aside at the bottom of the staircase. He then gestured to Josh to follow. "I hope you don't mind. It's just that when it gets cold like this, the fire feels nice. It's gas, not real like we'd get up in a cabin in Northern New York, but it does a nice job heating the small room."

Josh tripped up on so many words as James spoke— *sitting room, fire, a cabin?*—but he listened and followed, taking in parts of the townhouse he hadn't yet seen. It was still very beautiful, and with the lights dim, it felt cozy. And James was right. The fire did give off a fair amount of heat. The table was set, and Josh was about to speak when an older woman stepped around the corner, carrying a bottle of red wine. He blinked.

"Mr. Barnwell, your food is staying warm in the oven. I found that bottle of red wine you were looking for earlier." The woman was clearly from New York based on her accent. Josh estimated her to be his mother's age. As James took the bottle and thanked her, it was with surprise and a heat to his cheeks that he realized she worked for James—as a housekeeper or maybe a butler? Josh wasn't sure, but she was dressed as an employee and had obviously been rooting around somewhere for this particular bottle of wine, which Josh realized was very expensive.

Josh smiled pleasantly as her attention flickered to him. She gave him a warm smile and surprised him by winking at James. "I'll leave you two to your evening, Mr. Barnwell. Call me if you need anything. It's nice to have you home for a few days."

James' chuckle was genuine as he turned to watch her leave, "Thank you, Maggie. Are you ever going to call me James?"

"Not in this lifetime, Mr. Barnwell. Goodnight!" she called out in a sing-song, playful tone before the front door closed and locked. James turned back to Josh, grabbing his corkscrew.

"Maggie is my butler. She keeps up with this place whether I'm here or not—waters the plants, laundry, the whole thing," James explained as he opened the wine and began to pour two glasses. "I hired her when I first moved back to New York years ago. She's amazing. But she always calls me Mr. Barnwell and it just…makes me crazy." He shook his head with a laugh and Josh marveled at this man and his world for a moment.

"Probably just keeping it professional," Josh suggested lamely because he had no idea why she'd still call James that after years of service. James shrugged as he set the bottle down and picked up the glasses, handing Josh his.

"Probably. I just feel like I should know her better, y'know? She's been in my life longer than…anyone personally. She's seen me on some bad days. She has four daughters and never had a son. Sometimes I think that's why she mothers me the way she does from time to time."

"She only works for you?" Josh inquired.

"Oh yeah. I make sure she's well taken care of," James explained without hesitation. "I take care of the people closest to me." They maintained eye contact for an extended period of time, Josh trying to come to grips with what exactly that meant before a timer from the kitchen interrupted them. Josh jumped slightly, unprepared for the noise. "Oh! Let me get our food. Have a seat. I'll be right back." James started for the kitchen.

"Can I help? I can—"

"No, I've got it! You sit. You're my guest."

Josh wasn't sure if he should overstep and insist or listen, so he sipped his wine and settled down at the table in front of the fire. It was a table big enough for four but with a setting only for two. A black linen cloth with red napkins covered the table. He unfolded one and set it on his lap as he leaned back in the comfortable chair. He considered his evening, because *this* was unusual for him. His clients occasionally offered a drink or took him out to dinner as a showpiece, but they didn't wine and dine him before sex. He was still trying to decipher what was happening when James returned with a basket of warm bread and a plate of crispy calamari and sweet pepper rings. Josh's mouth watered. This was *definitely* welcome, he decided, regardless of what was the norm.

"So, whenever I'm in town, I *have* to eat at DeGrazia's," James began as he set down the food and settled himself in the chair across from Josh. "But since it's cold tonight, I figured we would eat here." He raised his glass, grinning so brightly that it made Josh's stomach flip.

He smiled too, just as wide, since James' smile was completely contagious. He raised his glass as well.

"To your schedule being clear tonight. And to a successful trip to Jamaica. I honestly couldn't have done it without you."

Josh let their glasses come together as he pondered that statement. He let it float between them as he sipped his wine. "It was honestly the best vacation I've ever had. I can't thank you enough." Josh's cheeks heated as he ducked his head slightly. "I'm glad I could be there for you," he added as he glanced up shyly.

James was gazing at him intently and with such utter kindness that Josh floundered inwardly. "I'm so glad I could give you such a good vacation. I hope you were able to relax as much as you wanted to."

"God, I was," Josh answered quickly, before shutting his mouth abruptly. He cleared his throat and ran his hand over his lips as James looked on with sweet amusement. "I mean, it was hardly work. Honestly. I felt relaxed and enjoyed every minute."

"Maybe you'd be interested in joining me in Italy for two weeks then?" James asked the question like he was asking Josh to pass the bread, and Josh gaped a little. James was busy serving himself calamari, but when he looked up, he immediately jumped to amend his invitation. "I mean, my staff thinks I have this boyfriend now, and it's a really important trip for me. You helped me so much in Jamaica, keeping me sane, and you know I'd pay for every expense. There'd even be time to sightsee if that's what you're worried about..."

Josh watched James ramble, the confident man of moments ago suddenly nervous and making Josh feel a little less so. *Italy? For two weeks?* It was the chance of a lifetime. He couldn't say no. Not to mention that he didn't *want* to say no.

"Absolutely," he replied after a brief moment of silence as he processed the invitation "I'd love to go to

Italy with you. Are you sure, though? I don't want to be a burden. I—"

"You're so far from a burden, Josh. Please. I really want you to come…if you want to."

Something about all this suddenly seemed so intimate to Josh. *"I really want you to come"* had made Josh's heart leap in a way it wasn't supposed to over a client. That was all James was, a client. He had to remember that.

It became increasingly difficult, however, as dinner went on. James talked about the trip to Italy and what it would entail. They'd fly over together this time— same fake relationship, same sexual arrangement. The money he offered Josh was obscene. Josh would have to cancel more than half a dozen clients, but it wouldn't matter financially. And when James was in meetings, he'd be able to explore and draw. It sounded like a dream, especially because the sex was so easy. Nothing about being with James was hard.

They shared chicken marsala and chicken piccata for dinner, with salads and vegetable sides. The food was decadent and to die for. The conversation centered around James, his recent visit to Miami and a silly scandal the local South Florida tabloids had posted about him. It wasn't true, and James took it all in stride, but Josh was entertained.

Josh ate more than he should have, he decided. James was right there with him, though, and they were both full as they settled down on the couch in the same room, having moved the table that apparently actually belonged elsewhere. Josh realized somewhere in the back of his brain that James had done that for *him. What world am I in?*

The couch was comfortable as they sipped their wine. The conversation had dwindled, but it was easy silence until James cleared his throat, seeming to be searching for words. "So…what's in your bag?"

Josh had forgotten all about his bag until that moment, slight heat blooming over his cheeks. "I'll tell you," he began, twirling the very nice wineglass in his hands, "but first let me say thank you for dinner. You didn't have to do all that."

"I wanted to. Trust me," James assured him quickly. "You deserve to be treated like that. But I'm dying to know what's in the bag."

Josh really enjoyed this about James — his curiosity and openness in bed. "Well" — Josh tried to focus on work — "I had a few ideas when you said adventurous." He licked his lips, nibbling on his bottom one. "I brought silk ties for your wrists and a pair of black panties I picked out just for you, because I know you'd look so fuckin' pretty in them."

Josh had expected that James would blush at the words but seeing it was so much more satisfying. James lit up, his cheeks bright, even in the dim light, and he chewed his own bottom lip, a tell he had for nerves.

"Panties, huh?"

"Mmm-hmm. If you don't want to wear them, I'll wear them instead. There's one other thing, too, but I'll need your explicit consent — and none of them will leave with me," Josh urged, turning to face James a little more on the leather sofa.

"Okay…" James motioned for Josh to keep talking as he sipped his wine.

"I brought a Polaroid and figured I'd take a few photos of you all tied up and looking pretty."

James blushed crimson, and Josh grinned. *Yes.* He was in. "I mean, I've never done that before, but..."

"You've never done any of this before," Josh reminded him gently. Suddenly the fullness from dinner was gone and replaced by a new hunger for James.

James chuckled a little as he shifted. The man was aroused. It seemed that not only did praise arouse the man, but so did the unknown. James was too much fun. "I-I guess you're right. I mean...if you want to. If you think I look good enough for that..."

"You *definitely* look good enough for that," Josh assured him with a low voice and a pointed look. James didn't need to know the copious number of drawings Josh now had of him.

"I probably shouldn't have eaten so much." James laughed, and Josh couldn't help but join in.

"I'm sure those abs will only benefit from the food." James kept a clean diet most of the time and worked out hard. His body would look just *fine.*

"Well, where are these panties? I should put them on, right?" James asked shyly and Josh saw James slip into his sweet, submissive role, right before his very eyes. Their dynamic turned him on just as much as James himself did.

"Follow me," Josh urged, setting his wine down and reaching for James' hand. James put his own wine aside, took his hand and followed. Josh absorbed James' warmth as they walked to the stairs and the waiting duffle bag. He only released it to open the bag and pull out the small, lacy scrap of material. It was a boy-short cut but made to fit a man of their size. James eyed it and Josh could tell he was shy and unsure. "No pressure, Jamie. We don't have to do anything you don't want to…ever. Okay?"

The gentle reminder seemed to soothe the older man. He chewed his lip and took a deep breath, taking the garment from Josh. "I'll go put it on. Give me a few minutes?" He looked so shy, which didn't suit the beard he wore at all. It made Josh's cock throb suddenly — and hard.

"Of course, sweetheart. Take your time. I'll finish my wine and be up shortly."

Josh leaned in to kiss him and James met him halfway. It was sweet and tender, but the wanting was just below the surface. He hoped it reassured him that this was okay, that this would be fun. He had James' best interests at heart. He'd take great care of him. He always would. It was his job

But it was also so much more than that now.

* * * *

James stared at himself in a full-length mirror in his closet. He was naked save for the lacy black boy-shorts that hardly covered his ass, let alone his full length. He was half hard simply from anticipation. He'd turned up the heat just slightly for comfort before he'd gotten undressed, and he was glad for it now. It helped…a little.

Josh Roberts sure knew how to put a confident man on the edge of uncertain territory.

The thing about it was that James trusted him. He trusted him to make sure this didn't go downhill. He trusted Josh to know what he was capable of. He was indeed ready for more. He wasn't sure *this* was what he'd meant when he'd thought about more, but he was willing to try this—all of what Josh had planned.

He had to give himself credit. He didn't look that bad. His Adonis belt abs slipped into the panties, his chiseled chest on display. If he was gonna wear them, at least he didn't look horrific.

He padded quietly out of the bathroom, running a hand through his wild hair. He'd mussed it as he'd paced prior to actually putting the little things on. He didn't really care. It was hardly something to be worried about when someone was about to tie him down and photograph him.

He knew he could say no—but he didn't want to. He'd charge through the nerves and let Josh show him a good time. He always did.

That was the real issue about all this that James was having a hard time confronting directly. Josh was becoming a problem. The man had become someone James needed. It wasn't hard to invite him in, to laugh with him. He was charming, sweet and when he blushed...it made James want to do it more, more than he was ready to even comprehend.

He would also continue to ignore the fact that by taking Josh to Italy, he was compromising his time. He would also continue to ignore the fact that if this man left him to sleep with other people, it was his job. It didn't matter if it didn't sit well with him when he considered it—so he ignored it and paid him a lot of money, a lot more money than he asked to be paid, to take him away from that for a while and have him all to himself. Thank goodness he didn't have anyone to tell him how wrong that was.

A soft knock came on the doorframe of the bedroom as James was just reaching the side of his bed. He stopped and took in Josh's eyes, which were wide as he seemed to be taking in James' new attire. James rubbed the back of his neck, feeling those eyes on him heavily and everywhere. "It fits."

"It sure as fuck does," Josh replied in a raspy tone that sent a chill up James' spine.

James flushed hard. "How... Where do you want me?" he asked as he ducked his head and looked up shyly through his lashes. Josh set his bag down as he rounded the bed toward him. Sometimes he was shocked by how easy this all came.

Josh stopped before him and James was surprised to feel his fingers along the lace trim at the top of the panties. They toyed with the material, not pulling or adjusting, just touching and caressing. James had been half hard in anticipation, but the small touches made his erection grow fully. He groaned quietly, letting his eyes fall shut as Josh gripped his balls through the fabric, caressing them.

"Lie on the bed, head on the pillows, arms above your head. I'm going to tie you down by the wrists," he explained quietly against James' ear. "The ties are silk. They're not easy to break but they won't hurt you either. Traffic lights tonight, okay? Once you're tied, I'm going to take some Polaroids and play with you. You're too fucking gorgeous not to play with."

James shivered and found himself thrusting into Josh's hand fully, groaning when he pulled away. He opened his eyes slowly and was surprised to find Josh staring at him with an utterly gentle gaze.

"Tell me that's everything you want, Jamie. Tell me so I can get my hands on you properly. I'm dyin' to." Josh's pinched eyebrows and needy expression told James that he'd meant his words. It filled him with a confidence that he didn't know he had to do this and made him desperate to see that expression more.

"Yes," he breathed. "God, yes. Please. It all sounds like just what I wanted, Josh."

"You're so good to me, Jamie," Josh replied quickly, leaning in to steal a kiss James was beyond ready to give him. It only lasted a few seconds before Josh pulled away, his expression dark with arousal. James shivered again. "On the bed, baby — on your back."

James didn't hesitate, pulling the comforter off and climbing onto the heather gray sheets. He hadn't planned it, but he knew now that the panties would stand out. Josh seemed very pleased with that as he grinned and approached with black silk in his hands.

"Arms up." James complied immediately, placing his arms where he knew Josh could tie them to his wooden headboard. Josh leaned over him, explaining how much he'd thought about doing this to James, and James wanted to squirm. *He has been thinking about this...* It made James' cock throb.

Being tied tightly to the headboard was a new experience but not one that James disliked. He felt vulnerable and exposed but also warm and comfortable in his own bed with someone he trusted. Josh stripped slowly, down to his own black Calvin Kleins, before grabbing the Polaroid camera. He loaded the small deck of film in, the camera the only noise in the quiet room.

As Josh approached, James' heart stuttered. Josh was all lean lines and chiseled muscles. He'd committed most of them to memory, but it was still something he couldn't get over. Josh's shoulder-to-waist ratio alone still floored him. He chewed his bottom lip as Josh hovered around him, seeming to prepare for the pictures and deciding which angles he wanted. "Close your eyes." Josh murmured it in that voice that James was starting to hear in his dreams. James closed them quickly, being very good at listening these days. "Good boy." He also heard the snap of the camera. The whirring followed and James knew the picture was printing. It was surreal — terrifying and yet exciting. "So fuckin' beautiful," Josh whispered moments later, discarding the picture on the table beside the bed. James cracked his eyes and Josh shook his head with a grin. "Roll your head to the left. Bury your face in your arm — yeah, just like that. God, you're so pretty, Jamie. Shit…" The last word was more of breath as Josh began snapping pictures.

He'd instruct James occasionally — sometimes his eyes open, sometimes shut. When James would squirm, he'd get a tap to his cock. He'd groan and try to hold still. It was exhilarating.

What felt like an eternity later but was probably a mere twenty minutes, Josh was crawling onto the bed, the camera and photos forgotten. "I've got to get my mouth on you, Jamie. I can't wait any longer."

James was a whimpering mess, a strangled 'please' leaving his lips. Anticipation had worn his resolve thin. He needed to be touched. Josh didn't disappoint as he nuzzled his face into the black panties and cupped his balls through the fabric. He shivered and James moved his hips, a groan escaping. James caught Josh's pleading grin and his face flushed. *Yes.* He loved this. There was no question. He was so glad he'd flown home.

Josh mouthed at his straining cock through the fabric. It was hot, wet and simply not enough. James hissed and tried to move so he could encourage something more. A strong arm settled across his hips and he sucked in a breath. "Hold still," Josh admonished with a dark look. James stilled, his heart pounding.

"Please," he whispered. He needed *something, anything.*

"You want me to suck you, fuck you with my fingers?" Josh asked as he lazily pulled James' length from the panties. He cried out at the first graze of his tongue.

"*Fuck...yes...*" He was in so much need that it seemed impossible to wait. Josh seemed to understand as he opened his mouth and engulfed James' length in the warm, soaked heat.

James felt the tear of the fabric more than he heard it, along with the rush of air on his skin as his balls and ass were now exposed. It was so many sensations all at once, but Josh kept a slow rhythm on his cock, simply massaging with his tongue and sucking. James didn't even hear the cap of the lube before there were slick fingers between his cheeks, rubbing his hole experimentally. He jerked, despite his best efforts, widening his thighs and biting his bottom lip with a vengeance. *Yes, right there, right there...*

Josh teased him with one, pressing forward to breach slowly as he sucked his cock harder. James would have been lying to say he hadn't used his toys lately, thinking of Josh the entire time. There was a quick pinch, but he relaxed into it, moaning loudly into the dark room.

He kept his eyes closed, riding down on the finger that stroked him slow and easy. Josh praised him for taking it so well, adding a second finger much quicker than he usually would. James gasped and drove his hips down on them deep. Josh chuckled against his inner thigh and he opened his eyes to find Josh staring at where his fingers were. James' face went hot, and he was feeling almost too vulnerable as Josh stared with great hunger. "Josh," he whined, not even sure what he intended to say.

"Shh-h, I got you, Daddy. Let me just take care of you." Josh's words were almost too much. James felt like an exposed nerve.

Josh took him back into his mouth as he added a third slick finger. He stroked deep, caressing the bundle of nerves that needed it as he sucked hard, relentlessly on James' cock. It was overwhelming. So many things to feel all at once, and *Daddy* rolling around in his head was more than he could handle. He wanted to touch Josh, wanted to run his fingers through that blond hair, wanted to yank it and fuck Josh's face like he liked to do. He writhed beneath the man as Josh began to truly finger-fuck him, hard and rough. He didn't care about the sounds he made, the incoherent words he knew he was babbling. He only cared about the man between his thighs and the heat building in his stomach as his balls began to tighten. If Josh would just stroke that…*oh fuck, oh yes, right…fuck.*

He hadn't meant to go off without warning or permission, hadn't meant to lose his mind. But Josh had pulled him over the edge so quickly and effortlessly that James lost control. He saw stars as he all but blacked out from the pleasure, coming hard and fast down Josh's hungry throat. He felt weightless, boneless and questioned his mortality as he finally stopped yanking on the ties and writhing against the man who was cleaning him up with his tongue. He was oversensitive, overstimulated and in need of a reprieve.

He shuddered with the licks, his heart still racing as he let out a shaky moan.

Eyes still closed, he could hear Josh's praise. "So good, Jamie. Look at you, so beautiful, wrecked like this for me," and, "You came so hard. So fuckin' good. I've missed tasting you." It was so filthy and so beautiful, and James didn't know what to do besides smile faintly as he forced his eyes to open.

Josh untied him and grabbed a bottle of water, urging James to drink. He gulped hungrily as soon as his wrists were free, as Josh discarded the ripped garment. It was surreal as he worked to focus again, and the first thing he saw when he did was Josh's own erection, protruding proudly from the boxer briefs. His face fell.

"You didn't..." he acknowledged. Josh glanced down then back up with a gentle grin.

"This isn't about me, James. It's about you," he replied, kneeling beside James on the bed. "I'll be fine."

"But I want you to. It's...important to me." He stumbled over the last part because it came flying out of his mouth. He hoped Josh just thought it was post-orgasm slurring. Josh was certainly capable of making him do that.

James wasn't ready for Josh to know just how important it was for him to get pleasure from all this too.

"Jamie, I really don't—"

"Come on me," James blurted again, because apparently he had no self-control. He tossed the bottle away and leaned back on his elbows. "Come on my chest, Josh. Let me watch you."

Josh, surprisingly, looked unsure as he stared down at James. "Are you sure you want that?"

"More than anything, Josh. Come for Daddy." His face was so hot as he heard himself saying the words, surprised by how the kink had suddenly blossomed between them once more. "It's not a suggestion. It's a request."

He watched the expressions cross Josh's face — surprise, arousal, acceptance — and something else he couldn't place. Those blue eyes hooded, he nodded and pushed the boxer briefs down to mid-thigh, shuddering as he wrapped a hand around himself.

The view was magnificent. Those lines that ran down his hips to frame his cock... His abdomen tight with the need for release... The dusting of hair and the freckles that lingered from the sun... He was utterly gorgeous as he began to stroke himself. He bit back a moan, but James wouldn't have that. He was getting every ounce of the show he'd asked for.

"Let me hear you, pretty boy," James urged, his gaze dancing from Josh's face to his cock and back. He tried to memorize how Josh touched himself, the way his pointer finger was loose, how his thumb rubbed across the head on every upstroke. It was mesmerizing. "You gonna come on me? Make a mess of me?"

It felt filthy and yet completely natural as he spoke to Josh this way, and he ignored it. All he wanted was to watch Josh's face as he let go. And he was close, his hands shaking, his free hand slipping up to ghost over his own pecs, tweaking a nipple and squeezing it hard. "That's it, sweetheart. Come on. Come for *Daddy*."

Josh broke and James watched it happen. It was beautiful. He cried out and shuddered, his hand stuttering before he spilled all over James' chest. It was a lot, more than he'd thought he'd see, and he couldn't get enough of the view. Josh threw his head back, his eyes closed as he moaned James' name over and over again. An 'Oh, *Daddy*' slipped out in a gasp and James' cock twitched. It was too tired for now, but James would have this man fuck him before he left in the morning. It had to happen.

Josh rocked back on his heels, releasing himself as he panted. He was shiny with sweat in the dim light, and James wished he could reach the camera to take a picture of this glorious aftermath. Josh was wrecked. James wanted to make this a usual thing. It was too beautiful to never see again.

Looking down at his chest, he swiped up a dab of the cum that was all over him. Curious, he stuck his thumb in his mouth. He couldn't help the groan. *Salty, masculine.* He tasted just like he would have expected Josh to taste. He looked up to find Josh watching him with wide eyes, his mouth hanging open slightly. James shrugged, another blush covering his cheeks. "I wanted to know how it tasted."

"I just… Fuckin' hot, sir," Josh stumbled out and James laughed a little.

"Kiss me then clean me up," James replied, adding a playfulness to his tone that came easily. Josh blushed and smiled before leaning down and kissing James so sweetly that James almost forgot they couldn't go again. A few more slow pecks and Josh was adjusting his boxer briefs and slipping off for a towel. James lay back, relaxing into the pillows as Josh returned with a hot towel to clean him up. He tossed it into the hamper and reached for his pants. "Get over here, Roberts." James wasn't letting this man leave. *Absolutely not.*

Josh blushed again and dropped them, heading for the bed. "Yeah, James?"

"You're staying," James replied. "I mean, if you can," he added, hoping he could and not wanting to be pushy.

"Oh, sure I can. I just didn't want to assume…"

"If you come over, you stay. Okay?" James added quietly as he sat up to grab the comforter he'd thrown off earlier. Josh helped him adjust the soft blanket.

"Yes, sir," he replied as he slipped onto the same side of the bed he'd slept on in Jamaica. James wondered if that was how he slept in his own bed. The thought was strange. He pushed it away.

They curled up around each other like they'd grown used to. Josh's head found James' chest and they tangled their long legs together. It was comfortable and familiar. James could feel sleep begging for him already. "Breakfast in the morning," he mumbled, squeezing Josh. "Please stay."

"I'd love to," Josh replied immediately, and James grinned as he drifted off. Finally, a good night's sleep was chasing him. He'd needed this. He'd needed Josh.

Once again, a thought he pushed to the back and a reminder that Italy was only a week away. Then he'd have Josh all to himself for two straight weeks.

Yes.

* * * *

Josh wasn't sure what time it was when he finally woke in the morning. Gray morning light filtered through the curtains and he briefly wondered if the snow had started. It didn't matter to him if it snowed a day early. He had nowhere to be. And he wondered briefly if maybe that meant James would be around an extra day. *Maybe we can spend another night together.*

It was becoming a bad habit, thinking about James like that, but Josh couldn't help it. James was sliding into his everyday thoughts far easier and more frequently than he should be.

Last night hadn't helped. Their evening had been nothing short of amazing in Josh's opinion. He was still floored by the fact that James had asked him to get off and to come all over him. He shivered as he thought about it.

Then there was the middle-of-the-night sex. He'd woken to James stroking him, slowly coaxing his cock to life. He'd been confused at first, the press of soft lips to his neck, the hand on his length insistent. But then James had murmured his name and arousal and need had slammed into him like a runaway train. They'd rolled together until James' back was to his chest on their sides, and with a little prep, Josh had slipped a condom on and pressed into James, fucking him long and slow from behind. They had lain together, their legs tangled, Josh's arms around James as they moved languidly against one another, heat building between them. It had been quiet and sensual, far more than Josh ever did with his clients. James was proving to be a whole other adventure entirely—one Josh needed to keep exploring.

He rolled to his back and blinked, slowly waking more. The bed was so warm and welcoming, but the smell of coffee and bacon was alluring. He heard the shower running, briefly wondering if maybe they could have another round. Those thoughts came to a skidding halt as the door swung open and James' butler, Maggie, stood on the other side, carrying a pile of fresh towels. Josh had pushed up on his elbows and they locked eyes, a knowing smile growing on her face.

"Forgive me, Mr. Roberts. I just wanted to drop these off for you and Mr. Barnwell. Straight out of the dryer. Still warm." She threw him a wink as she set them down outside the door. "I guess you didn't hear me knocking. I didn't mean to startle you. Get back to your sleep, and don't worry about me." She threw him another grin and wink before pulling the door shut again. His heart racing, he flopped back down on the bed and pulled the comforter up. *Having a butler would take some getting used to*, he mused.

Except he'd never have to get used to it because he'd never have a butler. *Don't get carried away, Roberts*, he scolded himself before rushing the thoughts away as the shower shut off and his interest piqued.

James emerged moments later with a towel wrapped around his waist. Josh had spent seven days in a suite with the man, but seeing him in a towel in his own home was a bit unnerving.

He noticed Josh immediately, slowing his gait as he headed for his large walk-in closet. "Good morning, sleepyhead," he greeted, making Josh's cheeks heat. "Sleep well?"

Josh pushed himself up to sit, rubbing the back of his neck. "Sorry I slept so late. You could have woken me. I would have—"

James raised his hand and turned, heading back toward the bed. "Shh-h. None of that. I asked you to stay for breakfast, remember? I was just teasing you." When James reached him, he ran his hands through Josh's bedhead and pressed a kiss to his forehead. It was intimate and made Josh suck in a breath. James continued without missing a beat. But Josh did suddenly feel better about sleeping in. "I made pancakes, bacon and sausage—and coffee, of course," he carried on as he went into his closet to dress.

That will be quite a breakfast, Josh mused silently as he threw his legs over the side of the bed and stretched. "I'm starving. That sounds amazing. Someone really made me work up an appetite," he threw back toward James, glancing over his shoulder to see the man naked in his closet, pausing as he grabbed a pair of jeans. His chuckle carried.

"I may or may not have had to sneak a few bites earlier for the same reason."

Josh let that wash over him, the warmth of knowing what he had done to James. He smiled and stood, finding his bag for a change of clothes he always packed, just in case. "Um…Maggie dropped off extra towels. I guess I didn't hear her knocking and she just opened the door." He straightened up, clothes in hand as James pulled a shirt over his head, his expression gentle and apologetic.

"I'm sorry she saw you. I promise she has the utmost discretion." He made quick strides toward Josh again, looking abnormally casual in a gray long-sleeved button-down and jeans with socked feet. "She doesn't know who you are or anything like that—just that I had you over. Hopefully, that helps?" He gave a lopsided grin that Josh found completely charming.

"Oh, it's fine," Josh assured him, not worried about all that and more about the fact that James had had him to bed. James didn't seem worried, and Josh tried to ignore the pit that stirred in his stomach. Did he have people over often enough that Maggie just ignored them? "I just wanted you to know it had happened."

"She's probably just happy to see I had someone here." James let his eyes roam Josh and a flush extended into his chest. "You're not the worst thing to see in my bed, by any means." James ducked his head and pressed a kiss to Josh's jugular, and Josh briefly wondered if James could feel how quickly his pulse was racing.

And he supposed that answered his worries about there being a lot of people coming through this bedroom. He shouldn't have been relieved by that, but...he was.

"Go ahead and shower if you want." James ran his hand up Josh's thigh to his lower back, settling a firm grip there. Josh felt like a mess in front of this well-put-together man. "I'll be downstairs waiting for you, and we'll figure out all the Italy details before I get Paul to take you home. I've got a few conference calls, or I'd keep you here all day." The last sentence was suggestive, and it made Josh's stomach flip again of its own accord.

"S-sure thing. I'll be down in just a few minutes," Josh began, his body already responding to the touch.

"Take your time, handsome. I'm not rushing you. Enjoy the shower." James dragged his lips over Josh's cheek one more time before heading out of the bedroom with one last smile.

As soon as he was gone, Josh had to close his eyes with a deep breath to find some self-control and balance. He had to rein himself in or this was going to get out of hand—and fast.

And if it already had? Well, he was going to prove Nadia and Andrew wrong and deny it for as long as humanly possible. Maybe forever.

If he could hold it together that long.

Chapter Five

One thing Josh hadn't even thought about was the press. Jamaica had been quiet, no pictures had been taken and James had never done any interviews. Landing in Italy was completely different. He would have appreciated a slight heads-up. Several people were waiting to catch a glimpse of them as they deplaned at the small airport and slipped into a car, though James seemed unfazed. He never let go of Josh's hand. For that, he was grateful.

Apparently, James was well-known there and the Italians seemed to love him, Josh realized as he watched James pose with two young women, the last of several. He couldn't blame them at all. James was sweet and handsome, and why wouldn't they want their picture taken with him? He just hadn't expected any of it.

A quick text to Nadia and Andrew as he waited with security by a private elevator got him an answer.

He does a lot of charity events over there, Google tells me. And a lot more magazine features. Read this article.

She'd sent the link for a Spanish version of *Architectural Digest*. James was on the front, standing before a resort Josh had yet to see, beardless and looking suave as ever. Josh made a mental note to translate the article with an app later.

Andrew chimed too.

Damn, your boy has dated some hot ladies.

Apparently that was what Google was telling him.

Nadia sent back several eye-rolling emojis as Josh pocketed his phone when James approached. He didn't need him finding out he was doing a little research.

"Sorry about that." James grinned as one of his security team members gestured for the stairs up to the lobby. Josh shrugged easily, smiling back.

"No problem… Can't blame them, really." The pit in his stomach was still there, but he mashed it down, adding, "I wouldn't mind a picture with you myself," in a teasing tone. James' grin grew.

"I'm sure we can easily make that happen." The man winked and Josh's stomach tightened in a different way.

"I sure hope so."

They'd flown in together, this time leaving New York on Singapore Air. They'd had a small suite for just the two of them, keeping up the relationship facade. It wasn't difficult at all, because midflight, James had slipped himself onto Josh's lap and kissed him like a starved man. Josh hadn't complained. His thoughts were consumed by this man far more than he'd like to admit. He went into these adventures now without expectation—but James always surprised him in the best ways.

They hadn't had sex on the flight. Well...not entirely. Josh may or may not have coaxed them both to orgasm by stroking them together on his lap, their cocks rubbing deliciously in his fist. Luckily, they'd both packed a change of clothes and no one seemed to care or question it. And Josh considered himself a new member of the mile-high club.

If this business relationship were only ever just that, which Josh was *sure* it would be, he was becoming a world traveler in every way, thanks to it—and wealthy. But that was something he chose to overlook, because when he thought about the money? Well, it put a damper on the high mood James gave him.

If he wished, deep in the dead of night when he was alone, that there was no money involved and James just took him along because he wanted him there? Well, no one had to know about that.

The resort was unlike anything Josh had ever seen. He had felt that way about Jamaica too, but this was something else entirely. As James approached the desk and said hello to the manager, Josh stared out of the windows overlooking the Italian resort. *Il Lusso Invernale* was located in the heart of Puglia, Italy. Josh could see so much of the town and the olive groves, and with a slight turn he could see the Adriatic Sea. It was breathtaking. He already loved it more than Jamaica, and that was saying something, because Josh had *loved* Jamaica.

"Josh," James called, bringing him back to the present. Josh ignored the immediate itch to sketch the landscape. There'd be time for that, he knew, if this trip played out like the other had. "Our villa is ready, if you are." He gave a gentle smile and Josh knew somehow that if he asked for something else, James would grant it to him. But James had his attention at the word *villa*.

"Yeah, sorry." He flushed, taking James' extended hand. "It's absolutely beautiful here," he complimented. James smiled broadly and squeezed his hand.

"This is one of my favorites. Wait until you see the villa. I always stay in this one when I come here. I think you'll like it." Josh knew there was no way he wouldn't, but he simply squeezed James' hand again and let them be led down to another waiting car. Stephanie was there, and Josh had to be honest that he was happy to see another familiar face. She waved excitedly as soon as she saw them.

"Josh! Ahh! I'm so happy you're here!" she exclaimed, and Josh separated his hand from James' as Stephanie approached, all smiles. She was still dressed immaculately, Josh noted, in a pencil skirt and a lovely light-blue blouse. Her heels made her his height but that didn't stop her from jumping into his arms. He laughed heartily, unable to stop himself at the sweet greeting. While he didn't know where he and James stood in their affections sometimes, the way she greeted him was genuine. It was special to him.

"Steph! Hi!" He caught James' grin as the man stood back and watched the reunion while their bags were loaded into the new car. "I'm glad to be here. And I'm glad *you're* here." He was too. She was a ray of sunshine and had been a huge help to him in Jamaica.

"I go everywhere with this guy." She jutted her thumb toward James with a laugh. "And I'm glad to see that it seems you do now too, except I missed you in

Miami. He's so much more relaxed when you're around." Josh set her back down and glanced quickly at James, who was blushing hard behind his expensive sunglasses.

"Well, let's see if I can keep him relaxed here then." He threw her a wink, and she was all smiles. "Then maybe I'll earn myself an invite to Miami."

"God, please!" She laughed and leaned in close, stage whispering, "He missed you, ya know."

Josh's own cheeks heated, and he took a moment to nervously glance at James. They'd hardly communicated while James had been in Miami, and Stephanie was to be none-the-wiser as to their real arrangement. But did that mean James was pretending to miss him? Or was that real? It was the one thing about all this that was making Josh's head spin on occasion. Everything felt confusing.

But James was blushing down into his white cotton shirt under his blazer and Josh had to question what exactly Stephanie had called him on.

"Look at him. He's blushing so hard," she teased before James was swatting at her playfully to quiet her and get her into the car. Josh laughed it off and followed, filing that all away for analyzing later. Maybe he'd text it to Nadia and ask her what she thought.

Or not, he decided, since he was sure she'd still fuss at him about it. He'd have to figure this one out on his own.

The landscape was stunning as they drove. It was exactly as he'd pictured Italy to look, which was like a dream. James' hand was settled in his own, tucked in his lap for the whole short drive as Stephanie chattered on about the week's upcoming events. Josh would only need to attend a cocktail party on Wednesday for some celebrity visitors and a dinner on Friday. The rest of this week was for him to simply sit back and enjoy. James had meetings, a few other stops to make and a few rounds of golf to play with investors and regional directors, but he made a point to promise Josh he'd be around as much as possible. And added, with faux disdain, "I guess when I'm *not* around, you and Stephanie will have to continue being besties so she can torture me with it later."

Stephanie gave them a mischievous grin that made Josh laugh and James roll his eyes. Josh was very thankful for Stephanie once again.

The car came to a stop, and while Josh was not ever prepared for these moments, it seemed, he was beyond unprepared for what was before him.

The driver opened the door, and as he climbed out, he pulled his sunglasses off to get a better, unobstructed view. The house towered before him, three stories and magnificent. It was a masterpiece — all hard lines and neutral colors, inviting in every way. Their suite in Jamaica had been amazing, but this was a whole other level of James' wealth and reach. Josh was about to stay in a *villa* in *Italy* for *two* weeks. He was sure he'd died and was literally in heaven.

"Stunned speechless, huh?" James appeared next to him and Josh could only turn and gawk at him.

"Jamie…this is…"

"This is how I do Italy. Just wait… I'll make sure these two weeks are two of the best you've had yet." The kiss to his cheek caught him off guard, then Stephanie and James were heading for the house, a security detail and concierge following with their bags.

Josh followed in shock. Stephanie had slipped back into work mode, laying out papers on the beautiful kitchen table for James to read over and assess. She was explaining more about the week's events as Josh wandered the expansive house on his own. There were three bedrooms, each with their own bath, including a master with a bathroom built for two, including the shower with two shower heads. The colors were completely neutral throughout, and the view was incredible from the balcony. He couldn't decide what he wanted to sketch first—or where he wanted to fuck James first. He was curious if they'd be rooming together for a brief moment, but as he walked back through the house, he found his luggage already settled in the master bedroom. It made him smile a little brighter than it probably should have.

When he finally arrived back in the kitchen, everyone was leaving. Even Stephanie was saying she had phone calls to return and emails to send. She paused as she passed Josh, wrapping her arm around his waist in an affectionate half-hug. "So good to see you again, Josh. My phone still works here too, so if you need me, call."

"You got it. Thank you." He squeezed her back before she waved goodbye and headed down to the waiting car. Josh realized quickly that they were completely alone then, no more security or concierge. James was gathering up the papers in the kitchen, sorting them as Josh shut the front door, flipping the lock out of habit. It felt a little weird for a moment, but then James looked up at him and gave him one of those smiles, and Josh was immediately at ease once more. "So…it's just us?" he asked, needing to make sure they were alone before he picked the first surface to lay James over.

"Yes, sir," James replied easily, closing the distance between them slowly. "There's a housekeeper who will come in the mornings to make us breakfast, make the bed and do laundry if we need it. But she won't be here until tomorrow at about eight a.m. So until then, pal, it's just you and me."

Josh noticed the way James spoke a little softer as he reached out to touch his chest. His touch made Josh's body temperature immediately rise. Josh wanted to ask if he really had missed him in Miami and if he really was more relaxed when he was around. But the words died on his lips as James met his eyes and murmured a small, "What should we do first, Sir?"

The fact that James slipped into his role so well, so easily, made Josh's cock immediately start to swell. He wasn't ever really sure how these adventures would play out, but it seemed James knew just what he wanted. Josh could follow that lead and take over, no question. He lived for it, honestly.

Josh let his hands slide up James' strong arms, a smile spreading across his lips. "You've been aching to get me alone, haven't you, handsome?" he asked. "The plane wasn't enough for you, was it?"

"Nope," James grinned, though Josh could see the desire in his steel eyes, the hunger. He was already working on Josh's belt. "Need more… That just took the edge off."

"Where do you want to christen first? The kitchen? The balcony? The bedroom? The shower?" Josh had far too many ideas as he turned James and pressed him back against the cool, cream colored stone.

"The balcony," James requested before he leaned forward and pressed his lips to Josh's in a slightly bold move. Josh didn't mind. In fact, he relished that James wanted to kiss him. He kissed back hotly, letting himself taste James' mouth as he loosened James' belt and pants, reaching inside to pleasantly find how hard James was for him already. One stroke and James was mewling beautifully against his lips.

"Good choice. Let everyone hear me claim this tight, hungry ass."

James whimpered against Josh, and it was such a beautiful noise. Josh backed off, pulling his hand away as James whined, this time in disdain.

"Go upstairs, take off your clothes and I'll meet you on the balcony. Touch yourself out there in the sunshine. Get warmed up. I'll find my things and be right out to fulfil your needs."

James' cheeks were flushed as he departed quickly, making his way up the stairs as Josh gathered himself. He counted to twenty slowly before climbing the stairs to find his carry-on bag and the contents he'd packed. He'd bought a new, high quality lubricant just for this trip and he pulled that from his suitcase. James' clothing was neatly laid out on the bed and couldn't help but grin. This man was something else. Josh could not wait to wreck him once more.

* * * *

Waking up next to James was something Josh could easily get used to. There was a comfort about it now after Jamaica and New York that made it even more enjoyable. Josh knew how he looked, his hair and beard a mess, his eyes closed, mouth opened ever so slightly. He tended to lie on his back and that opened up that expansive chest for Josh to cuddle up against, which he'd been about to do when he'd heard the door downstairs open. Pausing mid slide, he strained to listen for anything else as James shifted beside him. As if on cue, James' alarm started blaring and Josh became very aware that the lazy morning he'd been hoping for was quickly dissipating.

James groaned adorable and Josh flopped back on his own pillow. "Fuckin' alarm," the older man grumbled as he rolled to shut it off. Pans clanked and Josh suddenly remembered that it was the housekeeper downstairs. Well…at least it wasn't an intruder—or his imagination.

James opened his eyes and stretched, then laughed when he saw Josh's glum pout. "I've gotta play golf at nine with some investors. I'd take you with me, but I know it's not your thing. Plus, it's getting colder—and who wants to golf in the cold?"

James pulled the warm, heavy comforter up over them and let his hand splay over Josh's ribcage. "I promise we'll grab a late lunch around two or three. Then I'm yours the rest of the day."

Something about the way James made these plans, with every intention of actually spending time with him, made Josh's heart beat rapidly and off rhythm. It felt so domestic, so right, so *real* that if Josh just ignored the little conscience in the back of his head, he could pretend they were really together. He didn't, or at least he tried not to, but it was easy to let those lines blur.

Especially when James was staring at him right now with that little smile of his. "We could get wine, take a walk—maybe find a fire pit," James enticed Josh further, as if Josh had any intention of saying no to anything.

"I mean," Josh drew out teasingly with a faux sigh, "I guess I can manage this morning. Maybe my friend

Stephanie will meet me for an espresso and a danish somewhere on this gigantic resort of yours."

James laughed, and it filled Josh's soul. "Oh boy…I think you two are becoming actual best friends."

"We might be by the time this trip is over," Josh teased, rolling to face James and kiss him out of pure habit and desire. James' expression softened and he kissed Josh's forehead in return. It was affectionate and personal. Josh flushed.

"She's essentially my best friend, but I guess I can share," James huffed in playful exasperation, and Josh found that adorable as well. James moved all too far away and slid out of bed. Naked, Josh got a good look at the residual red marks along James' ass from their adventures the night before. After their quickie on the balcony, they'd explored the house further and ended up in the large shower. Josh had started by going down on James and hungrily sucking him until the man couldn't wait any longer, then they'd moved to the bed for condoms and lube and a rough fuck that had left Josh spanking James until tears had filled his eyes. They'd come at the same time, exhausted and satisfied. They'd had an order-in pasta dinner in front of the television, then they'd fallen asleep wrapped together.

It had been the most perfect evening ever, in Josh's opinion.

Josh stayed in the bed while James showered, messing around on his phone and texting Stephanie to meet for coffee. She agreed for ten and Josh figured he'd catch a ride in with James. Pulling himself from the warm bed, he made for the shower and stopped only long enough to appreciate the way a clean, shirtless James looked while brushing his teeth in a towel. It shouldn't have made him feel things, but... He was not a tin man.

They shared a sweet smile, then Josh turned the shower on and climbed in, losing himself to the heat and steam as he cleaned up. He had to hit the gym today too, wherever that was.

Climbing out, he grabbed a towel and decided he had enough to do to keep him occupied while James worked. It was strange that he felt such a need to spend time with someone while on one of these vacations, but he ignored it, drying off. James had already disappeared to get dressed, so Josh finished up, brushing his teeth and fixing his hair. He left shaving for last, slathering the cream from his travel bag all over his neck, jaw and lower cheeks.

James came back in as Josh was slipping the blade down his cheek and regarded him curiously as he fixed his collar. "Have you ever let it grow out?"

"Hmm?"

"Your facial hair. Have you ever let it grow? Had a beard?"

Josh chuckled as he rinsed the razor under the running water. "Nah. Wouldn't it make me look old?" He said it then immediately looked at James, who was giving him a look of playful warning. "You're older than me. It's okay for you to have a beard. I'd look —"

"Very attractive, I bet," James replied, crossing his arms and leaning against the counter. "I bet it would feel real good in *other* places too."

Josh's cheeks went hot. "Well," he considered, knowing he couldn't stop now after having shaved half his face, "I'll...think about it."

"You're attractive just the way you are, Josh. Don't worry. But I think a beard or some scruff would add a little extra...something special to you. Anyway, I've gotta go early, gotta meet the guys for coffee and a brief meeting before our round. Stephanie will come down to get you with your security." Josh tried to digest everything James had just said, from the genuine compliments to the fact that *he* had security, then James was kissing the side of his clean hair and running a hand down his back affectionately. "I'll text you in a little while. Have fun and enjoy the resort. Charge anything you want to the villa. Don't worry about cost."

And with a departing smile, he slipped away before Josh could form words. He stood there staring after the man, the water running and his razor in midair.

The kiss had left him floundering. His heart beat erratically in the best of ways, knowing that all of what James had just said was just for *him*. It wasn't about the money or security itself. It was about the fact that James had taken the time to ensure Josh had a phenomenal trip while James worked. It made him feel warm all over.

He ignored the rational part of his head that flashed attachment warning signs. He was fine. This was all fine, just part of the job.

Who am I kidding? Only myself, apparently.

* * * *

"You're sure this is enough?" Josh stood in front of the mirror on Wednesday evening, looking himself over as he considered his suit. It was a new one he'd bought just for the trip, and while it wasn't as expensive as the one James had bought him — he was saving that one for the dinner that weekend — it wasn't a cheap suit.

James was slipping on his black overcoat, adjusting the collar as he glanced up to look Josh over. Josh's cheeks flushed under his gaze.

"I mean," James began as he walked up to Josh, standing behind him as he admired him in the mirror, "I'd prefer you naked, but the suit looks *very* good on you."

Josh's flush ran down into his chest, heating him up under the suit. "Jamie…"

"What? I'm being honest." He shrugged like it was the easiest thing in the world to say, and Josh, once more, didn't know how this entire situation had fallen into *his* lap. This man would be the death of him.

"Thank you," he murmured, staring at their reflection in the mirror. They did make a handsome couple. It was almost as if they were really together…

"Hey, I have something for you," James interrupted his thoughts as he stepped away, heading for a drawer on the large dresser they shared. He pulled open the top drawer—he had the top three, Josh had the bottom three—and pulled out a very nice leather box. Josh's curiosity peaked as his heart began to beat rapidly.

James handed him the box and grinned confidently. "I saw this and immediately thought of you," was all he said, but something about it carried affection and made Josh's belly flip.

He untied the white silk ribbon and let it fall away. Opening the lid, he gasped.

"Jamie!" he whisper-yelled in surprise, staring at the expensive—beyond expensive—gift. "I can't… This is… I'm just… I can't, James." He was in awe as he stared at an IWC watch, something *far* out of his affordable range.

James didn't look deterred by Josh's panic. If anything, he looked pleased. Josh's gaze flickered between the watch and James' gentle expression. "Josh, it's a gift. I saw it and immediately knew it was perfect for you. And it'll go great with your suit. Let me take care of you for the way you take care of me," James urged.

Josh had trouble forming words. "I... But this, James. I c-could n-never afford this," he stuttered. His face was probably red as a tomato. No one had *ever* gifted him something so beautiful, so exquisite. And while the suit James had given him in Jamaica had been incredible, an IWC watch was something a man like himself only looked at through store windows. He knew this watch would cover at least a year of mortgage payments on his mother's house. It was white gold and leather perfection.

"That's why I'm giving it to you. I *can*. And I *want* to give you nice things, Josh. Please let me?" James reached up and cradled Josh's face gently, and Josh had to work to keep his facade from falling. It was becoming harder and harder every day. Josh was an actor. He was *good* at doing his job and remaining disconnected. James was ruining that with every look and touch...and *gift*.

It was confusing...and thrilling beyond anything Josh had ever experienced.

"James, I'm still..."

"Just say thank you." He was utterly gentle as he stroked Josh's cheek. Josh caved.

"Thank *you*," he emphasized, pressing a kiss to James' lips without thinking. James kissed him back quickly.

"Let me put it on," James murmured as they finally pulled away. He took the box and after gently extracted the watch, he slipped it around Josh's left wrist. It fit perfectly, latching with ease. The leather was soft, but James' fingers were what made Josh warm.

"I love it," Josh marveled. James just smiled widely.

"I'm so glad. Let's go show you off, shall we?" He extended his arm and Josh could not help but take it as they prepared to leave. Moments later, Josh had his overcoat on and they were headed to the awaiting car. While cocktail parties were something Josh was used to, he had no idea what to expect at this one. Celebrities, models and the like were awaiting James' arrival — and he was on James' arm. Staring at the watch that shone up at him in the moonlight, Josh realized how surreal this all felt. He pinched his thigh as they drove.

Ouch.

By the time they arrived, the party was bustling. James held Josh's hand as they slipped in, down a grand staircase and into a ballroom. Cocktail tables lined each side of a dance floor where a live band was playing jazz. Three full-service bars were set up, and Josh was enamored with the beauty of the room and, once again, how James put on a party. He was sure James had event planners for these types of things, but James put a lot of hard work into everything and cared about every detail. Everything about this party said James — or rather, James Barnwell.

Stephanie was waiting for them at the bottom of the staircase, looking stunning in a conservative black and white dress that landed just at her knees. They stopped to greet her, Josh taking a moment to embrace his new friend. "You look gorgeous." She blushed.

"So do you two! Hot couple alert!" She threw her hands up at them as she stepped away from the hug, her eyes flickering to Josh's wrist with a mischievous grin. "I see someone liked their present." She elbowed her boss playfully, who simply smiled at Josh as if he were the only person in the room. Josh flushed.

"He's so sweet and modest, but he accepted it," James replied, and Josh just chuckled a little, rocking on his heels.

"Thank you again," he murmured as James slipped his hand back into Josh's. Their eyes locked, and for a moment Josh forgot Stephanie was standing there, until she cleared her throat.

"Ooookay," she drew out with a breath, physically turning them both toward the waiting crowd of about fifty people. "Stop making eyes at each other and go schmooze. I'll make sure a waiter brings you drinks. Bourbon for you, James. For you, Josh?"

"Gin martini, straight up, please, with a twist."

She gave him a look of approval and dashed away to find a waiter. Josh gripped James' hand as they happened upon their first guest, a fashion designer and his wife. It carried on like that for most of the evening, until James disappeared for a cigar with a long-time interior design partner, leaving Josh on his own.

They'd been there a couple of hours and Josh had to admit he was feeling the effects of his second martini. He was now sipping on an Americano, wondering about what they'd be having for dinner to soak up this alcohol, when a handsome, dark-haired man approached him as he overlooked the small lights of the town of Puglia.

"Good evening," the man greeted with a thick accent that Josh detected to be possibly Spanish—definitely not Italian, based on the accents he'd heard the past couple of days.

"Hey," Josh greeted back, standing up from where he was leaning on the balcony and feeling a little awkward. He flashed the man a smile and finally caught a good look at him as he stepped closer, stopping a few feet from Josh. He was taller, maybe by a few inches, lean with gorgeous dark hair. He was tan, in a cream-colored jacket with a black sweater and khaki slacks. Perfect sideburns, a touch of scruff and Josh determined that this man *had* to be a model. If he wasn't, he should have been.

"Standing over here all alone?" the man began, glancing back at the party. "Not much for socializing — or taking a break?"

Josh chuckled a little, knowing he must look as out of place as he felt. "A little bit of both," he admitted.

"Ah. Understandable." The man smiled, and Josh found himself taken aback by how handsome he was. Josh was fully smitten with James, but he wasn't immune to a good-looking man. "Alejandro Garcia," the man said and extended his hand.

"Josh Roberts." Josh shook his hand, noting the man's grip was firm, his skin soft.

"A guest of someone?" Alejandro sipped his drink and just smiled easily, with nothing rushed about him. He had a sense of confidence and sophistication. Josh speculated he had ten years on him.

"Yes, I am. Are you?"

"No." Alejandro chuckled a little. "I was invited. I model for several of the designers present. If you were my guest, I wouldn't let you be standing up here all alone. Someone would surely think you were a prize for attending this evening."

The man looked Josh up and down and his cheeks went hot. *Oh.* He was being hit on. *Well…that's unexpected.*

"A prize, huh?" Josh countered through his blush. Josh was an accomplished escort. He was self-assured, confident. But something about being in Alejandro's sites was unnerving.

"Oh yes," he replied easily, and Josh was actually beginning to enjoy the accent. *Definitely Spanish*, if the name was any indication. "A very handsome one." He bit his lip as he stepped closer, albeit still keeping a foot between them. "What do you do, Josh Roberts?"

Josh took a long sip of his drink and wondered, not uncomfortably but just curiously, where James was. "I'm a consultant…and an artist." At least the last part made him feel like he wasn't lying *as* much. He was a consultant, sure, for sexual fantasies. He never planned on going into that much detail, especially when he was actually on a job.

"An artist? Drawing? Painting?"

Josh never talked about himself, and it seemed that this man had more than enough questions. He shifted from one foot to the next as he answered.

"Both. Mostly drawing. I prefer to sit with my charcoal and sketch. But I paint when I have time. But that's not nearly as interesting as your being a model. How long have you been in the industry?"

Josh sipped his drink as he tried to read Alejandro. It was a difficult task. Not only did the man want to stare at Josh like he was actually *hungry*, but he deflected the question.

"Ten years. But I would much rather talk about you, Josh. I'm intrigued as to how such a young, handsome

American ended up here, in Puglia, while whoever he came with is off with someone else."

Josh laughed, self-deprecating, shaking his head. "He's got a lot of business to attend to. And I'm a big boy. I can handle being alone."

Alejandro only seemed more interested as Josh stood up for himself and his date. "Oh, really? Well, now you have got me listening. Would you like to get another drink?"

Josh laughed again, not quite sure what was happening but feeling flattered nonetheless. "I shouldn't. He'll be back and—"

"Please. I promise that as soon as he reappears, I'll give you back without a fuss. It would be rude of me to let you stand up here all alone with such a lovely party going on."

Josh wasn't sure he agreed, but they were now on the same playing field and Alejandro was clearly attracted. He wasn't sure if it was his healthy buzz or his piqued interest that made him agree, but soon they were headed down to the bar. Josh kept looking for James, but he didn't see him anywhere. It wasn't like him to leave without Josh, but he also knew this night was important for him somehow. Josh never minded letting James work. And besides, they weren't *technically* together. Not that Josh chose to put much weight on that reasoning, because while he was very much being paid to be there, he would have gone by choice, no questions asked, if the opportunity had presented itself to be on James' arm in Italy.

Alejandro ordered them both another drink and they settled there, leaning against the bar as they talked. Alejandro was far more interested in Josh and his life than talking about himself. That put Josh on the edge a little, because one of things Josh hardly did was talk about himself, especially while he was working — and especially when he didn't have a very specific cover story.

Alejandro was very handsome, charming and all the things Josh would look for in a client. But Josh wasn't looking for a client or a partner. He was very pleased with the one he currently had, no matter the arrangement they were currently under.

Josh enjoyed the attention despite it all, blushing and answering Alejandro's questions as best he felt he could. James often came up, as he was there with him and for him, and they were boyfriends in this environment. Josh found it so easy to talk affectionately about the man, and Alejandro seemed to enjoy the way Josh lit up when he spoke about James.

The alcohol was helping Josh relax. It was rare that he let himself have so much. He wasn't drunk, but he was certainly enjoying the evening, despite James' absence. He caught Stephanie's eyes over Alejandro's shoulder and made a small wave with his left hand, calling Alejandro's attention to the very expensive watch on his wrist.

"Well, look at that. Not sure what kind of consulting you're doing, but I know that watch and I know it's not a cheap one." Alejandro reached out and grasped Josh's wrist gently, revealing the IWC *Portofino* James had gifted him earlier. He flushed once more and gazed at the watch.

"It was a gift. From my boyfri —"

The words died on his tongue as suddenly James was at his side, sliding an arm protectively but gently around his waist, his focus on Alejandro. "Hello, handsome," James said to Josh, turning to give him a sweet but pointed smile and a gentle kiss. Josh melted as Alejandro released his wrist. "Alejandro, nice to see you."

"Ah." Realization dawned on Alejandro's face and a smile crossed his lips. "Now I see who you're a guest of. You didn't tell me it was James Barnwell himself."

The implication made Josh immediately feel bad. He hadn't meant to hide such information, but James was swift to respond. "I do believe it's called privacy." He was cold toward the Spanish man and Josh tried to school his features and simply watch the exchange. "He doesn't have to tell you anything, as long as he told you he was seeing someone."

"Oh, he certainly did. But he was alone and looked like he needed the company, so I stepped in during your absence."

Josh bounced back and forth between the two, his face hot and his tongue a little too thick in his mouth to say anything. It was when James tightened his arm and he put his drink down that Josh suddenly realized what was happening. James was *jealous*.

"I had business to attend to and, luckily, Josh is very good at entertaining himself during that time. Aren't you, baby boy?"

Josh preened under the term of endearment, torn between feeling awful about the exchanges with Alejandro and being turned on by the sudden possessiveness James was showing. "Yes, sir," he replied, finally finding his voice.

Alejandro grinned and nodded. "I apologize, James. I was simply enjoying some time with him. No harm done."

James' smile didn't reach his eyes as he simply pulled at Josh's waist. "Have a good night, Alejandro. Come on, baby. Let's go back. We'll order in."

Josh left his drink and murmured a soft, "Nice to meet you," to Alejandro as James pulled him away. They bade good night to people they passed as they walked back up the staircase to their awaiting car. James was unusually quiet until they were seated inside the sedan, the panel sliding up between them and the driver. It was a couple of minutes before James spoke, Josh's nerves a little frayed the whole time they sat in silence.

"Did you have a nice time talking to Alejandro?" James kept his fingers threaded in Josh's but his gaze out of the window as he spoke.

Unsure of how to interpret the air between them, Josh licked his lips and replied, "It was fine. He was nice."

James scoffed at that as Josh felt his throat tighten. He was a little too buzzed to be trying to navigate his way through what had just happened, and he was also a little too confused about his emotions to be sure of James'. That last drink had been a mistake, he realized too late. But that was just always the case, wasn't it?

"He's nice all right. He seemed to be just about to charm your pants right off before I walked up."

Josh whipped his head toward James, because that was definitely *not* the case. The five-minute ride was quickly coming to an end, the car pulling to a stop in front of their villa. Before he could respond and defend himself, James was releasing his hand, climbing out and heading for the staircase to the front door. Josh scrambled to follow, and for the first time in their short arrangement, he was terrified he'd ruined everything.

Entering the home, James went straight for the stairs to their shared room. Josh shut the door and locked it, slipping his overcoat off and laying it gently over the back of the chair. *How can I fix this?* Sure, he'd flirted with the guy, but he wouldn't have ever done anything. Not to mention James wasn't *actually* his boyfriend, so what did he have to be jealous over?

Finding some comfort in his rational thought, Josh began up the stairs. He could just suggest James send him back to the States — or he could sleep in the guest room. They didn't have to pretend to be together all the time. In fact, that was more their natural progression than anything.

Feeling suddenly tired and still awful, Josh turned the corner into their room. "Jamie, listen. I — "

He was cut off as James practically pounced on him, slamming his back into the wall by the door. Josh's eyes went wide as his hands came up in a gesture of innocence, his chest suddenly bursting with anxiety. Their eyes locked, and for a tense moment, Josh wasn't really sure what was about to happen. James had an air of aggression about him that Josh had not yet experienced. His steely eyes were ablaze, his face tense and firm.

"Sweetheart," he began, further confusing Josh, "I'm so sorry you got confused back there." James drifted one of the hands he had on Josh's lapels to cup his cheek, rubbing his thumb over Josh's bottom lip. He shivered in response, willing his body to not react to the heat his touch. "I left you, and of course you could be seen as fresh meat to someone like Alejandro, who's notorious for one-night stands. He could have scooped you up and made an utter mess of you. I've seen the aftermath, with men and women. You're better than that, baby. And I *know* I make you feel better than he could."

His words were far more dominant than Josh had ever experienced, and it did *something* to him. His tongue snaked out of its own accord, teasing at James' thumb. The man chuckled darkly.

"Aww, there he is, my sweet, hungry boy," he cooed. "You realize how jealous you made your daddy tonight, right? I wanted to make you fuck me over the bar in front of every guest there when I saw you with Alejandro, to ensure there was no question who brought you, who you belong to." James pressed himself to Josh, and Josh swallowed his moan and willed his body not to react—but it was too late. His cock was quickly hardening, and James could undoubtedly feel it. James' expression told him so as he started to grin. "Mmm-m, did you like making me jealous, baby? Do you like knowing that you made me want to claim you?"

"Yes, Sir," Josh whispered, his throat suddenly dry as the dynamic between them shifted and James took on the dominant role. Suddenly Josh's cock was ready to go and needed friction or attention immediately. Something about the change, *not* having control, was making Josh needier than usual.

"Well, baby boy, let Daddy show you who you belong to."

Josh wasn't sure what that meant for a split second, then James was dropping to his knees. Josh's brain skidded to a stop and malfunctioned as he realized what James was about to do. He'd never done that before to anyone, let alone Josh, and—

Josh's brain sputtered as James leaned in and nuzzled his hard-on through his slacks. Josh jerked and groaned, suddenly unable to control his behavior. The groan was strangled and low, but there was no question James heard it and acted on it, bringing his hands up to rub him firmly through his pants. When he looked up, Josh noticed the first bits of insecurity showing, the James Josh was used to. *Oh no, no, Daddy,* he spoke silently in his brain to James, *you can do this.*

"Gonna suck me, Daddy?" Josh found his voice, gravelly and thick as he spoke, steadying himself with his hands on the wall. "Gonna taste my cock for the first time and make me forget his name?" He would do whatever it took to boost James' esteem. And he'd *beg* if he needed to, to get those beautiful lips wrapped around him. He felt weak with want for the first time in far longer than he could remember.

"Yeah, sweet boy. I'll be the only name in that pretty head of yours after tonight..."

James undid Josh's belt at that, unzipped the slacks and pulled them down around Josh's thighs. Josh's erection bobbed out, showing just how much he needed James. James was eye-level with his length for the first time and seemed to take a minute for him to appreciate the view.

Josh swallowed hard and found himself unable to stop begging. "Please, Daddy, suck me... Dying to feel your mouth... I need..."

"Shh-h, sweetheart. I've got you." It felt a little like they were playing a game, some kind of role change as James wrapped a tentative hand around Josh's length. Josh nodded and swallowed hard, needing more but taking what he was given with grace. James stroked him a few times, leaving Josh feeling exposed and a little nervous as he let his free fingers graze Josh's inner thighs and over his balls. Josh keened, needing more, very sensitive to the touch. James grinned, cupping his sac and squeezing as he started to stroke with more purpose. Josh didn't hold back on his noises. He let James know just how good it felt, just how well he was doing.

"So good," he groaned, swallowing hard. "So, so good, just —"

Josh's brain short-circuited as he watched James flicker out his pink tongue and curiously lick over his swollen red tip, and in that moment, it was the most erotic thing Josh had ever seen or felt.

"Mmm-m," James moaned, seemingly delighted with his first taste. He parted his lips and wrapped them around the tip of Josh's length, and Josh about lost it to the sight alone. Knowing this was James' first time was beyond exhilarating. Somehow, he'd gotten to be the first person James had experimented on. His heart raced as James played, getting a feel for the shape and curve of his length. He was slow — and Josh didn't mind one bit. The man could explore all night if he wanted to. The problem was that once James really got going, it wouldn't be long before he exploded. He could only hold on for so long. He was just human, and the closer that bearded face got to his hips, the harder it became to hold it together.

James was working his way down, taking Josh deeper with every bob of his head. He sucked and pressed his tongue to the underside, and Josh knew he was trying to recreate all the things Josh had done for him. He ran his hand through James' thick hair, the tendrils soft under his fingers. "That's it, Jamie." Josh kept his voice low and sweet, maintaining the dynamic they'd created. He let out moans as James took him deeper, swallowing around him before he coughed and pulled off for a moment. His cheeks were red, but Josh didn't focus on the floundering. He desperately wanted to come down that throat. He knew it wouldn't take much more. He was on the edge, just almost there... "Suck the tip, Daddy. Squeeze my balls. I promise I'm right there," Josh begged. "Please, please..."

James went back in for more and didn't disappoint. He did just as Josh told him to, wrapping his lips around his length about halfway down and sucking with intent. He squeezed and rolled the ball sac in his hand, no doubt having done it to himself, and Josh basked in the impending orgasm. He whimpered and moaned and gripped James' hair without forcing him. For a novice, the man was ambitious and determined. "I'm gonna... Jamie, I'm right there— I'm—" He tried to warn him, but James didn't move. Instead, he sucked with more vigor and had Josh's toes curling as he stared down at the glorious man on his knees in front of him, pleasuring him because he *wanted* to. Josh lost it. He bellowed and shook as he came hard enough to see stars.

James did his best to swallow it all, backing off to let a little more room in his mouth as Josh emptied himself. He was panting as he finished, a complete wreck against the villa wall as he forced his eyes open to find James licking him clean, still on his knees. Josh wished momentarily that his cock could respond already, because that was a sight he wouldn't soon forget.

James looked very pleased as he stood, brushing hair from Josh's sweaty forehead. "That's my boy," he praised, and Josh beamed tiredly. James kissed him deeply, letting Josh taste the saltiness left behind, and he pulled James in, wrapping his arms around him and holding him close. It was a dangerous kiss, the kind one could lose themselves in and that made one want to die happily having had the best kiss of their lives. Then Josh realized James was hard and heavy in his own slacks and, well, he couldn't let that continue.

Reluctantly pulling away from James' delicious lips, Josh turned them around and dropped to his knees in front of James, all innocence and want. James looked pleased and hungry, but Josh had other ideas. "Mark me," he requested in that destroyed voice. "Mark me and my suit and all that's yours. Prove that I'm yours…"

It was vulnerable and they hadn't experimented with this yet. James stared in something that was a mix of awe and desire, rubbing that thumb over Josh's swollen bottom lip once more. "Want me to come all over your face, handsome boy? Is that what you want?"

"Yes, Sir. Please. Tell me I'm yours. *Show* me."

James didn't need to be asked twice, it seemed. He dropped his hands to his slacks and pushed them down to his ankles, pulling his sweater over his head and tossing it aside. Josh swallowed thickly in anticipation, that hard cock he'd grown to have a deep need for standing just inches from his face. He placed his hands in his lap in the ultimate submissive pose, tilting his chin up so James didn't have to aim much. God, he wanted this so badly that it scared him.

James wrapped his hand around himself and let out sweet noises as he began to work himself over. He wasn't slow. He didn't tease. He was running toward his release, seeming to want to mark Josh up as much as Josh wanted it. He was always generous in his sounds and he kept his eyes on Josh's the whole time, the heat between them inexplicable.

Josh memorized the way James touched himself, the stroke he used, the grip of three fingers and his thumb. He stared at the way his skin moved, the glistening tip. Josh was so hungry for what came next that he found himself silently begging, *Please, Jamie. God, yes...look at you. Please, Sir. I need it, Daddy.*

James didn't disappoint. He let go with a low, long groan, his mouth falling open as streams of white covered Josh's face. Josh closed his eyes out of instinct but basked in the warmth as it landed on him, covering his cheeks, his lashes, his skin all over. It was personal, it was filthy and it was somehow the sexiest scenario with James that Josh had found them in yet. The afterglow resonated around them as both James and he were gasping, one from exertion and one from the thrill, and Josh knew that if he could rebound quickly, they'd be in trouble. He had every intention of rolling over and taking James in the night. He just needed to rest and soak up this moment between them.

"My God," James murmured as managed to crack his eyes carefully. His cheeks went red as James stared, but Josh could tell it was awe in his eyes. He swiped some off Josh's cheek and put his thumb to those lips once again. Josh hungrily licked it off. James moaned a low, "such a *good* boy."

It was different for James to be the one doling out all the praise, but Josh knew it was to ensure that Josh didn't forget who he was with — as if he ever could. He was sure nothing would ever compare to this.

Cleaning up was slow, methodical and sweet. James cleaned Josh's face with a warm cloth then they kissed until they both needed water and aspirin. They undressed and slipped into more comfortable clothes before raiding the kitchen for peanut butter and biscotti. James brewed them decaf espressos and they collapsed into bed not long after, both getting rid of their clothing to sleep skin to skin.

Josh couldn't then be held responsible when his cock woke him, hard and hot and pressed against James' round ass. Josh didn't tease him and simply slipped on a condom, coated his cock and pressed himself against that tender, hungry hole. James, barely awake, consented with moans and cries for Josh, the stretch apparently a little more than normal but nothing unbearable.

Lying on their sides together, Josh peppered James' back with kisses and nips until he was fully seated. They moved together, slow and rhythmic. James held on to Josh's hand, gripping tightly as he whimpered. Josh angled his hips, knowing just where and how to make James lose his mind, even slowly like this. *In and out, deep drags, an extra thrust just before I pull out.* Wrapping a towel from the bedside table around James' length to avoid mess, Josh fucked slowly and deeply into him until they both released. Curled against one another, hot and sweaty, Josh almost forgot to rid himself of the condom.

For a brief moment, he wished there would be a time they didn't have to use the protection anymore. His hazy brain reminded him that would probably be never, but he pushed the thought away as he cleaned them up thoroughly and slid back into bed, wrapping himself around an already-asleep James. He didn't blame him and didn't even wake him, pressing a kiss to his cheek before letting himself fall back asleep as well.

* * * *

Sitting in the sunlight on the resort terrace, sunglasses on and a third cup of coffee at hand, Josh remembered why he preferred not to get drunk. His head was finally no longer pounding, now just a dull ache behind the eyes, and he was feeling less sluggish than when he'd first woken up to an empty bed and a sweet note left by James.

Josh,
I have a nine a.m. meeting. I wish I could have woken up with you, enjoyed breakfast then some time in the shower. I'll make it up to you later. More aspirin and water on the table. Take it. It's not a suggestion.
See you later this afternoon.
James

Josh had lain in the bed with a dopey smile and reread the note at least five times like a lovesick fool. Somehow, he was able to not focus on that, to ignore the lovesick part and simply call himself a fool as he dragged himself to the bathroom. He looked like death and felt very close to it.

Now he was getting some sunshine outside a cafe, sucking down hot coffee and eating fruit in hopes he'd be alive by the time James found him. Still in a black tank top and cotton sweatpants, he wasn't exactly a fashion statement. Luckily, no one bothered him, though — or seemed to care.

He sketched the cliffs from where he sat, able to catch a lot of the town below, the sunrise and the ocean. It was therapeutic to sketch, his portfolio full of different projects from Jamaica, New York, Italy and now James. He'd begun a new one upon meeting James, leaving his other sketches at home and using a new leather-bound portfolio with a new class of nice paper and pencils. He'd used some money from what James had paid him to indulge. While he didn't use that money for much, traveling with someone like James made him feel the need to portray the lifestyle. At least when he carried this beautiful folder around, he felt the part he was playing.

Emptying his cup, he decided he needed more. He slipped the latest sketch back into the folder, not bothering to zip it as the loose-leaf papers lay inside. He was just going to grab another cup and head back outside, get a little more sun and maybe take a nap. By then he'd feel better about seeing James, and maybe his cheeks would be pink enough to let James think he wasn't as hungover as he still felt.

Shit, he cursed himself as he rushed through the open-air doorway into the cafe. The change in light messed with his eyes and he blinked rapidly. Unaware of his proximity to the woman passing him, he bumped her roughly with the arm carrying the folder. Not only did he drop the coffee cup while trying to catch the woman from falling on her tall heels, but he dropped the folder too, sketches fluttering all over the marble floor. He successfully grabbed the woman's arms, holding her up, despite the mess he'd made otherwise.

"I am *so* sorry!" Josh exclaimed, helping to steady her on her feet. A stream of expressions crossed her face, surprise to horror to...*is she blushing?*

"Goodness! Has anyone ever told you that you're built like a brick wall? I think you broke my —" She stopped and was gazing down, and Josh's eyes followed then widened in his own horror. "Is that...? Are you...?" The woman looked between the several sketches of naked James Barnwell and Josh, recognition dawning now on her face. Josh wanted to melt into the floor and disappear from his life at that very moment.

"Umm…" was all he could muster as he dropped to his knees, frantically — but gently — gathering up his artwork. The woman seemed frozen for a good thirty seconds before she dropped down to help, picking up three pictures in particular.

This is terrible. Awful. Like someone seeing into his soul. He shouldn't have been sketching pictures of James, but it wasn't against the law. And the man was beautiful. He shouldn't feel bad about it, but a pit sat heavy in his stomach. If she knew James…

Josh was sliding the rest back in, hiding the pictures of James under several landscape pieces. When he finally looked up to see the woman holding a few, he tentatively reached out. "May I — "

"These are incredible." She spoke with a fierceness he hadn't expected. "You drew these?"

She turned the pieces so Josh could see them. One was of the Jamaican resort, the new area James had just opened. Another was James, naked and face down on the bed, his visage hidden by his blankets. It was a personal favorite of Josh's, drawn in Jamaica as well. It was an explicit piece of James' backside, as Josh had sat in the chair at the foot of the bed and drawn from that direction, every detail memorized and saved to paper. Josh's flush intensified dramatically. The last piece was the one from this morning, of the Italian landscape. He swallowed hard and nodded.

"Yes, ma'am. Every piece is mine," he answered meekly, that hangover no match for her gaze of steel.

"Are you a commissioned artist? Do you have a gallery? What's your full name?" She peppered him with questions like fast balls and Josh hardly noticed the barista cleaning up the broken porcelain behind him.

"Josh Roberts, ma'am. And no, I don't. I'm not. I sketch for fun. I mean, someday I hope to open my own gallery, but I don't think that will happen anytime—"

"Do you sell your work?" She was back to staring at the sketches. Josh's forehead was furrowed so hard it hurt. *Why is she asking so many questions? And why is she still staring at James' ass?*

"I-I haven't, no. I don't really show it to—"

"Come with me. *Now.*" She stood swiftly, spinning on her heels and heading for the elevator.

"Ma'am? I'm—"

"Come, Mr. Roberts! We have a lot to discuss."

Josh made sure to zip up the folder as he stumbled to his feet, grace to be desired in his flip flops. He scurried after her, feeling the adolescent, small and sickly version of himself, being dragged to the principal's office for punching a bully in the eighth grade. A terrible thought overtook his brain as he watched her turn the corner toward the board room that he knew James and his team were occupying that morning. She was going to tell. She was going to expose Josh for drawing James and accuse him of selling the works. There was no way he could let her tell James—

But she was flinging the door open before her could reach her, but he stumbled in soon enough to see her set the three images down before James himself. Josh stood in the doorway, his shoulders hunched and panicking. "Ma'am! James! I can explain—"

"I just ran into your freight train of a boyfriend, James. Quite literally. It seems he's an artist. How come you didn't tell us about his talent?" The brunette woman leaned on her palms against the table, looking at James with what Josh decided was a cross expression. James looked utterly confused and flushed as he stared at the middle picture, which most certainly was his ass.

"Hello, Maria, Josh." James' gaze flickered to Josh's for a split second—and not nearly enough to settle Josh's anxiety.

"Did you know? Were you hiding this from me?" Maria demanded, switching the order of the sketches so the Jamaican resort was in the middle. The dozen people around the table were all peering at the art, and Josh was sure this was the end. He'd be shipped back to America on the next jet out of— "You *knew* what I was looking for and it was right under your nose. This"—she tapped the picture—"needs to be hanging up front and center in the lobby in Jamaica! It's *perfect*!"

Wait…! She said what? Josh's mind tripped over her words.

"Maria, I had no idea he was an artist. I can assure you." James looked up to Josh and their eyes locked. Josh shrugged helplessly.

"It's a private hobby, honestly," Josh finally interjected, his voice sounding small to his own ears. "I don't really tell people about it."

"A hobby? Mr. Roberts, what you have here… You should be selling this. In fact, James, we need to get him under contract. I need these. I can see it now…" She stood up, looking around the room. "If he can do pieces for each resort, for the suites even, the lobbies, it would give such an authentic, personal, *family* feel to each location. A theme." She was enthusiastic as she spoke, and Josh's jaw was dropping with every word she said. "Barnwell, I'm having it drawn up. Mr. Roberts, can you do this? Can you see my vision? I want *this,* and *this*, and maybe even a little of *this*." She tapped her finger over each picture, James' being the last. "With less nudity, of course, for each resort. Several. Can you draw people? Faces? Do you use color? Paint?"

Josh was gripping his portfolio so hard that his knuckles were white. Everyone was staring at him, including James. He was not dressed for a business meeting, not even showered, and somehow something *huge* was happening to him right before his eyes.

"I um... Yes ma'am. I do all those things," he managed to squeak out. A grin was pulling at James' lips.

"Perfect. Bruce" — she pointed at another man Josh had yet to meet, but who looked strangely uncomfortable and was staring at the naked sketch of James — "draw it up. Mr. Roberts, we'll meet at two o'clock. James" — Maria patted the man's shoulder and Josh could tell it was affectionate, like they knew each other well — "you should check out *all* the sketches your boyfriend has drawn of you. He leaves out *no* details."

Everything from Josh's face to the tips of his ears grew hot as James shifted his gaze back to him. Their eyes met again, and James offered a warm smile that was a balm to Josh's very frayed nerves. "Oh, I plan to."

Josh managed a smile back before he mumbled something about excusing himself to get ready. "May I...uh..."

"Oh, sure. We'll need these in pristine condition to make prints." Maria gathered the art and handed it back to Josh. "I look forward to meeting later."

"Yes, me too," Josh was quick to reply, a little more excited now that impending doom had made way for an amazing opportunity. Even if he made an abysmal amount, it was additional income to support his mother. And this was his *art*! His real passion!

Catching James' glance one more time, he excused himself, slipping away as quietly as he could as he hurried back to their villa. It was only Thursday and the first week had already been a whirlwind.

Chapter Six

Josh had just signed a contract—one that stated he was to create original pieces for all Winter Luxury Resorts for the next calendar year, and it had a clause that stated they could renew the contract at the end of the year if his work was well-received and exactly what Maria Harding, Director of Interior Design for Winter Luxury Resorts and all things J. B. Barnwell LLC, wanted from him. Apparently James also owned four boutique coffee shops and an office building in Miami. *Who knew?* He had signed several contracts since he'd become an escort, but none of them had been for a job like this or for the amount he'd just signed on to receive, starting *now*. As he stood, still in his best suit, on the terrace of their villa, the chilly evening wind cooling his overheated body, he wasn't sure if he was going to be sick or cry with joy.

He'd signed on to create two thousand pieces at a minimum of five hundred dollars each. They were already making travel plans to send him all over the world to explore the resorts. He'd be in Miami starting in January. They'd take care to make prints, all complete with Josh's signature, and if anything sold, he'd get three-quarters of each sale. That was fine with him, because the base alone was enough. He could easily create two thousand pieces. He wasn't overwhelmed by the prospect of what he was creating and how many. He was overwhelmed by the amount of money and the fact that his art had garnered him that at the tender age of twenty-four.

Maria said that if he had enough pieces by mid-December, she'd have a gallery set up for him in New York, with a studio he could work in. She had big-picture plans. Josh had stared at her, starry eyed, as she'd explained. It was far more than he'd ever dreamed of.

He wanted to call his mom. He wanted to call Nadia. But he really wanted to talk to James *first*. And as the car drove down toward the villa, he knew he was finally about to get his chance.

They hadn't spoken since that morning short of a text exchange.

I'm so sorry. I ran right into her and I dropped my folder. I wish I had an explanation, but I don't. I think it's pretty obvious that I sketch you, and I should have told you. I'm sorry. I'm also sorry she disrupted your meeting. I feel like we need to talk before I sign anything.

Josh, you have nothing to be sorry for. I expect nothing less of Maria. She has worked with me for years. I was surprised by the sketch, but I'm more surprised that you're an artist and you didn't tell me – not for any other reason than I just want to know what brings you joy. Don't wait for me. If this is a good opportunity for you, take it! I can promise we will uphold any end of the bargain she brings you.

Who used punctuation that well in a text? Apparently a businessman… Josh had laughed a little to himself.

People don't pay me to talk about myself. That's why I didn't tell you.

I do. I want to know everything you're willing to tell. We'll talk more tonight. Sign the contract. Good luck! If you don't like the package, negotiate. If you still aren't pleased, call me. I'll make whatever you need happen.

Josh hadn't needed to call James. The package had been perfect — good pay, great insurance, bonuses and perks he'd never be able to fully use. Once more, though, he felt himself anticipating the end of their arrangement for the third time in less than a week, and why did it overshadow the amazing day he'd had? *Oh, right.* He knew. But he wasn't about to say *that* out loud.

The car stopped and James stepped out alone. After James shut the door, he caught Josh's eye as the car began to pull away. Josh only turned to go inside once James headed inside.

They met in the kitchen at the same time. Josh was already blushing and felt wholly unprepared for whatever was going to happen. But James was simply grinning as he slipped off his jacket and loosened his tie. "You are the talk of the town, young man." He chuckled and shook his head, leaving the tie over the back of the chair and heading for the wine rack. Josh winced.

"I'm so —"

"Don't you dare apologize again, Josh." It could have been snapped or shouted, but James was gentle and smiling as he offered the words, pulling out a bottle of white from the chiller. He grabbed two glasses and the opener. "How did the signing go? I didn't hear from you, so I assume you're pleased?"

Josh wanted to beg for forgiveness, to grovel and panic and all the things he felt internally. But James seemed to content to pour them wine and talk about the contract. Josh cleared his throat. "It went great. Maria is very straightforward." Josh picked up his copy from the table, where he'd laid it upon arriving home to process. "You can read it over if you want. You have great benefits and perks." He set it back down in front of where James stood.

"Good. I'm glad she was thorough. I try hard to take care of my people, and you just became a very important asset to our next phase." He smiled as he handed Josh a glass, lifting it up in a toast. "To you, the artist. Congratulations, Josh!"

There was a genuine spark in James' eye. The fact that this had been his first thought upon arriving — to celebrate his new job — was sweet. Josh raised his glass, tapping it against James'. "Thank you! You have no idea. This is a dream, honestly — something I've wanted my whole life."

James' expression softened at Josh's words. They each sipped their wine before James stretched out his free hand. "I cancelled our dinner reservations. I have food being delivered at eight p.m. There's a charcuterie in the fridge that was prepared for us. We're celebrating alone, together, and you're going to tell me all the things I should have asked about you long before now. And for that, *I'm* sorry."

James had guided him into the living room, gesturing for him to sit, but Josh was so enamored with his words that he simply stood while James started the gas fireplace. When he turned around and saw Josh still standing, he frowned. But Josh was just surprised and a little in shock. It had already been a long day and his brain was hurrying to catch up and absorb such kind words. "Jamie, you don't have to. I'm —"

"Josh," James shushed him, closing the distance between them to place a hand to his cheek, thumb caressing his skin. "Tell me everything. I want to know everything there is to know about Joshua —" He paused, waiting. Josh's cheeks heated.

"Grant," he supplied quietly. James' smile grew.

"Joshua Grant Roberts. I want the autobiography. Sit." He pressed a kiss, chaste but no less inviting, to Josh's lips before gesturing once more to the plush couch. Josh did as he'd been told, and James sat close. And thus began a night of Josh talking about himself, something he was far from accustomed to.

He told James about his youth, his father dying overseas in a training accident with the Army before Josh's birth. It had only ever been Josh and Sarah, his mother, from then on out. She'd worked hard as a nurse until she'd retired at fifty-two after a health scare. Josh shared how he'd started drawing as a young child. Since he'd been small and sickly as a child with a knack for getting into trouble, it had been a good way to spend time when grounded. Puberty had been good to him, as had weight training in high school and college.

"And escorting?" James asked a couple of hours into their evening as they drank their third glass of wine and ate the delicious charcuterie provided by the head chef at the resort. Heat flared in his cheeks, knowing the question had been inevitable.

"So that's kind of a funny story," Josh began, laughing at the memory. "I had really no concept of what exactly any of it was. I was a twenty-one-year-old in a fancy bar downtown one night because I'd had a date and she'd stood me up—which is unsurprising because I'm not *that* charming." James admonished him quietly, but Josh waved him off. "Anyway, this older woman approached me, started flirting with me and asked if I was going to accompany her home. She asked for my card and, confused, I told her I didn't have one. She just laughed and patted my cheek. I mean, I had been flirting back and she was absolutely stunning, like *gorgeous*, all curves and red lips. I've always been bisexual, but up until that point, I had only ever been with women—and she topped that list, by far. Still does, to be honest." Josh chanced a look at James, who seemed very interested, grinning a bit, so he continued.

"So anyway, she took me back to her brownstone and asked me to fuck her, so I did, because what else was a guy to do? She was *very* sure of herself and I was young and not about to turn down the opportunity. Afterward, she asked how much I charged. Confused, and now exhausted, I must have just looked like a lost animal because she grinned, handed me five hundred dollars and a piece of paper to write my number on. She called me again a week later and every week after. She referred her friends to me, and soon I was knee-deep in the business." He shrugged and slipped a piece of rich cheese into his mouth. James looked amused and affectionate.

"Do you still see her?" he asked, and Josh couldn't figure out his neutral expression.

"I did, every week, until *you* happened." Josh purposely caught James' eyes for a short moment before looking away.

James licked his lips, a smile still slipping through the motion. "And men? When did *that* happen?"

That made Josh run a hand over his face, laughing a little. "So, unlike with you and Margaret, my first client, I usually screen them. She referred an older man to me. I had to nervously explain that I hadn't ever bottomed — or even been with a man. He was very pleased by that and promised he'd take his time. If I'd had a friend I trusted, I would have tried something else first — but I didn't. So I, um, bought some stuff and practiced, then…yeah." He shrugged, his face as heated as the hot pepper jelly on the tray before him. James pressed on, though, to Josh's embarrassment.

"Yeah? Did you like it?"

Josh ran a hand over his face, unsure why he was suddenly nervous talking about something that made him very, very good money. "I did. A lot. I think by nature I prefer topping most of the time, but…I mean, you know what that penetration feels like. To be so full and stretched and…" The air in the room shifted and Josh's belly tightened as he thought about that *particular* feeling. "It's been a while. God, a really long time actually, now that I think about it, but I *do* like it."

James nodded his head, his gaze so focused that Josh could tell he was very engaged. "And do you still, ya know, practice?" James' tone had dropped just slightly as he reached for the second bottle of wine.

"I…um…I always have the supplies with me for clients, but I haven't done it to myself in a while."

James nodded again, biting at his bottom lip as he seemed to consider what Josh said. "This guy, your first... He took care of you?"

Unsure of why James asked, he went with it, "Mm-hm. Taught me a lot about it, actually. I haven't seen him in over a year. He got married and obviously no longer needed my services. But he always took his time and talked me through it. Probably taught me a lot of stuff I wouldn't have known otherwise."

"Did you top him too?"

"Oh, no. A referral from him, actually. The guy only bottomed. So I applied what I'd learned and what I knew — and that wasn't nearly as nerve-racking. Blow jobs, rimming — the more I did it, the better I got." As soon as the words left his mouth, he scrunched up his face. *God, way to make yourself sound like a whore, Josh.* "Sorry... That was...unattractive."

"Without your talent, knowledge and guidance, where would I be now?" James replied easily, rubbing Josh's back through the dress shirt he still wore. Josh dropped his eyes and shrugged.

"I guess that's true."

"Do you still see him?"

That question again. "No, also a year and also got married." Josh finished the last bit of his wine, feeling tipsy but very good. "He still refers people, but my schedule tends to be full of regulars. The night I met you had been a rare night off."

James' eyes offered remembrance and he smiled fully. "You preyed on me."

"I saved you from the nail-polish queen," Josh amended. "I remember it differently."

They laughed and it was easy and freeing for Josh. Somehow he wondered if what he'd told James had changed how the man viewed him. "I don't ever talk like this with clients," Josh spoke quietly. "I hope it wasn't too much."

James was quick to shake his head and assure him. "Absolutely not. I have loved hearing about you…and your job. There is *one* thing I'm still curious about, though."

Josh swallowed nervously at that, whipping his head around to face James. "Yeah?"

"Can I see the sketches? Of me?"

Yep. He'd been afraid of that. Pursing his lips then biting the bottom one, he nodded slowly. "Let me, uh… Let me go get them for you."

"Take your time. The food should be here any" — the doorbell rang and James chuckled — "minute. I'll get this settled. You go on."

Josh stood, a hand to the back of his thigh stopping him. The squeeze made him look back and down, and James was tilting up his head. "C'mere," the man murmured, and Josh wasn't about to neglect the request. He leaned down and kissed James happily, the kiss turning hungry quite quickly, before the doorbell rang again. They separated with sheepish grins and Josh disappeared for the stairs to get his art.

James' head was full of Josh — so full of everything Josh. He had so many questions still, and yet the more Josh said, the more James wanted to know.

He still felt terrible for not asking sooner. Hearing Josh talk about being a sickly kid in Brooklyn, hearing about his father? It made James just want to take care of him more than he already did. And hearing him talk about his escort adventures only made him want to do more with him, to experience more.

And the inexplicable pride he felt for Josh having been given a huge opportunity today? Well, that was just something he couldn't decipher. He hadn't even known about Josh's talent until Maria had thrust it in front of him. And he'd been more distracted by Josh standing adorably embarrassed at the conference-room door as if he were trying to shrink himself down with his rounded shoulders.

Though he had to hand it to Josh. While James had seen his ass in those Polaroids, seeing it on paper, sketched in full detail...? Well, that had been beyond flattering.

Josh descended the stairs minutes later, bringing James out of his thoughts. He rounded the corner carrying the leather folder from that morning and James had to admire the portfolio. It looked well-made and taken care of. He wondered if some of his money had contributed to it. That gave him a rush of joy.

The Italian meal, complete with pasta and delicious bread lay waiting for them on the table under warmers. But James was far more interested in seeing the drawings. He wanted to truly understand and appreciate Josh's passion. "Let's look at these first, then we'll eat," he suggested. Josh nodded silently, following James back into the living room.

James sat first and was glad he'd cleared off the coffee table. He set their wine aside and rested his hands in his lap, waiting as patiently as he could. He'd waited all day. He could wait the thirty seconds it took for Josh to open the portfolio and lay them out.

One by one Josh slowly — *maybe hesitantly? Reluctantly?* James wasn't sure — laid them out on the table. Not just the pictures of James — of which there were several — but pictures of landscapes, trees and sunlight and snowy mornings. There were sketches of fishermen on their boats, children on the beach… James was sure many of them came from Jamaica and New York, and he could see a few from Italy. And Josh was incredibly talented, capturing such small details to bring each picture to life.

But the ones of himself… They demanded his attention.

James studied the pictures — nude, clothed, awake, asleep. How had he kept these from him? Sure, he was often busy, but to keep this talent from him? When had he been drawing? Josh had captured every detail, James was sure, down to freckles and birthmarks and the absolute curve and detail of his length. It was like looking into a mirror. He was in awe. One in particular stood out. James looked wrecked, on his back, naked, his eyes closed. His cock was curved up against his body — but judging by the mess of his hair and sheets around him, they'd just finished. James studied it, catching a glimpse of Josh studying him.

"Is this what I really look like after?"

Josh cleared his throat twice and James had to admit that watching the man be vulnerable turned him on in a way he couldn't yet describe.

"Yes," Josh answered, and James knew he was being honest. The man swallowed hard, his cheeks a beautiful shade of pink.

"What do *you* look like?" James asked, as he looked square at Josh.

Josh balked and shook his head for a moment, his forehead pinching. "I'm not… I don't… I only focus on you," he got out, and if he were any more adorable in his state, James would die.

178

"Well" — James leaned back, resting one arm on the back of the couch and rubbing his beard with his other hand — "you're fuckin' talented, and I can't believe you never told me how much. You deserve everything you got today. I'm proud of you, Josh."

Josh's blush only darkened as a smile appeared on his face. "Thank you, James," he replied earnestly, his gaze on his hands as he sat before James. James couldn't have that. Watching him squirm under the attention was becoming addictive.

He pressed forward, using two fingers to gently lift Josh's chin. His head came willingly, those big blue eyes on display just for him. "Attention makes you nervous?" He pressed, searching Josh's eyes. "Don't take compliments well?"

Josh made a small noise, licking his soft lips. "I don't...uh, ever share my art. It's been a big day, and you just saw every piece I've drawn of you. I'm just a little..."

"Shhh-h," James countered, shifting closer. "Bask in it, Josh. You deserve nice things. You deserve to be on the end of good things. Let me show you how it feels, how *you* make *me* feel."

It was a big statement, and he couldn't ever know that he meant it even deeper than it had come out. But as he closed the gap and kissed a shell-shocked Josh Roberts, he was determined to uphold his words. He didn't know exactly how this would work, but he had the confidence in himself and the determination to take care of Josh, to lay Josh back and show him just how good he was — make him squirm and cry and prove he deserved it more than anyone.

Josh was melting. He was melting into a puddle of blushing nerves at the hands of James Barnwell. The man had single handedly twice now changed their dynamic in a natural way that left Josh floundering in the best way. It wasn't like he cared necessarily who topped or how it worked. He was more professional than that and only wanted James' pleasure, whatever that meant. He just hadn't realized how easily switching could come in this moment, how easily he could be reduced to the stammering young man he was underneath his professional exterior. Something about James' words spoke deeply to his soul, and he couldn't stop himself from grasping James' thick hair like an anchor or the way he begged 'please' into James' sweet lips.

They found themselves tangled on the couch before long, James' hips flush with Josh's, Josh writhing below him like it was the most natural thing in the world. James was no inexperienced man. He'd been with woman far longer than Josh had, and Josh would bet *more* than he had, despite his job. James knew just how to cant his hips to press against Josh's arousal, how to drag his mouth down Josh's neck like it was meant just for that. He sucked hard on Josh's pulse point. There'd be a mark tomorrow, but like hell if Josh cared. James could leave love bites all over his body and Josh would show them off like they were a gift.

Their slacks were in the way, and Josh had chosen a poor time to wear briefs. His erection was trapped, and James was taunting him in a way that was half what Josh had taught him and half just James. He gripped with rough hands at Josh's short hair and at his hips, his nails biting the skin to show Josh how much James wanted this. And to Josh's surprise, he'd never been more anxious to submit, the anticipation of being under James making his heart pound.

James left no exposed skin unkissed. Josh was sure his pale complexion was red and scraped by James' beard and part of him wished for a mirror, to see and to watch. James wasn't ready for that yet, however. He needed to do it once without an audience. If it went well, however, there was a large mirror in the guest en suite that would be perfect for just that activity.

Open-mouthed, hungry kisses left Josh whimpering. His cock was drooling in its confines. Josh knew where this was going and needed to hit the brakes for just a moment. He wasn't ready to bottom just yet, hadn't prepared himself, and if that was what James wanted…

"Jamie," he gasped, the name coming out more noise than anything. James grunted against his lips in reply, but Josh had to get this out, had to make sure this went right. "James…I. Hang on." He was gentle as he cupped James' face, finding his eyes to make sure they were in fact on the same page.

"Yeah? You okay?" James immediately asked once the kisses had stopped, concern evident on his forehead and in his eyes. Josh couldn't stop the smile that pulled at his lips.

"Tell me what you wanna do, baby," he said, pressing his hips up, their clothed cocks rubbing together. James' eyes fluttered for one brief moment, a strangled sigh escaping. "Tell me."

"I wanna fuck you," James replied in that husky, hoarse tone that went straight to Josh's need. "I wanna lay you down and fuck you, deep and slow. Can you handle that? You want that?" James nudged Josh's chin with his nose affectionately, and it almost didn't fit the moment. But it warmed Josh to his soul and licked heat up his spine because…

Hell yes.

Josh closed his eyes for one small second, his body clenching at the thought of James' intrusion. "Fuck…*yes*, yes I do," he replied through a groan, drifting his hands from James' cheeks to his ass, pressing them together. Both men bit out hard groans and James took the hint beautifully.

"You're gonna come now—first, with me. Then we'll shower separately and reconvene in the bedroom. Sound good?" Josh needed the orgasm, God, he did, and James needed the edge off or he'd come the second he slid home. Josh would be *tight*. It had been a long time. Josh wanted to make this as good as possible for James. And he wanted to be good *for* James. The thought sent a chill up his spine.

"So g-good." Josh shuddered and James began an onslaught of thrusts that had him holding on. It was delicious, not enough and yet just barely what he needed to get there. Hearing James' moans into his lips, the primal yet simple act of dry humping on the couch like horny teenagers, knowing he was about to come in his expensive slacks? It was all sending him close to the edge. Then James started to talk and Josh's brain short-circuited.

"I can't wait to fuck you, to be inside you. Wanna make it good, want you to remember how my cock feels inside you. You ever fantasize about it?" The words were so heavy against his ear that Josh couldn't quiet his replying moans, his words taking hiatus for a moment. They rutted against each other almost wildly now, moving with the comfort of knowing one another well. "I didn't know I needed it until tonight, but God, Josh, sweetheart, I need to be inside you."

The nickname, new and something no one had ever called him, made his breath hitch and his hips jerk. It was affectionate, personal and he'd be replaying the way it had sounded on James' tongue until he said it again, sliding a hand under Josh and pressing them together.

"Come on, sweetheart. Josh, make a mess for me so I can take my time learning you tonight."

God, Josh didn't need to be asked twice. He held on to James as his mouth fell open and he came, hard. James fell over the edge with him, their foreheads pressed together as they made a sticky mess between them. It was erotic, oddly intimate and almost just the right side of humiliation for Josh, his blood running hot as he emptied himself for what he knew would be only the first time that night. They lay panting and sharing breaths for several long moments, until James started peppering Josh with kisses, pulling him from his daze. "I'm just getting started, baby boy," he murmured low into Josh's cheek. "I can't wait to fuck you. Don't make me wait, please…"

Josh knew he'd be as fast as possible at cleaning and preparing himself, because like hell was he wasting any time before that cock was buried inside him.

He didn't allow himself to focus on how the lines between need and obligation by job and contract had blurred. He ignored the flutters in his chest as James kissed his nose and grinned like Josh held the moon. He filed them away like little scary secrets, because if he went there, if he let those moments consume him, he'd be a goner for good.

And if he already was...? Well, he didn't want to know about it.

James shouldn't be nervous.

As he lit a few candles, padding across the room lightly in only his white cotton boxers, he knew he shouldn't feel the nervous tightening in his stomach. He shouldn't feel out of his depth. But something about what was about to happen, the dynamic they were about to change, left him feeling jittery.

After leaving one lamp on by the bed, James surveyed the room. Josh always made sure to take ambience into account — and James would do the same for him. He felt like the room held a certain glow now, a certain sexual appeal. He was mostly satisfied, as he pulled the comforter off the bed they'd been sharing.

The thing that caught him the most in these moments was that it was never about the money. It was never about what Josh cost, how much it cost to have him there. James never even considered the price tag that came with these experiences, and he always paid Josh above and beyond what he was asked to pay. They didn't discuss payment, either. James made sure the generous amount kept that conversation at bay, because he honestly didn't want to have it. He didn't want to think about the fact that every kiss and every tug of his dick was bought and paid for. He wanted to live in his pretend bubble that the gorgeous man on the other side of the bathroom door was as interested in him as he was in return.

It couldn't ever be different. There was no way Josh could ever be just *his*. But that didn't stop him from pretending, from wishing, from monopolizing Josh's time and whisking him away to far-off places to keep him all to himself. He just denied that was what he was doing in his own mind. If he could keep the separation, if he could continue to deny his emotions, no one would get hurt.

And even if he *was* about to fuck the guy, to top him for the first time in hopes of wrecking him to the best of his ability, that didn't mean he had to tell himself or anyone else the truth. *Nope.* He'd save that for a rainy day.

He just hoped Josh's new job didn't stop things between them. They hadn't discussed it and Josh had seemed content with his future, so maybe they wouldn't need to. Maybe they could continue their arrangement and actually spend more time together. Maybe...

The bathroom door swung open slowly, yanking James from his thoughts. Josh emerged, his skin pink from a hot shower, blond hair wet and slicked back on his head, a towel wrapped around his waist. He looked every bit as delicious as he had just a little while ago, albeit the pink hue across his cheeks was left over from earlier. He was surprised by how much he wanted tonight, how much he wanted this man writhing under him. He was always more than content with their current arrangements, but something about the pride he felt for Josh, the way Josh had fallen apart under him, made him want to take care of him in a way he hadn't yet.

"Hey," Josh greeted, a small smile forming on his pretty face. James shook his head, grinning as he approached him, and wasted no time.

Cupping the man's cheeks, James kissed him feverishly. There was no preamble. He simply went in for the kill, because if he had to wait a second longer to get his hands on Josh, he was going to explode in frustration.

Josh stilled under the kiss for just a moment before kissing back full force. He released the overlap where his hand secured his towel and put both hands on James' flanks, gripping hard. James knew then he had him, knew this was going to go his way. He mashed down the nerves and pulled Josh closer.

"I may need you to walk me through this a little, but I'm a quick learner," he mumbled into Josh's lips. He groaned in reply, darting his tongue out and rubbing James' in a way that made him gasp.

"I'll help however you need, but somehow I don't think you'll need much instruction," he replied, and James grinned into the kisses, pulling Josh back toward the bed.

They'd see. He hoped he had as much confidence in himself as it seemed Josh had in him.

Josh was seeing stars just kissing James. He was really in for it tonight.

And James wasn't taking his time, as Josh found himself naked on the bed, his towel gone long before his back hit the sheets. The sultry smell of spiced vanilla carried through the room, and to James' credit, he knew how to set the mood. If Josh didn't know better, he'd think James was seducing him for *real*. He'd never say it, but thinking it made his dick jump between his legs, already well on its way to being fully hard as James shed his boxers easily and climbed over him, kneeling above him with his hands on either side of his neck and looking at him in a way that made him feel *very* vulnerable.

"God, Josh," James breathed, and Josh shivered at the tone he used. "I can't believe I get to go to bed with you every night." He dropped his mouth to Josh's collar bone, mouthing at the flesh as Josh's breath caught in his throat. The onslaught of touch, James' hot mouth and tongue mixed with those words had Josh completely hard and reaching for the man above him.

"Jamie…you don't have to—" Josh flushed hard, his cheeks heating under the affections and words of the man above him.

"Don't have to *what*? Tell you how handsome you are? Tell you what you do to me? Tell you how much I enjoy waking up to you in my bed? You've gotta know by the way my body reacts to you." James' hot breath washed over Josh's chest as the man slid south, nipping at Josh's defined pectorals. Josh's lungs expanded, making him feel like he was floating off the bed with every word James spoke.

James didn't mean the words, Josh's brain argued. This was just the arrangement talking. Josh did his best to maintain that as James kissed his way down Josh's abdomen, nosing at his cock that was swollen and ready, lying against his belly. Josh's breath hitched again, and his words were forgotten as James wrapped his hand around the base of his cock and slowly took his length into his mouth.

The heat and the sight of James taking him in inch by inch made his toes curl. He didn't even try to suppress his moans, letting them fall out of his throat easily as James began to work him. It was sinful, so good, and knowing his cock would always be James' first made his stomach tighten relentlessly.

Josh barely heard the cap of the lube, the snap and click just audible above his moans. But when he felt the wet fingertips rubbing around his rim, he knew that was what it had been. "J-Jamie," he stuttered, forcing his eyes open, "I prepped a little in the shower for you."

"Well, look at you, eager boy." James grinned but there was sudden, slight apprehension in his features. "You wanna feel me inside you, don't you?"

Josh nodded eagerly, as that had been his reasoning. He'd also wanted to make sure he was clean and to speed up the process, because he didn't want James to have to start from scratch when it had been so long for him. Not tonight. Not James' first time...

Josh swallowed hard, his gaze softening at James. "I can take two," he informed him through a soft sigh, his body empty and clenching in anticipation. The fact they'd been together so many times and it was still this thrilling, if not more so than the first time... Josh couldn't get over it. He squirmed a little as James massaged his tight rim, teasing and learning his body. James' thumb rubbed the flesh between it and his balls, making his eyes roll back in his head. It was at that moment that James pushed two fingers in, slowly breaching him.

The air rushed from Josh, not necessarily because of the twinge and sharp tingles but due to the act itself, and that James had slipped two thick fingers inside him because he *wanted to*, because he wanted to see what Josh felt like. Josh had half a mind to fuck himself down on his fingers and beg James to forego the condom. To have him unsheathed was something of his fantasies. It was wrong and he wouldn't do it, but the desire was there. It washed over Josh like hot water on a summer's day.

James ran his free hand down and gripped Josh's cock, stroking him slowly but tightly. Josh keened, squirming beneath the man, unable to stop himself from digging his heels into the bed and chasing the intrusion. "Feels good, huh?" James rasped, thrusting his fingers slowly, twisting his wrist around to open Josh up for him. They went easy now, the lube and the prep letting his body open beautifully for James. "Feels so good to be full, to be played with, stretched open. You always made me ache for you, wish you could just stay inside me for hours. We'll have to try that sometime, huh? What do they call that? Cockwarming? God, to have you inside me, just throbbing and making me wait... *Fuck*."

Josh met James' groan with his own, uninhibited as James' words washed over him. His cock was aching, his body clenching hungrily around the fingers inside him. James added a third before Josh could respond, rendering him speechless for a moment as his mouth fell open and his body adjusted to the change. He had to give it to the man... He wasn't afraid. He was going for it.

A crook of his fingers and a turn of his wrist had Josh seeing stars. He cried out, grasping the sheets below him as his legs shook with arousal. James just grinned, pleased that he'd gotten that right, Josh was sure.

"God, Jamie...need your cock...*p-please*."

Josh could hardly breathe, his chest rising and falling rapidly. If James didn't stop stroking him with such vigor and stop fingering him so well, he was going to lose it before the main event. And while he'd been fucked long after orgasm before — on request — it wasn't his favorite. He wanted them to experience this together. He was about to grab James' wrist when the man pulled off and slid his fingers out.

"Is that how you ask, beautiful boy?" James murmured as he wiped his fingers on a towel. Josh chewed his lip, catching his breath as he watched James slide the condom down over his cock, the need making him crazy.

"Daddy…" His voice cracked, his lips dry from his gasping at James' ministrations. "Daddy, please fuck me. Let me feel your cock." Josh let the words slide right off his tongue. He couldn't stop them. He needed this. He'd had no idea how much.

James smiled, seemingly more relaxed as he leaned down and peppered Josh's chest with kisses. Josh ran his fingers through his hair, whimpering in desperation. James chuckled against his sweaty skin. "Guess we know what makes you weak now, don't we?" he mused as he took himself in hand and grew slightly more serious, lining himself up.

"*Please*," Josh begged one more time, grasping the sheets below him as he watched James' every move. His own cock jumped at the first touch of James' slick, rounded tip. It drooled all over his belly as James teased him, making Josh moan incessantly. It was pressure everywhere but where he needed it, until finally, *finally* James pushed against the loosened ring of muscle, gaining entrance after slow and steady pressure.

As soon as the crown of his thick cock pressed through, Josh was gasping. The stretch was more than James' fingers, the shape less forgiving but in the best way. He forced his eyes open to watch as James took his time, pressing into him gently. James' hands were on his hips now, and he held Josh still as he slipped his cock inside him, making Josh's mind go completely blank of anything but obscene pleasure.

"Holy *fuck*," James groaned, and Josh forced his eyes open to glance down at him. James was focused on their joining, his eyes wide and dark, his face red with tension and pleasure. "You should see yourself...f-*fuck*." His words stuttered as he pressed forth, Josh's body slowly accommodating him. It was erotic, sensual and somehow something Josh hadn't experienced in the times he'd done this before. He felt open and vulnerable, but also like James would take the best care. It was a heavy feeling that weighed over him until James bottomed out and began to pull back, making Josh moan wantonly because... *No, not yet, I need...*

James pulled his cock out and Josh gasped at the loss. He traced his finger around Josh's hole, humming to himself in a way that made Josh shiver. Then he plunged back in slowly, that initial notch of his cut head inside making Josh see stars. The drag, the twinge of stretch mixing with the insane pleasure of being penetrated was going to make Josh go mad. "Fucking hell, Jamie." He stretched his head up and back, pleasure ricocheting off every nerve, "S-so...*oh*," he huffed in surprise as James began to move, a slow rock of his hips that was sinful. Josh gripped the sheets tightly, his biceps and abs flexing as pleasure drowned him.

He caught James, hands on the bed on either side of his hips, rolling his into Josh with purpose, roaming his gaze over Josh's body. Josh felt like a prize under his scrutiny. He let the sounds fall freely, let his body move as it wanted to, meeting thrust for thrust until James was repositioning them, bringing Josh's legs up and over his shoulders. This gave him more leverage and the curve of James' dick allowed his head to scrape Josh's prostate every time he pulled back, until he was almost completely out, driving Josh mad. Then he'd thrust back in, pushing a whoosh and a groan from Josh's lips. The man knew how to fuck—it was evident—even if he'd never fucked a man before. Josh was so close to losing his mind, so full and stretched, his toes curling, every muscle tightening...

"Jamie... *Jamie... Daddy... Please*," he chanted, letting himself fall into the well of pleasure. James nodded, on the edge himself.

"Touch yourself. Come all over yourself while I come inside you. *God...fuck...*" It was punishing now, and between that and James' words, Josh was in a mad dash to come.

"Come inside me, *please*," he said as he jerked his cock frantically. Their moans mingled in the hot air between them, their bodies slick and sliding together with practiced ease. Josh didn't want this to end, but God, he had to come so badly or he'd die. He was sure of it. "I'm...oh, God... Jamie, come inside me, please..."

"Good boy. Come on, beautiful boy. Come *on*. *Come* on yourself and I'll come inside you, just like you want." James knew just what to say, it seemed, and Josh didn't question it. He did as he was told, basking in the praise as he came hard. He clenched down on James hard cock as cum covered his chest, his chin and his abs, his moans broken as he rode the waves.

James followed him right after, but Josh was barely aware. With three more punishing thrusts, he stilled with a shuddering groan that Josh *felt* more than heard, then pumped his hips a few more times, slow and shallow.

Shockwaves traveled through Josh for several moments before he opened his eyes again. James had his forehead pressed to Josh's right calf, his own labored breathing evident. Letting go of the rumpled sheets, he slid his hands down to rub at James' thighs. That grabbed his attention, and he raised his head to grin down at him.

"Hi." James blushed hard, and Josh couldn't help but flush in return with his own small hello. They chuckled a little, the passion of the moment fading and leaving aftereffects in its wake. "That was…"

"My best bottom experience ever," was out of Josh's mouth before he could stop it. He slapped a hand over his mouth and actually laughed, his cheeks flushing. James snorted.

"I'm going to think you're actually serious since you reacted that way." He chuckled, rubbing his beard against Josh's calf. "Honestly… That was fucking *amazing*."

Josh nodded, letting his hand fall away as he ruffled his sweaty hair with his other hand. "I'm serious, though. I shouldn't have said that, but *fuck*. I felt that in my toes. I might be dead."

James flushed a beautiful crimson as he pulled out of Josh slowly, both men groaning at the separation. James shuffled unevenly off the bed to dispose of the condom and Josh contemplated a second shower. There was no way he could go again, not for at least an hour. Maybe James would join him…

James returned with a warm towel and a cup of water and Josh had to blink. People did not take care of him. Aftercare was never in the agreement. But James swiped the warm towel over Josh thoroughly, disposing of it and climbing back into the bed. Josh reached for James and they locked their hands together as they slid their bodies close.

"You're sure you're okay?" James asked quietly, nuzzling against Josh's ear. Josh's cheeks went hot and a smile formed as he nodded.

"Far beyond okay. You're…that…wow, Jamie." He turned his face toward James, their eyes locking as their faces were level on the pillows. James roamed a hand over Josh's chest absently, and it was warm and calming.

"You are, Josh," James replied softly before closing the distance and kissing him slow. Josh's heart fluttered and his body gravitated toward James without a second thought.

It was apparent that somewhere in his post-sex rush, somewhere in his addled mind that he was falling for his client. And there was seemingly no stopping it.

* * * *

The sun made the day outside look deceiving as it came through the lace curtains. James knew it was no warmer than New York outside, but the sun made it seem like spring. And the shape it illuminated on the bed made it seem all the warmer.

Josh was curled up on his side, one arm curled under the other, his face tucked against them. The sheets and comforter had fallen to his waist as he slept, leaving his bare upper body on complete display. His blond hair tousled, a barely there shadow of scruff on his jaw, his pink lips parted just slightly, eyes still very shut with sleep, he was the picture of handsome peace. James didn't want to wake him, but the fresh pastries and coffee would get cold if he didn't.

He'd woken before the sun, wanting to get emails out of the way so he and Josh could spend time together with Maria, working through this new job opportunity and Josh's future. He wouldn't normally be involved in such matters, but this was *Josh*—not only his faux boyfriend but also someone he cared about. He wanted to make sure his company did right by Josh—and that Josh was prepared.

That in itself was enough to wake him before dawn—the worry about the why he cared for Josh so much. He had boiled it down to their arrangement, their friendship and close proximity. He was determined to only see it as that. He was paying the man, for goodness' sake. There was no way to back out of this arrangement without someone getting hurt or something being ruined. They were in this now, and James was determined to keep things the way they were.

Even if last night was more than incredible.

Setting the tray down on the side table, he sat on the bed beside Josh, folding one leg under himself as he contemplated how to wake the sleeping beauty. He couldn't stop himself from brushing the soft hair off his forehead, trailing his fingers down the light strands. Josh's long eyelashes fluttered, and he let out the softest sigh James had ever heard. His heart clenched. And *that* was why he had to stay focused *off* his heart.

"Good morning, sleepyhead," he murmured, letting his fingers run down Josh's arm. Josh opened his eyes, blinking a few times in the bright morning light. James couldn't help finding him utterly adorable, all youth and clean, hard lines blinking like a sleepy puppy. The yawn he tried to cover solidified that comparison.

"Hey, Jamie," he rasped, shifting under the covers to stretch. James couldn't tear his eyes away as the sculpted arms rose over his head, his long legs stretching under the covers. His abdominal muscles shifted, his pectorals hardened and James' cock was growing more interested with every second he stared. He was literally insatiable for this younger man. It was still shocking sometimes.

"Brought you some coffee and pastries, baked fresh this morning," James offered, unable to pull his hand away when Josh slid his fingers into it. It was a tender gesture that warmed him more than the sun could.

"Yeah?" Josh shifted again to lie back on his side, assessing James' own morning hair and sweatpants. "I think that's my shirt." Josh sounded amused and didn't hide his smile. James glanced down at the soft gray T-shirt and chuckled, his cheeks heating.

"Huh. You know, I didn't remember buying it, but it was too soft to take off." James ran his free hand through his hair, surprised at not feeling awkward in the slightest as Josh smiled up at him like a ray of sunshine.

"You can keep it. I don't mind. I have like ten of them," Josh offered without hesitation. "Looks better on you anyway." His free hand fell to James' thigh as he spoke and James knew then that they were on the same page. "Like the way it fits your arms, across your chest." Josh dug his fingers into the muscle there, caressing as the words grew quieter but heavy with intent. "You should come closer. I'm hungry…"

James scoffed in mock surprise but moved closer without waiting more than a beat. "Your coffee's gonna get cold," he teased, though he suspected the man didn't care. And as he rose and flipped James to his back, pinning him to the mussed sheets, his suspicions were confirmed.

"Ain't coffee I want." Josh's Brooklyn slipped out and James shivered, gritting his teeth with anticipation. With the top sheets shifted, it was obvious that Josh was *very* aroused. It was a pleasant surprise and something he never grew tired of seeing.

"Well, far be it from me to stop you from having what you're in the mood for," James replied, trailing his hands across Josh's round shoulders as Josh worked on getting his sweatpants off without much fuss. He licked his lips as James' cock sprang free, also very interested in the morning's turn of events. James' heart rate jumped.

"Don't mind if I do," the younger man all but growled as he wasted no time wrapping those beautiful pink lips around James' cock. Yes, this was the way every morning should start. James had zero questions about that.

Josh couldn't believe their trip was almost over. Ten days ago, he'd arrived in Italy as just an escort away on a job with one of the most eligible bachelors in the world. Now he was an artist contracted with a billion-dollar company, about to embark on a whole new journey. He hadn't quite figured out what he'd do with the rest of his life when he got back to New York, but he wasn't worrying about it. He was soaking up the Italian sun, wine and all the sex he and James had been having since they'd arrived. This was the best trip of his life.

He looked at James over his tiny espresso cup as they sat at a small coffee shop in Otranto. They'd taken a day to go exploring, driving a little over two hours south. While Josh was at a loss with the language, James was completely content, touring them around, speaking to the locals like he belonged. It was a little more than Josh could handle after spending so many nights in bed with the man.

James finished ordering another espresso from the young waitress and turned back to Josh, raising his eyebrows as Josh knew he'd been caught marveling. "Need something?"

"No, no." Josh shook his head, setting the tiny cup down to choose his words wisely lest he say more than he wanted to. "You're just so...comfortable here. It's nice to watch. And you didn't tell me your Italian was that good." He added the last part because he couldn't help it, their banter still holding up outside the bedroom.

James laughed a little and Josh enjoyed the way his cheeks turned pink. "Well, when we built the resort, I spent a lot of time here — got to know my favorite spots, learned to speak the language. I enjoy being here a lot." He sipped the rest of his current espresso before a small grin took over. "I've enjoyed being here with you. Thank you again for coming."

"Stop thanking me." Josh laughed off the part of James' enjoyment, because if only... "I should be thanking you. This has all...changed my life. I can't even begin to — "

"Don't. You don't need to thank me for anything. Having you here has been more than a joy. I'm still sorry Maria accosted you the way she did, but honestly, getting to know you has made this even more fun — and not just sexually, the *real* Josh."

The way James said the last part made Josh's body flood with goosebumps. It was such an intimate thing to say, and of everything Josh was sure of, he knew

James was a genuine person. He wouldn't say it if he didn't mean it that way in his heart.

"Well…feel special, because everything I told you, I hardly tell anyone. I mean, I have my roommates, but…" He drifted off with a shy shrug, smiling a little as he thought of his friends.

"Tell me about them," James pressed with interest. Josh chuckled a little.

"They're not *that* exciting or anything—Nadia and Andrew, my two best friends and roommates. Nadia I met through…work." He cleared his throat a little then laughed. "And Andrew is normal." The word made him laugh again and they settled into easy conversation as Josh let James in on more of his personal life. It was far too easy, but Josh never questioned it because this was James.

Once they finished their coffee, they continued exploring. Hand in hand, they walked the streets, James' security not far behind but giving them distance. It was still sometimes strange to Josh that no one in James' camp knew they weren't together, but it didn't bother him, because deep down inside he knew that being real was becoming the one thing he really wanted. He couldn't have that, so pretending was the next best thing. And pretending without anyone else knowing they were pretending…? Well, that was the best it was going to get, Josh knew.

* * * *

The next morning brought more of the life Josh had grown accustomed to in Italy, mixed with meeting Maria and ordering supplies, setting up trips and planning his work through March of the following year. Josh had texted his friends the news, and much to his appreciation, they seemed genuinely excited. He had yet to tell his mother about any of it—Italy, Jamaica, the job—because how was he supposed to explain all this to her? He kept up with her via text, the occasional casual exchanges to keep her from worrying about him and to keep him aware of what went on in her life. She could handle her own affairs. She was as strong as Josh himself, stronger really, but he looked out for her as her only child. He'd sent her flowers two days prior as a gesture and because he was feeling guilty about the lies and omissions, so when his phone rang midafternoon, he smiled and figured she'd finally received them.

"Hey, Ma," he answered as he shifted on the couch in the lavish living room of their villa where he was sketching. He continued mindlessly shading in one of the people in the picture as he held the phone to his cheek.

"Joshua Grant, explain to me why you're in Italy."

His hand stilled, charcoal against the textured paper as her tone and words hung over the line. "Umm-m…I can explain."

"I'm sure you can, sweetheart." Sarah Roberts wasn't beating around the bush, and Josh honestly didn't expect anything less. "I can't wait to hear about why I'm staring at a picture of you and a handsome, older man strolling hand-in-hand down an adorable cobblestone street overseas and why you didn't bother to tell your mother you were leaving the country?"

Picture…? He didn't remember anyone taking pictures of them, and he was momentarily distracted as he set the pad down and grabbed his laptop roughly off the coffee table that his feet had been resting on moments ago. "Pictures? Where?"

"I went to get my hair done an hour ago and Shelly had that *Daily Mail* website up on her phone and she said 'Sarah, is this Josh? Who's he with?' and sure enough, it was you and this resort designer I had no idea you were seeing. Care to enlighten me on when you got a very wealthy, much older boyfriend?"

Josh put her on speaker as he typed rapidly, googling James' name and *Daily Mail*. Sure enough, there they were, a feature article for that day. A dozen pictures had been taken of them, and he was silent as he scrolled, his heart racing in his chest.

"Joshua? Are you there?"

"Yeah, yeah, Ma, I'm here! I'm just... Hang on. I can explain," he said, scrubbing a hand over his face. He held the phone closer to his mouth, not afraid to keep her on speaker as James had gone up to the main building for a meeting two hours before. He scrambled to concoct a story, though he knew his mother would see through any lie he spewed unless he was utterly convincing in a way he'd never managed to be before. "I...met James — James Barnwell — a couple of months ago back in New York. We started seeing each other a little after that. I didn't tell you because" — he closed his eyes and leaned his head back on the couch, hoping the heavens would forgive him for the lies he was telling her — "he's much older than me and I didn't want you to know until we were serious, in case it didn't work out. If I'd known someone would publish pictures of us, I would have told you. He's wonderful, Ma. I promise." Well, at least most of that was actually true, he realized as he held his breath and waited for her reaction.

"Josh, honey, he's much older than you." She repeated his words, and there was concern in them. "You're a handsome boy, and if he's taking advantage of you—"

"No one is taking advantage of anyone. He...he treats me like a gift, Ma. You should see the place we're staying, the food we eat. In Jamaica, he—"

"Jamaica? Joshua, when—?"

"Shit... *Shoot*," he amended quickly, sighing heavily as he realized his mistake as his mother used his first and middle names again in admonishment. "Sorry. He just... He's so good to me. I promise. If he weren't, I wouldn't have flown here with him."

"Are you two serious now? I mean, you're in Italy, for goodness' sakes! I just wished you'd mentioned him to me. I saw you a few weeks ago, and when I asked if you'd met anyone, you said you hadn't. It says here he's bisexual and out. I know you are too, so why would you lie? Is he making you lie?"

Josh winced at her hurt, worried tone. He'd always told her everything, except for his escorting. He couldn't very well tell her now and that it was how he'd met James. Chewing his lip, he was careful but honest with his next words. "He'd never ask me to lie. He's a good man, really. He's kind, and he's so generous. He always makes sure I'm comfortable and happy. We laugh. I— We're not serious. I mean...not yet, I don't think," he said, because even the thought of someday ever being serious made his stomach tumble. "But he's great, Ma. I swear... He makes me so happy." The more the words came out, the more Josh realized how true they were. He leaned his head back on the couch and closed his eyes, smiling. "I'm sorry I didn't tell you. But I know you'd love him."

There was silence on the line and Josh managed to rein his smile in as he waited for her reply.

"Sounds like you really like this man," Sarah replied, hesitance evident in her voice over the line. "I just don't want my baby getting hurt by some powerful tycoon-type. Are you sure he's taking care of you? If you're… Are you safe with him? He's not into any of that—"

"Mom!" Josh exclaimed, his face flaming, despite him being alone, "Yes, we're safe, and yes, he takes care of me. I wouldn't put myself in something that wasn't safe. You know that!"

"It's my job to worry about you, sweetheart. As soon as I saw these pictures, I had the worst fears. You have to understand that. You look awful happy in them, but I couldn't be sure without hearing your voice."

Josh looked back down at the computer in his lap, and she was right. He *did* look happy. Actually, they both did. They were walking hand in hand, and Josh could remember the exact moment. He was smiling at James as he explained something about the architecture of the building they were next to. Josh actually looked like he was in awe as he listened, which showed just how evident his affection for James actually was. Josh's cheeks grew hotter the longer he stared at the photo. "I'm sorry I worried you. I didn't mean to. I was trying *not* to by not telling you. I'm good, I promise. I'll be home in two days, and I'll come right over and tell you everything."

She seemed to accept his apology and his words as they chatted for a few more minutes. As he hung up the phone with an *'I love you, I'll see you in a few days,'* he let himself stare at the paparazzi photos for another minute. He was just about to close the laptop when

James' voice startled him out of his daydream about their previous day's adventure and how actually *true* his words had been to his mother.

"I want you to know that I know. I shouldn't have listened, but I walked in and she was on speaker and I heard everything. I'm sorry."

Josh jumped out of his skin, his laptop sliding off his lap as he stood quickly, spinning to face James where he was standing at the entrance to the living room. He looked sheepish as hell, his tie hanging undone around his neck and his suit coat in his hands. "I didn't hear you come in," was all he could muster. James offered him a gentle smile.

"I figured."

They stood and stared at each other for a long moment before Josh cleared his throat, rubbing the back of his neck. "Listen… About what you heard, I—"

"No, no." He waved a hand, shaking his head. "I shouldn't be making you lie to your mother. I'm sorry."

"You didn't make me do anything. She doesn't know what I do, and if I told her it would break her heart. I just had to keep it up for her" *And I meant everything I said*, screamed itself inside his mind, the words dying on his lips as he stared at James and tried to read his expression. On impulse, Josh walked around the couch, running a hand through his wild, messy hair as he ignored how un-fancy he was in his ripped jeans and white T-shirt next to James' business attire. "She just worries about me. And I'm the one who didn't tell her I was going overseas. She's protective." He shrugged a little and offered James a half smile. "Did you see the pictures?" he asked curiously.

James nodded. "I did. I was going to tell you about them when I got home. My PR team is working to have them removed and to maintain your privacy. I'm really sorry that happened. Some amateur photographer sold them. This stuff happens occasionally." James sighed heavily and ran a hand through his own hair, and Josh suddenly wished to do the same. "I'm still sorry." Josh could tell by his tone and that gentle, wounded expression that he was sincere.

He took a step forward, resting a hand on James' forearm, out of second nature at this point. "Seriously, it's *fine*. It was good to hear her voice, and I know she still loves me." He laughed, trying to lighten the situation with some humor. "She called you handsome, at least, so there's that." Josh smiled hopefully, trying to ease James' concern. He wasn't worried about it negatively affecting his life back home, since his name wasn't written in the article and his clients knew he was away. He'd have to send the pics to Nadia and Andrew later, if for nothing other than a laugh.

"Yeah? I missed that part. I came in around the time she was calling me your '*wealthy, much-older boyfriend*'." There was finally humor in his eyes, but something else Josh couldn't place. Josh flushed, knowing everything he'd said after.

"Well…as far as everyone knows, that's what you are. Those are just facts." He shrugged, feigning seriousness.

"And everything else you said?"

Josh raised his eyes immediately to James, a little surprised by the forward question. While he couldn't remember every word he'd said, he had a general idea and flushed hotly. "Yeah," Josh replied a little more wistfully than he'd intended, knowing that no matter how much he meant it, it wasn't about to change anything. "I meant all of it. You're wonderful, Jamie. There's no way around that."

James stood quietly for a long moment, long enough to make Josh start to worry he'd said the wrong thing. His cheeks were pink as well and Josh admired that as he waited for a reply, holding his breath. "Nah. I'm not that great," James replied, a noticeable change to his voice—a little lower, a little huskier. Josh felt it to his very core.

"Pretty sure I've already made up my mind on that one. I'm the one who's been in your presence almost nonstop for the past two weeks," he replied, letting himself close the gap between them. James stayed where he was, but his body language invited Josh closer, the jacket leaving his hands as he reached for Josh.

"I've just got you tricked." A ghost of a grin lit James' features slightly as Josh made sure there was minimal distance between them. James was a magnet he was drawn to and there was no denying himself the man when they were in close proximity and alone. James didn't seem to mind as he found Josh's waist and gripped tightly. "I ain't that good, pal," he murmured softly, caressing the skin under Josh's shirt. He shuddered.

"I'll fight you to the end of the line on that," Josh replied before he shushed James with a slow kiss, ending the discussion with something he'd been craving since the man had left that morning. It was slow, almost tentative, as if he were prepared for James to bolt. That didn't happen, though, as James wound his arms around Josh and he pulled their bodies together, chest to chest, as their tongues danced, the taste of James making Josh need him even more than he already thought he did.

James didn't reply with words, but his kisses were telling. Josh took the reins, backing James gently against the archway where they stood, pressing himself against the man as their deep, languid kisses continued. James' beard was scraping his face as they both groped, letting the kisses take over. Josh forgot about the pictures, about his mother's call and his own internal confession. He focused solely on James, on making him groan, on getting him to let out those whispery little noises he made when Josh found a particularly good spot.

Josh pushed his thigh against James' hardness, making the man shake. "*Fuck*," he gasped into Josh's mouth, grabbing Josh's ass to knead. "Kissing you is… *Oh God…*"

Josh wanted to press for what exactly he was going to finish that sentence with, but the friction on his own cock from their grinding position against the door was making him groan instead. He chased the feeling while rubbing his leg against James, letting his mouth wander low on the man's neck. James happily and eagerly granted him access, twisting his head up and away so his whole neck was bared to Josh for the assault.

"You keep doing that, and I'm gonna need you to fuck me right here."

Josh chuckled darkly against James' throat. "I've got something better in mind," he said as he took James' hand and pulled him off the wall and up the stairs to the bedroom.

They were already half naked once they made it there. It was a short trip up the stairs, but they'd been busy. Josh's shirt was on the stairs, James' somewhere in the foyer. James' shoes had been discarded, his tie and belt gone. Josh was already stroking him with a tight grip through open pants and James was rubbing Josh through his jeans, fumbling with the button because Josh had him absolutely wrecked against the wall inside their bedroom.

It was so easy for them, Josh realized amid the passion and need. They just *did* this. It had never been this easy before, always a little awkward and contrived with other clients. But with James it all clicked into place. And Josh's body wanted nothing more than to react to James' every touch and noise.

They kissed frantically as James tried to get Josh's jeans down his hips. His grunts of frustration only made Josh's heart clench in that odd, adorable way. It was a joint effort until they were pooled at his feet, revealing nothing underneath. James looked very pleased as he leaned back to survey the sight.

"Mmm-m, need to taste you, sweet boy," he murmured with intent before he pushed off the wall and shoved Josh into the room. Their laughter was natural through more kisses until Josh found himself flopping onto the bed. He positioned himself in the middle as James shed his pants and boxer briefs, making Josh's mouth water.

"God, I love when you're feisty, Daddy," Josh groaned as James climbed over him, kneeling between his spread legs. His cock was already weeping against his belly, begging to be touched. James didn't seem to have the patience to wait.

"Can't help it. You make me this way, baby boy," he replied before he leaned down without further ado and took Josh into his mouth with no hands. Watching that bearded mouth work him over was something Josh knew he'd never get tired of. Sliding his hands in James' hair, he didn't push or fuss, simply gave in to the assault that was James' mouth.

It was hot and wet and perfect, and Josh could hardly keep his eyes open to watch. Straining, he held it together as best he could. He felt more than saw James' hand on himself. When he finally cracked an eye open, he took in such a pretty sight. James was working himself open while he sucked Josh down deep and hard. Josh jolted and pulled James off by his hair, panting and struggling to keep it together. "Holy…fuck…"

"Getting myself ready for you, baby boy," James rasped, wiping his mouth with his hand as he adjusted his position and arched his back. Josh's mouth fell open in awe as he watched James prep himself. It was something Josh hadn't known he'd needed to see. It was exceptionally sexy.

"You gonna get on my cock, Daddy? Ride me?" Josh purred, dragging his hands up and down James' arms and shoulders, hungry for more. James' groan was broken as rocked harder onto his own fingers.

"B-bare," he began, stuttering over his words as his face flushed. "I wanna ride you with nothing between us. D-dying to feel you… Please, Josh, please…"

Desperation filled his voice, heated and hungry, and it was evident in the blue gaze he lifted that he meant it. It was filled with pleading.

Josh didn't break his rules. It kept him safe. It kept him separated. But with James looking at him like that, it made his heart clench in a way he wasn't ready for. His body went hot. *Oh fuck.*

Even though his resolve was fracturing already, he still muttered a weak, hesitant, "Jamie…"

"Please," James begged, looking Josh in the eyes and making his heart race even harder. "I want it so bad. Can't stop thinking about it. Do it all the time…"

Josh couldn't say no to this man. Even though he knew better, that crossing this line would lead to no good, he simply could do nothing but give in.

"You wanna feel just me, handsome? Want my cock inside you with nothing else?" He couldn't believe himself, but something inside him cracked. *Oh shit, I'm in so deep…*

"God yes," James all but moaned, and his entire body shuddered as if his words alone had sent a rush of pleasure through his veins. "Want you to come inside me, *Josh*. Wanna feel it…"

It was almost enough to make Josh lose it right there. "You're killin' me, Daddy," he groaned, grabbing at James to pull him closer. "C'mon, baby. Come get what you want."

Grabbing the towel Josh hasn't even known was near, James stopped his prep quickly, wiped his wet hand and moved up Josh's body. Peppering kisses as he came, Josh found himself tensing and eagerly awaiting the feel of a hot body surrounding him. It had been so *long*, and he just prayed he'd be able to last long enough to get James off, because this was going to feel *that* good.

He reached for the lube and was surprised when James handed it to him with a shy smile, having obviously used it to open himself up. He popped the lid squeezed the slick liquid over the red tip of his length, watched as it dropped down to cover his flesh. Josh grasped himself and heaved a sigh. *Oh, oh, this is going to feel so good, and it will be with James.* Josh was sure he would not survive.

James stared with those starved eyes as Josh made sure his skin was slippery. James hovered, occasionally dropping kisses to Josh's lips until Josh reached between them to stroke James' cock. "You sure you're ready, handsome?" Josh asked quietly but with great concern. James nodded adamantly.

"Beyond fuckin' ready," he assured him, and Josh drew him down for a kiss. It was desperate but deep, and Josh felt like his soul would jump out of his body.

"Well, take your time anyway." Josh needed this to last. He needed to memorize every inch of James' body enveloping him — and the way James looked while taking his cock...

James chuckled a little as he positioned himself, one hand on Josh's broad chest and the other on one cheek, separating himself for Josh's length. Josh held his cock up and still, his breath hitching as he waited for the feeling of heat. James dropped his hips, seeking out the wet head and letting it probe against his loosened hole. It was a tease that made him gasp, and James did it a few times, enough to make Josh wonder if he could *feel* the slit in his tip. Josh was about to crawl out of his skin if James didn't sit down on him in the next few seconds —

Then he did and... "Oh fuck, oh fuck," James chanted as his body opened to allow the head of Josh's cock inside him. Josh stopped breathing at the sensations. James' body was *tight*, despite how James had gotten himself ready, and Josh had a brief moment of wondering why in the hell was he sleeping around when he could have *this* every night with James — no condoms, no need for anything but their bodies together. It sounded like heaven and it *felt* even better.

While the thought was a fantasy, it was the fantasy Josh craved.

Josh's focus bounced from where their bodies met to James. James was flushed, glistening from sweat already. His cock was hard, jutting out as he held himself just on Josh's tip for a moment. Josh roamed his hands up his thighs, caressing in a gentle form to let James know it was okay to take his time, even though he might explode. "F-feels so g-g-ood," Josh stuttered. The view was exquisite and the feeling of James' body slowly wrapping around him was...*incredible*.

James was panting, both hands now on Josh's chest as he slowly started to ease down. Their gazes met and Josh reached up immediately, overcome. "So beautiful," he whispered. James' broke out in a smile, before his mouth fell open in an O as he sank lower.

"G-God, Josh... It's so... I'm... It's..."

"Different," Josh finished, stroking James' cock twice. "It feels better than anything," and it was true. To be inside him bare was so *wrong* — and yet it felt so *good*. "Take it all, handsome. That's it, good boy."

James' settled against Josh's thighs, their bodies flush as they both panted. Josh wanted to come right then, and judging by the tight look on James' face, he did too. Instead, Josh pulled him down into a hungry kiss, as their bodies stayed joined and still.

Then somewhere mid kiss, James started to move. Josh saw stars as James rocked his hips experimentally. Josh gripped his waist encouraging but not demanding. James had the control for now. He needed to warm up.

Thus began a slow crescendo. They began to move together, Josh following every sway of James' hips as he rode Josh harder and harder. His movements gained momentum and their groans mingled with the sounds of sex throughout the room. It was surreal for Josh, being engulfed by the wet heat of James' body over and over, knowing nothing separated them. When he'd fantasized about this, it was always with someone he loved—a fact that subconsciously hit him square in the chest. He ached for the man above him, who whimpered *his* name and who held on to *his* chest for dear life.

Josh surged up and caught James in a rough, sloppy kiss. James groaned loudly into his mouth, holding himself up with his arms around Josh's shoulders as they continued to move together. It took only a moment before Josh's primal need took over, burning under the surface. He needed to make sure James would never forget this moment between them. And he hoped that maybe... Maybe this was the shift he'd been looking for.

He flipped them over, rolling so James' back hit the mattress while Josh's cock stayed inside him. After only a moment of adjustment, Josh parted James' legs and began to *pound* into him, the words spilling from his lips as he chased their end.

"You're mine," he grunted, words punctuated by heavy thrusts. "All mine. No one makes you feel the way I do. No cock will ever fill you like mine does. Say it. *Say it.* Tell me you're mine. Tell me you want me to come inside you..."

James was blissed out. Josh could see it. He was grabbing at Josh, holding his lower back tightly as Josh gave him everything he had, using every ounce of muscle in his body to fuck him. James took it all, whimpering and moaning loudly. "Make me yours, *Josh*, please. G-God...*oh*, *God*." Josh knew he was close. He pressed his knees into the mattress and pushed them to the end with everything he had left. "Come inside me. Be my first. I wanna feel it… Wanna be yours," he begged brokenly. Josh dragged his lips across James' as he dropped to his elbows in a sloppy, heated kiss, forehead to forehead, James' cock between them getting all the friction Josh knew it needed. "Wanna come with you." James gasped as James' words touched Josh at the center of his soul. It was too much. He couldn't hold back. He had to give the man exactly what he'd asked for.

"I—" Josh cut himself off, his lips against James' ear. He pulled up and away enough to find James' watery eyes and pressed their foreheads together again. "Come with me, Daddy. Come all over us while I come inside you, fill you up, call you *mine*…"

James let go with a harsh cry, clenching Josh as he let his orgasm rip through his body. Josh stuttered and let go himself. He spilled inside James with a shout, the feeling of coming fully uncovered sending sparks through his veins. James' body obviously welcomed the warmth and milked everything he had as James thrust up against Josh's abs, making a complete mess of them both—which was exactly what Josh wanted.

There were several moments afterward where they lay there panting and still joined. Josh didn't care about the sticky mess or the fact that he was completely lax atop James. All he cared about was the fact he was *still* inside him and basking in the warmth that James' body provided. It was welcoming, and Josh had zero interest in leaving his arms.

Which seemed fine with James, who had buried his head against Josh's neck, soft breaths in and out as they both regained composure. Something about *this* time felt special and…exposing.

Josh lifted his head from where it was buried against James after what was probably too long, his softened cock slipping on its own from James' body. James shivered beneath him as it happened, and Josh groaned at the loss of heat. He found James' gaze as his eyes opened, almost shy and unsure. "Hey," he murmured and immediately felt like an idiot. James just smiled sweetly beneath him.

"Hey, yourself," he replied quietly, stroking Josh's back.

"Are you okay?" Josh whispered. James nodded, long and sure.

"That was...everything I'd hoped it would be," James replied without a shred of uncertainty. Josh blushed hard and grinned.

"I don't... That's not... You're special. You know that, right?"

It was the closest he'd come to saying anything about his feelings toward the older man. For a moment he wanted to drag the words back inside his mouth and mash them down. But James cupped his cheek. "I just don't do..."

"Shhh-h, Josh. I know. And I'm not taking advantage of you, I promise." He pulled Josh down, kissing him slowly. Josh melted into it, James' words reassuring. They lay there and kissed for several moments before Josh pulled back, their bodies all but stuck together.

"I need to get us cleaned up," he started, their skin pulling as the dried cum stuck to them. They both chuckled at the sight, Josh on his hands and knees above James.

"Maybe a shower? Together? It's our last night," James suggested, bringing up the information Josh didn't care to remember. He didn't want it to be their last night at *all*.

"I'd like that," he agreed, dropping kisses along James' collar bone. James groaned low and lazy.

"And maybe more of *that* after some food," he added. Josh grinned wide as he moved back, reaching for James' hand.

"Absolutely."

* * * *

Josh didn't talk about it, didn't talk about the lack of condom the next two times he fucked James. They didn't talk about their situation at all in between.

Josh cleaned James up in the shower then ended up eating him out to orgasm once more. They indulged in cookies and cake brought down by the chef and his sous chefs in towels, gifts for Josh to celebrate his achievement. They followed them with wine, which only helped them end up back in bed, with Josh fucking James slowly and lazily from behind until James was a flushed, tearful mess. Josh woke James in the middle of the night for one more round, spooning him as he pressed into his loose hole, taking his time to bring them to orgasm naturally. James came first then begged for Josh's cum once again. "Make me yours. Make me yours," left his mouth over and over. It was everything out of Josh's wildest dreams. They fell back asleep just like that, Josh still buried inside James until his body softened enough to slip out.

Josh didn't question any of it. It was as though none of the arrangement existed. They laughed, they slept together, they *talked* the rest of their time together like there wasn't an envelope filled beyond its brim with cash buried safely in his bag—an envelope James had slid in there two nights prior. It was more than twice the amount he'd paid for Jamaica. While James surely knew he wasn't hurting for money now, that didn't stop him from showering Josh with what he could. A set of Tiffany's Cabochon cufflinks in sterling silver with turquoise sat in a Tiffany's signature box next to the envelope. James obviously didn't care what they'd cost.

* * * *

"Fuck," Josh muttered through his mouth full of toothpaste and toothbrush. "Fuck!"

"I'll call the private jet. There's no need for you to rush like this," James urged him, still clad only in his comfortable linen pajamas. Josh shook his head.

"No more gifts or favors from you, James. You've done enough. You already paid for this ticket. I just wish I hadn't overslept."

Josh quickly rinsed his mouth then tossed his covered toothbrush into his toiletries bag with everything else, zipping it hastily enough to almost break the leather bag's zipper.

James just smiled. "If I recall—which is difficult because it feels like it was a dream in my mind, though my ass sure knows it wasn't—you were the one who woke *me* at sometime a.m. to fuck *again*."

Josh choked on air as he tossed the small bag into his larger one and began to zip it. "It's not my fault that ass begs to be fucked every five minutes."

James helped carry Josh's bags down the stairs, admiring the way he looked in his jeans and blazer. He looked every bit the contracted artist he'd become. James was so damn proud of him. He couldn't ignore the heaviness in his chest though, but he wasn't sure why it was there.

"I'll text you when I get home," Josh told him as if it was the most natural thing in the world. James grinned and stepped closer as the driver knocked on the door.

"Be safe. Call me if you have any trouble." James leaned in for the kiss, though it took everything he had inside him to keep it from turning into more. Josh stole two more of his own accord before pulling away with apparent reluctance. "If you miss your flight, just come back. I'll make sure you get home."

"I'm *not* gonna miss it," Josh assured him, stealing one last kiss before heading out of the door at a sprint.

The cloud now hanging over him could have been seen from a mile away if he'd been paying attention instead of falling in love, he was sure. There Josh went, with thousands of dollars of James' money and James' whole heart.

This couldn't continue. James had to stop it there before he couldn't turn it around.

Chapter Seven

Josh had the messaging app pulled up as he sat sideways on his bed. He was sweaty from a long session at the gym, but no less anxious as he stared at the last message displayed, which had been sent a long eight days prior...

I made my flight and just landed at JFK. I feel like I keep thanking you, but you have no idea how incredible this trip was for me and how much I enjoyed our time together. Text me when you get back. Hope you have safe travels

Complete with a smiley emoji and everything, the message Josh had rewritten ten times eight days ago sat unanswered. And it wasn't like James had died in a plane crash or some unforeseen circumstances had occurred, because Josh had been copied on an email announcing his own joining of the team the morning after he'd arrived home. To say Josh was puzzled was an understatement.

He'd replayed every second of their last twenty-four hours together, obsessed about them even. Nothing but the conversation he'd had with his mother and the condomless sex stuck out to him as potential for disaster. They'd even kissed several times on Josh's way out of the door. He would have predicted an increase in correspondence but not an end to it completely. And while eight days wasn't long in the grand scheme of life, it was in fact the longest he had gone without talking to James in *weeks*.

Chewing his lips, he typed up five different versions of *Hey, Jamie, hope you made it home safely* and discarded each one. His emotions pulled at him. Maybe giving in to not using a condom had been foolish. He was sure his mentor would call it an amateur move, and Nadia would never stop making fun of him if she knew. Had that been what had made James not respond? Josh scrubbed a hand over his scruffy jaw.

Sighing, he tossed his phone away and made himself take a shower. Every minute his phone didn't buzz with a text from James was agony in a way he couldn't describe. He'd *never* cared about clients before in this manner. Sure, he looked forward to certain ones, but they were few and far between—and nothing like Jamie. But Josh knew the real root of the problem with the lack of communication from James, and it felt humiliating.

He'd fallen for Jamie. He knew it. He'd known it for over a month. But with each passing day that he didn't hear from him, the elation turned to a painful ache he couldn't get past. His sleep was terrible without James beside him. He missed that smile over morning coffee, no matter how rushed, and as he had started work upon his return, he found his hand wanting to sketch

James more than anything — so he didn't forget the details. And because he missed him…like hell.

The shower did nothing to ease the pain in his chest. Checking his phone to find no notifications didn't help either. One more day without word from James Barnwell… Well…maybe he wasn't so important to the man, Josh told himself as he stared into the small mirror of his non-luxurious Brooklyn apartment bathroom.

He shaved his neck but kept the scruff he'd been growing for six days. Something about not shaving made him feel better — or maybe it was just that he didn't have the effort to do so knowing James wasn't around to see him.

Pulling on jeans and a gray Henley, he didn't bother with a product for his hair. He had a regular client he hadn't seen since before Jamaica, and there was a comfort level with her that didn't make him feel the need to doll himself up. Despite his inner turmoil, he had a job to do. While he technically didn't need it anymore, thanks to his art contract, it was still good income and he hadn't quite decided to give it up yet. And if James was no longer in the picture, as his dramatic heart was telling him was the case, then why stop?

He brushed past Nadia in the hallway, his bag slung over his shoulder and sulking. She did a double take and made a face that he ignored. "Excuse you," she snipped. He kept going.

"I've got a client. I'll be home late."

"You've got an attitude too. Maybe work on that before you get home." She called him out and he didn't even slow down on his path to the door, yanking it open.

"Ignore me if you don't like it," he replied, slamming it behind him. He knew his anger was displaced, but he wasn't able to blare it at the person causing it, so it seemed everyone else in his path was at risk. He mentally chided himself on the way to grab a taxi and shot Nadia a quick *Sorry I'm an asshole* text. She replied as he gave the driver his client's address, spouting off two middle finger emojis and *We were friends first. Just because you're making money doesn't mean you get to be a douche.* He winced because she had it all wrong. He'd talk to her later and at least set that record straight. While he couldn't tell her all about James because his wounded pride wouldn't let him, he could certainly tell her his struggle about what to do next. She'd at least understand that much.

The taxi ride was over forty-five minutes in traffic, but he finally didn't have to worry much about money. Still ten minutes early, he paid the driver and hopped out as the sun was setting. It was cold now, December in New York, the snow beginning to fall. He'd had naive dreams about seeing the Rockefeller tree with Jamie, strolling down crowded streets hand in hand. He admonished himself and shook away the thoughts as he pressed the doorbell on the familiar brownstone just one neighborhood up from Jamie's.

A voluptuous older woman answered the door promptly with her dark hair tied up perfectly in a chignon and her lips as red as berries of mistletoe. The smile that spread across Josh's lips was genuine for the first time in a week. "Josh, darling," Margaret Carter greeted warmly in her crisp English accent. Josh stepped past her as she widened the door for his broad shoulders.

"Hey, Margaret," he greeted in that boyish tone that always made her grin. Today was no exception as she walked around to face him, bringing her hands to his jaw immediately.

"What's *this*?" She ran her fingers over the dark blond beginnings of a beard, and he flushed with a laugh.

"Just a little something I'm trying, I guess," he replied a little self-consciously. Her gaze was playful as she looked him up and down.

"I'd say it's working." She grabbed him by the lapels of his heavy peacoat and brought their bodies together suggestively. "It's been far too long that you've been out of the country and I've missed your company. Let's get to it, shall we?"

Josh focused on the feel of her full, round breasts against him, keeping his mind in the game by reminding himself of all the things she preferred, all the spots that made her whine and thrash, and how she preferred him to start at the top and work his way down—meticulous, practiced, memorized. *This will work*, he chanted inside his mind as he tried to force himself to forget his phone and his heartache and to give Margaret all his attention.

Thankfully, his body rose to the occasion. The rest of him was, of course, another matter entirely. It didn't work. It just didn't work.

Josh usually didn't rush off after Margaret, and tonight was no exception. Sitting in her parlor, she lit a cigarette and poured them each a Scotch. It had become a tradition of sorts, since their second time together.

Josh listened to her stories about her latest travels, how the man she'd been seeing was a dud. He was quiet, nodded and laughed genuinely, but his smile wasn't true. His heart was still aching, and he'd had to rein himself in to keep from crying Jamie's named when he had come.

Margaret stood to pour herself a second drink, and when he agreed to stay for one more, she abruptly put the decanter down, eyeing him with suspicion. "All right, Roberts. What's going on?"

Panic flooded his chest as he looked up at her, trying desperately to cover his tracks. "What? Nothing."

"Right." Her voice was laced with sarcasm as she finished pouring the drinks and came to sit beside him on the expensive leather couch. "You forget how well I know you, darling. You've never had a second drink with me. And tonight, despite your stellar performance as usual, you were not yourself. You were all work and no play. So spit it out. What's got you all out of sorts?"

Josh should have known she would see right through him, and yet for some reason, he'd thought he had this one in the bag. Sighing, he rubbed the bridge of his nose and considered how to respond. Apparently, she didn't need any further explanation.

"Oh, *Joshua*, you fell in love with a client, didn't you?" Her voice was full of empathy as she spoke. His gaze flew to hers, his eyes wide with surprise as he absorbed her words. She cocked her head as she realized she was right. "Oh dammit." Her tone told him immediately how much understanding she had for him. He let his head fall into his hands, unable to hide it for one more moment.

"I fucked up, Margaret," he admitted for the first time out loud. It hurt, stinging him into his soul.

She ran a hand over his back, rubbing in comforting circles. "You did no such thing," she said. "You're human. I'm honestly shocked you made it this far without a hiccup."

He huffed a humorless laugh, rubbing his eyes wildly as emotions he'd managed to mash down began to bubble up to the surface. "He's... There's nothing like him. And I could have sworn he felt the same, but..." He trailed off as one lone tear escaped. This was heading downhill quickly, and he felt small, like a child, as he tried to regain control.

"Oh, darling," Margaret began, putting her drink down to let her hand rest comfortingly on his knee. "What happened?"

Josh didn't even know where to begin. And while Margaret was his client and it shouldn't have been okay to talk to her about this, she was the one who'd started this all for him. And at the moment, he had no one else to turn to. "We've been traveling a lot together. He took me to Jamaica and Italy. God, we've been together more in the last three months than I see some of my clients in a year. He—uh—lied to everyone. We played make believe for four weeks, basically. And I—" He took a breath, ran his hands through his fluffy hair. "I got attached. Bad. And when I left Italy, I texted him to say thank you and he just...never responded. It's been over a week and I just thought... It wasn't even sexual, you know? I was just saying thank you because I work for his company now and—"

"You *work* for his company *how*?"

Josh immediately recognized her protective tone and he sat up to defend himself.

"I'm doing art for his resorts now," he explained. "His designer saw my art and she pulled me into a meeting and now I'm contracted to produce—"

"What's this man's name, Joshua?" She was blunt and Josh's eyes widened in panic.

"Margaret, you know I can't—"

"If this is who I think it is, I will personally—"

"Margaret, *no*! I can't tell you anything. You *know* that!" Josh's emotions took a back seat as he tried to talk her down. "It's all confidential, and besides, telling you won't make it hurt any less."

"It will when I beat his arse from here to England," she snapped, her own emotions written all over her face. Josh frowned, briefly wondering if they were, in fact, talking about the same person and how in the hell he'd even allowed himself to talk about this.

He scrubbed a hand over his face, sighing. "It's probably just me. I'm the idiot. I fell for the guy and he didn't have the balls to actually end the arrangement. He just…ditched out. Which would normally be fine, he doesn't owe me anything… I just thought—"

"If he doesn't respect you enough to end it properly then he's a coward and he most certainly doesn't have any balls worth talking about."

Josh tried to laugh but it was lacking, and he dropped his head back into his hands as more tears slipped out on their own accord. "I can't believe I fell in love with a fucking client." He sighed heavily. Margaret rubbed his back once more.

"Happens to the best of us, honey. It'll be all right. I promise. And when I find him, I'll give him a piece of my mind."

"Please don't." He sniffled, not bothering to look up.

"Don't worry about it, Josh."

Somehow, he knew that if she ever did find Jamie, she'd rip him to pieces. Josh hoped he'd be there to see it.

* * * *

The Miami sun beat down on the open balcony of James' penthouse suite. Three models — one female and two male — lounged in the pool with drinks in hand while James answered a few work emails from under an umbrella at a pool-side table. They'd been there since the night before, when he'd met them down on Ocean Drive at Nikki Beach. He should be thrilled, having them all at once like some kind of rock star.

He wasn't.

Filling the hole Josh had left in his life and heart was proving impossible. He'd been at this for two weeks now, burying himself in work and other people, trying to erase the void. The text from Josh still sat in his messages, read the moment he'd received it. But by then he'd already decided he had to stop. He had to step away. He didn't want to, though — absolutely not. He wanted to pull Josh in and never let go — but he couldn't. Josh was so young and had his whole life ahead of him. And James was on the verge of settling down. Josh had made him crave that more than anything.

Watching the three people make out in his pool, drunk on his liquor, hardly made his dick swell. It was inevitable that he'd end up back in bed with them again, but for the time being, he was thinking about Josh and wishing things were different.

The strange thing about all this was that Josh was now employed by the company, working directly for Maria. So while James knew he could get away with avoiding him for a while, seeing him was also inevitable. And seeing him again…? He knew *exactly* what it would do to him. Just the idea of laying eyes on him again, of being in the same room as Josh and hearing his deep voice and meeting those blue eyes? It made his heart skip a beat and his stomach lurch, all at once.

He missed Josh so damn much that it made his skin crawl, like a perpetual itch just under the surface that nothing could scratch. The sex with his current companions was filthy and fun, but it was every bit as empty as James' heart. It didn't matter how attractive they were or how good they were in bed. Nothing could compare to Josh and to the memories that James clung to from their time together — every kiss, every touch, spending every night in each other's arms and waking up together like it was somehow the most natural thing in the world...

The sound of a newly arrived email stole Jamie's attention, and he only then realized he'd been staring off aimlessly as his mind had drifted. He sighed and gave a slight shake of his head to focus, then clicked on the message from Maria and began to read.

"This is a company-wide reminder. The opening of Josh Roberts' exhibition is set for December sixteenth at the Whitney Museum of American Art. Business attire requested. The exhibition opens at seven p.m. Light hors d'oeuvres to be served with champagne, wine and beer. Please RSVP by the seventh. This is our first event of this nature, and we'd really love to see you all there in support of our very first in-house artist."

There were a few more details, and a picture of Josh and one of his pieces at the bottom. It had to be recent, James realized, as his heart simply ceased function in his chest, giving up the erratic beating of moments before. Josh's hair was a little longer, a little less gelled and controlled — fluffier by James' standards. And he'd grown a beard in the last two weeks. It covered his jaw perfectly, as if he'd been meant to grow one all along. It was a dark blond, an addictive shade. He looked tired. Jamie's throat was suddenly dry.

He hadn't even remembered receiving the first email. Had he? He started to search when a splash of water was sent in his direction, wetting his toes. His gaze flashed up behind his sunglasses, but the young brunette woman didn't seem to notice the daggers he shot through the lenses. "Are you ever going to stop working?" she whined, her young voice high pitched. "We've been waiting *hours* for a repeat of last night." She batted her lashes at him as he glanced back at the email still on the screen — the young man who owned his heart staring back at him with broken blue eyes. James slammed the laptop shut.

"Don't splash me again and I'll take you inside and fuck you until you can't walk." He stood up and headed for the sliding glass door as the models excitedly followed in their little herd. It wasn't like he would go to the opening, anyway. How could he show his face when he hadn't even dignified Josh with a platonic response or goodbye?

* * * *

The office was quiet as James followed the hallway to his office in downtown Miami. Most of the staff had already left for the holiday and anyone who hadn't was prepping to go to New York for the exhibition opening. James had seen the forum, heard the guest count and was aware of how excited Maria was for the particular event. Stephanie had assisted from afar in event coordination, and James was surprised to see her coming toward him from the direction of his office that afternoon.

"I figured you'd left already." He laughed a little, though it sounded hollow and harsh. Stephanie eyed him but kept her professional demeanor.

"Catching a flight this afternoon. Are you doing okay?" She let her eyes slip up and down, concern filling them. "You're coming, right?"

"I'm fine." He ignored her second question. "Just tired. Long weekend."

"It's Wednesday…" She raised an eyebrow, sighing. "Are we ever going to talk about it?"

"Don't you have a flight to catch?" He brushed past her, but she wasn't bothered. She turned on her heel and followed him. James sighed, pushing the glass door open and propping it open with the door stop as she followed him inside.

"I have three hours, so if you want to talk about the elephant in the room or the crack in your heart, I'm here to listen." She took a seat in one of the plush chairs on one side of his desk when he sat down at his computer on the other side. The office was clean, modern, and sunlight poured in through the windows. It was almost too sunny for his dark mood.

He sighed heavily, rubbing his face with both hands. "I don't wanna talk about it, Steph."

"Have you talked to him? You won't tell me what happened and that scares me, because it's not like you to *not* talk to me about things." James looked up at her and he understood that she only meant well. "Look at you. You're a mess. I've never seen you look like this and I'm genuinely worried. What did he do? Do we need to fire him? I'll talk to Maria. I'll—"

"You'll do nothing of the sort." He squashed her mini rant, shaking his head. "Josh did *nothing*. He's perfect. This is all my fault, and there's nothing we can do now to fix it, okay? So let's just let it go. And no, I'm not going."

"Jamie—"

"Stephanie," he warned her, "go to New York. I'll see you the week after New Year's. Do *not* come back any time before then. We're due in New Zealand February first to oversee the beginning of construction on the *Whitianga* resort and I'll need you fresh and ready. Your bonus is in the mail and your Christmas present will arrive to your mother's on the twenty-third. Do *not* open it until Christmas, understand?"

For all his personal drama, James never failed to take care of his people. Stephanie's gratitude and appreciation shone in her wide-eyed surprise. "Jamie, I—"

"Get out of here." He pointed toward the door and tried to contain his smile. "Behave yourself with Alejandro. I don't trust him as far as I can throw him."

Stephanie stood and scooted toward the door. She did blush at his words though. "Listen... He's a gentleman," she defended, but James made a loud *pfft* sound that made her laugh. "You're a jerk."

"Hey, I'm just looking out for my best girl, all right? You can't blame me for that. You call me if he does anything awful and I will personally see to it we never hear from him again. Got it?"

"Are you...telling me what I think you are?" Her eyes widened but he acted casual, fighting a grin.

"I don't know what you're talking about. Now *get*," he urged, letting a smile loose as she wished him a Merry Christmas and saw herself out of the office. As soon as she was gone, James reclined in the chair, the email from a few days ago still staring at him from his inbox. The picture of Josh still haunted him. To go to New York was foolish — possibly even unprofessional. Josh didn't want to see him. Why would he?

Pursing his lips, he closed his eyes and rubbed the bridge of his nose.

If he didn't go to New York, he'd be letting his own pride get in the way of supporting someone he actually *loved*. It was also a big deal for his company. The company *he* owned. As much as this was the *last* thing he personally wanted to do, maybe it was the *right* thing to do. He didn't move, however. He continued to stare at the computer like it would make his decision for him — until he finally picked up his phone and called his sister. Maybe it was time for a confession and to ask for advice.

"Jamie-o! Calling me on a Wednesday afternoon?!" His sister's shocked voice filled the office as he stared down at A1A through the large office windows. "To what do I owe this surprise?"

"Hey, Bec," he began, heaving another sigh. "I gotta tell you something, but you have to promise not to tell Ma."

"What'd you do?"

"I hope you have a few minutes. It's a long story."

* * * *

Josh couldn't believe the turnout on his behalf. The third floor of the Whitney Museum of American Art was filled with people — and they were all there to see his work. It was humbling and a dream come true.

His pieces adorned the walls. He'd poured his anxious energy into creation. Pieces were ready to be shipped off to their new homes and the originals displayed here for all J. B. Barnwell LLC employees to see. He'd been given ten tickets for guests and was a little embarrassed that he'd only invited four people then given the rest to his mom to invite her friends. His mother, Nadia, Andrew and Margaret had all accepted their invitations and promised to make appearances. He'd arrived early in the navy-blue suit Maria had insisted on, fussing with his tie every few minutes. He was beyond nervous. But one thing put him at ease.

The fact Stephanie had *assured* him that James wasn't coming.

It was a huge weight off his shoulders, knowing James wouldn't be there. His mother was still under the impression that he and James were still together, and he didn't have the heart to tell her they weren't. He'd gone to her home for Thanksgiving the week he'd gotten back from Italy, and all she'd done was carry on about how excited she was that Josh had a serious man in his life. That had been back when he had been still waiting to hear from Jamie. Now he'd long since given up.

And it hurt. It *killed* his heart. But there wasn't anything he could do about it. And he loved this new job so much he wasn't about to risk it by attempting to contact the CEO of the company. He'd been the guy's escort, nothing more. And while it was a slap to the face every time he thought about it, it was his own fault that he'd fallen in love. There was no one to blame but himself.

"You look awful pensive for someone who's about to have the biggest night of his young life yet."

Josh looked up from where he'd been absently staring at the program to find Nadia and Andrew waltzing toward him, arm in arm as friends. The smile that grew on his face was natural.

"Just counting my blessings is all," he replied, stepping forward to meet them as they crossed the immaculate space. He embraced Nadia first, tightly. After his conversation with Margaret that night, he'd come home exhausted, an emotional wreck, and had unloaded to Nadia and apologized. She'd been prickly at first, but upon learning of his plight, she'd been much softer to him. And he was much less aggressive now that he'd talked a bit about his situation and sorted out his next personal moves.

"You do have a lot to be thankful for." Andrew chuckled as they embraced as well. "The Whitney? Man, this is a whole other level. You're gonna ditch us soon, huh?"

Josh smiled wide and shook his head, his hand on Andrew's shoulder. "I could be making a million and I'm still staying in our apartment," he confirmed. They all laughed.

"You're a damn fool," Andrew teased as a waiter carried over a tray of champagne. They each accepted one as Maria approached, politely stealing Josh to introduce him to some higher-ups from the company. Josh excused himself and let the night carry him wherever it was destined to take him. He was determined to embrace every moment of the evening. He'd spent his whole life dreaming of this moment. He was going to live in it wholly.

As the evening wore on, more people came. Josh's mother arrived with a few of her neighborhood friends, excited to show off her son's new endeavor. She gushed over him, raving about how proud she was to her friends as she embraced him. Josh blushed wildly — making his mother proud was one of the best feelings in the world. He'd been working a job for years that he couldn't tell her about and now he finally had something he could share with her. It was special in ways he couldn't put into words.

Stephanie and Alejandro showed up next. Stephanie launched herself at him as though they were they oldest of friends, embracing him tightly. He laughed and held her. He'd missed her company over these last few weeks. She was a ray of sunshine. It was evident why James kept her as his assistant.

"I've missed you!" she exclaimed, leaning back to cup his cheeks. "Look at this beard! You handsome stud." She ran her hands over the bristles on his jaw, grinning widely. He flushed.

"Thanks, Steph. Trying something new, I guess." He shrugged, unable to admit he was doing his best to get past James and the heartache. She seemed to read it in his eyes, her expression turning to one of comfort.

"I know you got my emails and I know you know he's not coming, but he's a mess without you, I swear." It felt out of place for her to share such personal information, but Josh's heart clenched and wrapped up her words in some semblance of satisfaction and self-preservation.

"Well…that's his own doing, I guess," Josh replied curtly, swallowing the lump that had suddenly formed in his throat. Stephanie squeezed his arm. "At least he's not coming." He forced a smile, albeit a pained one.

"What happened between you two? I know it's none of my business but—" Her words were cut off by a wave of hushed reactions coming from the crowd around them. They both turned their heads toward the entrance to the exhibit and Josh's breath caught.

No. *No.*

Maria was greeting James warmly, shaking his hand and welcoming him into the exhibit. J. B. Barnwell employees talked among themselves as their CEO made his presence known, waving at some he recognized and introducing himself to those he didn't. Josh wanted to look for Nadia and Andrew, wanted to find a way to ground himself but he couldn't tear his eyes away. Every bit of ease and comfort he'd had about the night flew out of the window.

"You said—"

"I know!" Stephanie rushed out. "I *just* talked to him before I left Miami, and he said he wasn't coming. I swear! I would have told you if he was!"

Josh knew she would have. He trusted her. And the fact that James hadn't told her was surprising. It didn't help settle Josh's nerves one bit as they now raged within him.

Oh shit. My mother.

Glancing around, he found that she'd already spotted James and was looking between him and Josh with a sweet, almost-excited expression. She would expect a big introduction, and she would expect him and James to act like they were still together. He had *no* idea how to get out of this. Panic and anxiety began to flood his system. He had to get to James before she did.

Except he wasn't prepared for that gray-blue gaze to land on him after weeks of silence. James looked exhausted but his focus shook Josh to his very core. Josh was just barely aware of how Stephanie looked back and forth between them and how she tried to stop him from taking the steps he was apparently making toward James without even realizing it.

He moved through the crowd, a thousand different scenarios and statements running through his mind. He wanted to rip the man apart and demand answers. He wanted to cry. He wanted to walk right past him and out of the door then run as fast as he could in his fancy dress shoes as far away as they would carry him.

Josh did none of those things. He kept his expression as neutral as possible as he walked right up to Jamie. He hardly even registered Jamie's unsettled eyes.

"Josh, I —"

Josh raised his hand, not wanting to hear whatever poor excuse was about to leave his mouth. And he had to ask this before anything else happened and the barely stitched seams that were just holding him together ripped permanently. "I need a favor. And I'm hoping that regardless of what happened between us, you can do this *one* thing for me, because it's *really* important."

James blinked, stepping closer. Josh hardly registered the surprise that crossed his face. He was sure he was just doing his best to remain detached, knowing that if he allowed himself to feel...

"Anything, Josh. Name it."

"My mother is here. I didn't —" He cleared his throat, rubbing his hand over his mouth and bearded jaw. "I haven't been able to tell her that we weren't — aren't — whatever. She still thinks we are, and I didn't have it in me to take it away from her just yet. But she's here and she knows who you are, and if I don't introduce her to you —"

"Yes," James answered immediately. It was Josh's turn to be surprised.

"Yes?"

"Yes. I'll be your boyfriend. It's fine." He offered the smallest of smiles and reached for Josh's hand. Josh's heart jumped, the touch sending his emotions into a tizzy. "I'll make sure she knows everything is great," he assured Josh as he caressed his thumb over Josh's knuckles. Josh stared at the contact before his gaze flickered back up to those cloudy blues that had been haunting him. They were so soft that it was unfair. How could he look like this after ignoring him for weeks?

"You will?" Josh asked, shocked. James nodded, smiling wider now.

"Yeah, I will. Congratulations, by the way." James leaned up and pressed his lips to Josh's cheek, further confusing Josh and earning a murmured *aww* through the crowd.

Josh frowned as James leaned away, smiling the smile that lived in Josh's dreams. He kept Josh's hand and turned to face Sarah, seemingly unaware of the evening's photographer, who was snapping photos for the company newsletter and press releases. Josh followed, almost numb. He held himself together, forcing a smile as they approached his mother and she approached them, a confused Nadia and Andrew in tow. Josh met Stephanie's wide eyes over the crowd and he just shrugged one shoulder then focused solely on his mother as she practically squealed with joy.

"You must be Jamie," she greeted him, even though they all knew that she knew exactly who he was. "It's so wonderful to finally meet you."

Sarah Roberts was nothing but warm sweetness. She gave James the biggest of smiles as he only released

Josh's hand to lean into Sarah, kissing her cheek fondly. "Mrs. Roberts, it's my pleasure. I'm so glad to finally meet you. Josh raves about his mother. I'm so sorry I couldn't make Thanksgiving," he offered with a wide smile of his own, shaking her hand with both of his. Josh had to fight to keep his jaw from dropping at the scene because... *Thanksgiving?*

"Oh, it's all right. You're a busy man," she accepted easily.

James flushed a little and Josh couldn't help but wonder why. Was it because he felt bad? Josh wished that were the case but didn't hold his breath.

"Why don't I make it up to you by touring you around your son's incredible work? And you can tell me all the embarrassing stories of his childhood?"

Sarah laughed, delighted. "Oh, Joshua, he's as much the charmer as you said." Josh wanted to give her a deadpan look but he kept it in check.

"Ma, I —"

"Shush, Joshua." She patted his arm and looped hers around Jamie's. "What's your favorite piece? Show me," she instructed, and without missing a beat, James took her right toward a painting of the night sky over the Italian resort. Josh watched them go, glued to his spot for a moment as Nadia approached, turning to face James and Sarah as well.

"What the hell is that?" she muttered.

"I asked him to pretend for her. And he just... agreed," he replied just as quietly. Nadia's eyes widened a fraction.

"You better get the story on what happened."

"Oh, don't worry. I fuckin' plan on it."

The exhibit's opening went off without a hitch. The evening was incredible. Everything about it was a dream come true for Josh, including watching James woo his mother the entire evening.

Josh knew Jamie's skills, how charming the guy could be. He understood firsthand how James could make someone feel like they were the only person in the room. Sarah clearly felt it and Josh did still, every time the man looked at him, every time they made eye contact. It made his insides light up and his heart flutter.

But it also made him more upset as the night wore on. Josh was confused and hurt, and seeing the man he knew he was in love with carrying on with his own mother made it hurt worse. He couldn't deny it if he wanted to.

"Staring at him like that isn't going to get you answers."

The voice pulled him from his hard staring, drawing his attention to the spot beside him at the edge of the room. Margaret stood next to Josh looking absolutely gorgeous, dressed up for this special occasion. The red dress she wore hugged every ounce of her curves and Josh knew she was aware of just how good she looked. She also looked like she was ready to make James Barnwell pay for every sin he'd ever committed.

"You don't look particularly impressed either," Josh replied quietly, a small smile quirking his lips.

"Oh, sweetheart, I am most certainly not. I know that man—and his behavior is atrocious." She sipped her champagne, her red lipstick leaving a mark on the glass. "And if you don't say something, I absolutely will." Judging by her tone, Josh had no questions that she would follow through on her word.

"I'm going to," he replied, albeit weakly. He had no idea what to say or how to say it. She gave him a hard look.

"You better, Joshua. You deserve far better than you've been given as of late." She patted his arm and gave him a softer smile. "Before I leave you to your brooding, who's the redhead who's been making eyes at me all night?" Josh's forehead furrowed until he followed her gaze. Nadia stood close to his mother with Andrew, keeping tabs on James as Josh worked the room. She was also looking their way with unabashed interest. Josh's smile widened.

"That's Nadia," he began. Margaret nodded.

"She worked with you?"

"Well, she's independent, but yes. She's *very* good at her job."

"Well, excuse me, darling. I need to introduce myself. Be sure you make that man understand how he mishandled your feelings. If you need me, let me know." She pressed a chaste kiss to his cheek before making a beeline for Nadia, who was ready and waiting for such an interaction. Andrew smirked but kept his eye on Sarah, trailing behind her and James as they moved from artwork to artwork.

Josh considered Margaret's words and decided he'd confront James once his mother was on her way home. This needed to be between them. He didn't want her witnessing it. And he'd never dream of making a scene or embarrassing James in such a public place.

It was an agonizing two more hours until Josh was kissing his mother's cheek and saying goodbye. He'd spent the time walking around with her and Jamie, occasionally holding Jamie's hand or conversing over a particular piece of art. He couldn't contain his emotions when he looked at the man. He imagined it was written all over his face just how much he cared. For the sake of the facade, it wasn't a bad thing. For Josh's aching heart, however, it was terribly painful.

The crowd dissipated as Josh said his thanks and good-byes to coworkers and friends. James stayed, talking quietly to Maria about business until the last of the visitors were gone. Gathering his jacket and bag, Josh wondered briefly when the best time would be to grab him. But the longer he stood and waited, finally able to focus on the fact he was about to confront Jamie, all the pent-up anger and hurt was bubbling to the surface. Frustrated, he hit the elevator button three times, deciding that waiting for James maybe wasn't the best idea.

The doors opened and he stepped in, lost in his thoughts until a hand stuck into the closing door. He lifted his eyes from the floor to find James stepping in, his own winter coat over his suit jacket. He met Josh's gaze and waited until the doors shut behind him to speak.

"Josh…" he began, his tone laced with some kind of emotion that Josh didn't allow himself to dissect.

"Jamie," Josh greeted him curtly, clearing his throat. "Thank you for what you did. I'll break the news to her — mutual decision and all that, so no one is at fault." The elevator came to a stop on the ground floor, the doors opening swiftly with the bell. Josh didn't wait for James to say anything, striding out past him. The museum was closing, and only employees were around. James was following, and with every step they took, Josh was closer to a breaking point. He had a thousand questions, but could his heart take the answers?

He waited to hear the door click shut behind him as he all but bolted out onto the slick sidewalk in front of the Whitney. Snow fell in heavy flakes as he began walking away, ignoring the taxis and Jamie's waiting town car.

"Josh!" James called out. He kept going until he heard his name a third and a fourth time, the last time more frantic than the others. He stopped and turned on his heel, not realizing James had been chasing him until he discovered him just a few paces behind.

"I don't know what you want from me," he began, his hands shoved deep into the warmth of his pockets, him scowling hard. "I can't even believe you showed up tonight." Even though his emotions were bubbling, Josh worked to keep them at bay.

"I owe you an apology," James explained, coming to a stop a few feet from him. "I owe you a lot of apologies." The snow fell on his hair and shoulders, the dusty light making him look angelic against the darkness. Josh suddenly wanted to cry.

"You do," he replied angrily. "I broke every rule for you. I dropped everything for you."

"I didn't—"

"Yes! You did!" Josh advanced on him, but had to credit James with the fact he didn't back down. "You *begged* me to fuck you raw. I gave parts of myself to you I've *never* given anyone, let alone a *client*. You *let* me!" His throat tight, Josh forced the words out, finally letting everything pour out of him. He'd been holding it in for weeks. He could no longer do that. Jamie's eyes were wide as Josh continued, "I can't believe I let myself fall for you. I can't believe I actually thought you were a good person. Your blatant disrespect for me—"

"Now just hang on a second," James snapped as he held his hand up to stop Josh. "Disrespect? We were *both* there, and you could have denied me. I'm sorry for hurting you. I'm sorry for going radio silent, but I had some of my own baggage to work through. I was your *client*, after all. I paid you a substantial amount of—"

"Do *not* make this about money!" Josh suddenly shouted. "I'll pay you back every fucking cent you paid me if that's what you think this is about. Condoms"— he dropped his voice low briefly, aware they were on a public street, though no one else was around—"were a non-negotiable with me and you knew it! You took advantage of—"

"If they were a non-negotiable, why in the hell would you break that kind of rule for me, Josh? I can't be the first person to ask for that! Why would you give that to me if you weren't supposed to?"

"Because I have *feelings* for you!" Josh blurted the words loudly, throwing his arms in the air with exasperation. "I fucking fell for you and I would have given you *anything* you asked for. I was incapable of saying *no*. I gave you the one thing I'd never given anyone else, and you never called me again." He choked on the last word, the hurt he'd felt over the last weeks rearing its ugly head. James stood before him, his own eyes wide with surprise, his jaw slack. *Of course he's surprised*, Josh thought sadly. "You know what? Forget it." Josh turned again, desperate to get away from James before the tears began to fall. "Don't call me ever again. I don't do that anymore," he called over his shoulder as he began to walk away.

"Josh! Josh, stop! We need to talk about this." James ran up to him, catching Josh by the elbow. He pulled him back, but Josh was quick to shake his arm from his hold.

"There's nothing to say, Jamie," he replied, crestfallen. "I made an amateur mistake. I fell for you and it clouded my judgment. I'm sorry."

"No! No, *I'm* sorry," James tried, pulling at Josh to face him, "Listen to me. I got so caught up in my own feelings that I couldn't see the arrangement anymore." Josh's focus shot to Jamie at the confession, and he was dumbfounded. James didn't seem to notice. "I stopped calling you because I couldn't keep pretending. It was a shitty thing to do, especially considering everything that happened in Italy—and I'm sorry. I'm embarrassed by my behavior in a lot of ways." James squared his shoulders and softened his eyes as he gazed on Josh. "But I had to see you tonight. I had to tell you how I feel and how sorry I am for what I did. I'm an idiot—probably should have warned you that first night." He attempted to lighten the mood with a huff of a laugh, but it fell humorless between them.

Josh stared at Jamie, wide-eyed and taken aback. This was unexpected and a shock. He shook, his mouth opening and closing as he tried to process what James had said. "Your own feelings...?" Josh pressed, needing to understand, needing clarification. James didn't touch him, but his hand extended out as if he wanted to. It fell short, falling back to his side.

"I care about you, Josh. I didn't see it for a long time, but...what we had was the best thing I've *ever* had. I..." He stopped, drifting off, and Josh waited, holding his breath, praying that whatever came out next wasn't worse. "You gave me things I'd never had, made me feel things I didn't know I could. You...you're incredible, Josh." The softest of smiles pulled at Jamie's lips and Josh's heart ached. "I don't know what to do. I don't know how to figure this out, and I've been an absolute dumbass since Italy. Come home with me? Maybe we can talk this out more where we won't freeze to death?"

The invitation was all Josh had dreamed about since Italy. The man before him, graying temples and handsome lines, admitting his feelings and asking Josh to work it out. It was as though the entire exchange was a dream. If his toes hadn't been beginning to burn with cold in his dress shoes, he would have written it off as a dream.

But as Josh opened his mouth to say *yes*, the hurt he'd felt rose back to the surface with a new vengeance. Because if he said yes and gave himself to James one more time, only to be left behind again... He couldn't. He *wouldn't*. His heart throbbed but he hardened himself, setting his jaw.

"No." It was forced. It *hurt*, but he wasn't about to do this all over again. "I can't."

Jamie's face fell as though Josh had punched him. The hope, the soft smile, the gentle wrinkles around his eyes faded into shock as he stared at Josh. "Why?"

"I-I can't," Josh managed, shaking his head. "I know you probably didn't know you hurt me and I'm going to give you that because I need to sleep tonight, but it *hurts*. You hurt me, Jamie, and I haven't recovered. I'm not going to do it again if I can help it."

"Josh, just give me the opportunity to fix this," James pleaded.

Josh simply shook his head, his Adam's apple bobbing with words he couldn't say. His heart screamed *okay* but his head knew better. He hadn't protected himself before now — and he had to. Running back into Jamie's arms now was foolish. He didn't trust his voice so he turned, walking away from the one thing he wanted most.

"I'm not going to push," James called out, "but if you change your mind…"

Josh knew that was an open invitation. And he'd hold on to it—for now.

* * * *

Josh wasn't even sure how he ended up there. He wasn't sure how far he'd walked or how many hours it had been. But his slick dress shoes were ruined as he stood on the stoop in the heavy snowfall, hoping the person inside would answer the door. Not because he was frozen—which he was, since he had no idea how long his toes had been numb for or when he'd lost the feeling in his fingers—but because he had so much to say, and he didn't want to lose his chance.

The door pulled open after what felt like an eternity though was probably only a few minutes. James stood squinting on the other side, clearly half asleep. His white T-shirt was wrinkled, his sweatpants slightly off center. He looked adorable and every inch the man Josh had fallen in love with.

"Josh?" Josh sniffled, his nose running now that he had spent several hours in the cold. "You must be frozen! Get in here!"

This time Josh didn't protest and allowed himself to be pulled into the house. It was warm as soon as he entered, heat enveloping him as James shut the door and locked it. Josh turned to face him and caught Jamie's look of trepidation.

"Let's get your jacket off. I'll make some hot chocolate and start a fire. Have you been outside all night?" He held his hands out to Josh, letting Josh stay in control of his jacket and bag and how quickly he removed them. He was slow but managed, handing the heavy, snow-covered jacket over with his messenger bag. James hung it up as Josh bent to remove his shoes, untying them. His socks wet, he removed those too.

"I'm sorry. I shouldn't have come. I'm a mess. I—"

"Nonsense. Come in. Go into the living room, I'll get the fire going and we'll have you warm in no time."

And that was how Josh found himself thirty minutes later, wrapped in three blankets, fresh warm socks and with a second steaming cup of hot cocoa in his hands. James sat across from him on the other couch under a blanket of his own with another cup. They hadn't talked much, just simple sentences to get to where they were now. The air had grown heavier because Josh knew it was time to confess his reason for being there, no matter where it led.

"I lied earlier," he began slowly, not lifting his eyes.

"About what?" Jamie's voice was curious, neutral.

"I said I couldn't be here, and I couldn't do this again." Josh's words rolled around in his head as he tried to make sense of his thoughts. "I want to be here, and I want to try. But I…" He lifted his gaze to Jamie's. He found comfort there and pressed on. "I don't know how to do this, and I don't want to get hurt again," he finally confessed.

James nodded and didn't hesitate as Josh had expected he might. "That's fair after what happened," he began, turning the mug slowly in his hands. "I am so sorry for how the last few weeks have gone. I wanted to text you, but I didn't know how and so much time had already passed because I was panicking over my own feelings. I had ignored it for so long then suddenly I couldn't, and I thought pushing you away and seeing other people would help."

Jealousy roared through Josh's veins — but who was he to be jealous? He was a fucking escort, for goodness' sake.

"It didn't. I missed you. So much."

Jamie's heartfelt admission helped to ease Josh's sudden jealousy, and Josh knew James was genuine. The man hadn't been anything but. "I came tonight to talk to you and to celebrate you," James continued when Josh didn't speak. "Meeting your mother was a bonus. She's wonderful, Josh. I see so much of her in you now that I've met her. It was easy to be in love with you in front of her because I wasn't acting."

Josh's focus shifted from Jamie's hands to his face, the words sinking in with a distinct importance that Josh hadn't been ready for. Jamie's gaze was soft, his smile forgiving. "Don't worry," he went on. "I don't expect you to say it — and I won't say it until we're both ready, if you want." He was halting as he finished, as if worried Josh would run. The only place he wanted to run was across the room and into Jamie's arms. But he restrained himself, if for no other reason than to prove to himself that he was stronger than that.

"You're saying —" Josh began then stopped, clearing his throat to steady his shaky voice. "You're saying you want to try this? Us? And see where it goes?"

Jamie's expression was nothing short of loving as he gazed back at him. "Josh, sweetheart, it's all I want. *You're* all I want. I know I have lengths to go to prove I'm worth it, but I promise you I'll do anything to try. You're it for me, pal. And maybe it won't work, but what if we don't try and we never know?" There was a hint of desperation in Jamie's voice and it broke Josh.

He set the mug down and let the blankets fall as he stood on unsteady legs and rounded the ottoman between them. James looked panicked at first and Josh figured he thought he was leaving...but he wasn't.

He felt like a child, his youth in Jamie's wake showing as he sat down beside him. He took the mug from the man and set it down and away like he had his own. Then he looked James square in the face. "You promise you're not baiting me?" It wasn't how he intended to start, but if they were being frank, he had to ask. "This isn't about the sex?"

James chuckled to Josh's surprise, his eyes dancing in the firelight. "I mean, don't get me wrong, the sex is incredible. I had no idea how much until you were gone." James winced as he said it but kept on. "But no, it's not about the sex. And I'm not baiting you. This is real. I'm real. What I want is *real*. With you...if you'll have me. If you want to try. But this has to be on your terms, Josh," he said with conviction. "This won't work if you don't call the shots. I hurt you. I know that now. If we try, you set the pace. Everything is in your court."

James still didn't touch him, and Josh was grateful. But now it was up to him. And as James stated, it was all his to determine. So Josh reached out and touched James' hand, lacing their fingers lightly. "I want to try. I'm terrified, but I want to. I want to be with you."

"I'm terrified too," James confessed, the emotions written all over his face. "But I want to be with you too."

Chapter Eight

That first night was unlike any other night Josh and James had spent together. Upon their revelations to one another, they'd shared a few small kisses and Josh had asked to sleep in the guest room. James had respected Josh's wishes, even though he made it clear that it wasn't what he preferred. Josh wanted to start fresh and do things differently this time around.

"We've had a lot of sex with hidden feelings." Josh had blushed. *"I want to try things the real way and take them slow...if that's okay with you."*

James couldn't argue. How could he with that kind of reasoning? And something about them learning how to be together without that physical aspect was exciting. A new Chapter was unfolding. And as James had fallen asleep that night, he'd finally felt at peace. Things were looking up.

The next morning, over coffee and homemade waffles — Josh was fairly decent in the kitchen, James had pleasantly discovered — they discussed their next step. Sitting at the breakfast bar in their pajamas, they drank cup after cup of hot coffee as the snow continued to fall outside. James had given Josh a pair of long johns to keep him warm while he slept and they fit him deliciously. And the beard...? The beard, albeit short, was exceptional.

"Are you listening to me?" Josh poked James' arm, jarring him from his staring contest with said beard.

"Uh yeah," James attempted to recover. Josh laughed and shook his head. "Sorry" — James flushed — "how am I supposed to listen to you when you have all *that* on your jaw?"

Watching Josh blush, knowing it was genuine and that he had caused it, gave James chills.

"I can shave it if you —"

"No!" James blurted, startling Josh and making him laugh again. "Don't you dare," he added quietly, wrapping his fingers around Josh's arm. "I love it."

Their morning went on just like that. Flirtatious but soft. James needed to make one appearance at the New York office and Josh needed to meet Maria to talk about deadlines for the new year before Christmas break. They agreed to meet for dinner later that night, and as Josh waited for the car to take him home, now wearing sweatpants, a T-shirt and his jacket, they kissed by the door like true love birds — soft, sweet kisses that warmed against the cold outside.

If Josh spent the night, it would be in the guest room for now. He would spend Christmas with Josh at his mother's and New Years with his family in Florida. Then they'd arrange their travel plans in the new year so that Josh could do many of James' trips with him. It was a working plan, nothing set in stone, but both he and Josh were both pleased with what was to come.

Being together was the main thing. He'd take the rest as it came.

* * * *

He and Josh spent the ten days leading up to Christmas getting to know each other better without sex. They already had plenty of proof that they were compatible between the sheets, so he and Josh spent time together doing anything but that. All the walks through Central Park Josh had been wanting, the visit to the Rockefeller Center tree, snowy mornings having coffee and danishes downtown — James made sure that Josh got it all. It was a dream come true as far as he'd told James — and James didn't have any complaints.

"It's eight days before Christmas and you don't have a tree," Josh said incredulously as they weaved through the lot full of trees. "I can't believe you don't have a tree."

James laughed as he held Josh's hand and allowed himself to be dragged along. Josh was looking for the perfect tree for the brownstone, and James wasn't about to stop him. The sheer joy on Josh's face was everything. "Well, I was in Miami until the sixteenth then seeing you was top priority. I didn't realize a tree should have taken that place."

Josh made a *tsk* sound and continued looking as he spoke. "Second top priority," he replied. James continued chuckling.

"I only just learned that Christmas was your favorite holiday, Josh. I'll do better next year."

The grin Josh shot back at James over his shoulder melted his heart. He knew it was the slight promise of the future that caused it. He hoped there'd be a next year — and a year after that and every year to come.

They came to an abrupt halt next to tall, very full Fraser Fir. It had at least four inches on Josh and it was a beautiful dark green. Josh was practically giving it heart eyes as James looked between him and the tree. "This is it," he said almost breathlessly. James bit back his laughter. Josh was adorable.

"You're sure?" James prompted. Josh nodded without hesitation.

"This is her. She's coming home with us."

Twenty minutes later they were enjoying homemade cider as James had scheduled delivery of the tree for later that day. They were headed to the store next to buy decorations, and they'd do that together too. James hadn't realized how much he'd been missing these domestic moments in his life. He had done them with Becca a few times throughout the years, but this was different. This was personal and about *him*…and Josh. It was a new opportunity for James to discover things in life he had yet to have, he soon realized. It warmed him to know they'd have many more firsts like this together.

* * * *

The private plane touched down at Opa Locka Executive Airport the day after Christmas. It was early afternoon. The sun was shining, and the temperature and weather were much more inviting than New York had been. Josh's linen pants and crisp white button-down fit in against the tropical landscape as he and James stepped off onto the tarmac. He was thankful for the light clothing against the hot weather and looked back up the steps to take in the view of James in his own resort casual wear as he slid his sunglasses on.

Ever the businessman elite that he was, James' gray slacks and white button-down made him look delicious against the blue sky and white, shiny plane. Carrying a leather backpack and with a sport coat over his arm, he couldn't have looked any more professional or handsome, in Josh's opinion. His soft dark hair blew in the light breeze and Josh ached to touch him in ways he hadn't let himself since they'd been back together.

"Like what you see?" James broke his reverie with a knowing smile. Josh flushed but hoped the South Florida temperature was hiding it.

"Always," he replied sweetly before they shared a quick kiss. A bright blue Audi convertible pulled up as the crew worked to take their luggage off the plane. Josh let out a low whistle and looked to his boyfriend with a surprised, yet teasing, grin. "You sure do know how to travel in style. I don't think I'll ever get used to it," he remarked. James laughed as he shook the driver's hand and thanked him.

"Like it?" James asked, setting his bag and jacket down in the back seat. The gray leather interior shone in the sun. The car looked brand new.

"It's gorgeous." Josh took a moment to gaze at the car, knowing James had a growing collection and wondering what else lay hidden in his garage. As James popped the trunk and let the crew load the bags — something Josh also wasn't yet used to — he approached Josh and held out the keys.

"Good. Merry Christmas, baby."

Josh stared at the keys, his brain stuttering and unable to comprehend what was happening. "Huh?"

James laughed. "You're adorable. Merry Christmas," he said again, holding the keys closer to Josh. "She's yours."

Josh's bearded jaw was almost on the ground as he stared at the keys in James' fingers. "B-but we s-said no p-presents," he stuttered. James shrugged.

"Yeah" — he drew out the word — "about that. You're all I need, but you know I can't help myself when it comes to giving. I saw her in this color and knew you'd look handsome as ever driving her. So here... She's yours. You can drive us to my parents."

Josh took the keys more out of reaction than anything else, still staring at James as he rounded the car to the passenger side and climbed in. His heart was pounding. A car. *A luxury car?*

"Jamie, I don't know..."

"Just test drive it. If you don't like it, you can swap it out for something else in my garage."

How am I supposed to say no to that? "James, are you sure?"

"Josh" — he said his name with such tenderness and sincerity that Josh's heart ached — "I'm sure."

Josh slipped into the driver's seat. He took a moment to look over at James and absorb the handsome, beyond-generous man next to him. "Thank you."

James reached over and took Josh's hand, squeezing. "You're amazing. You're doing amazing things. Enjoy it."

Josh swallowed down the overwhelming lump in his throat and put his hands on the wheel, adjusting the seat before fixing his mirrors and getting comfortable. The car purred beautifully when he started her up and he had a moment of wild elation. This Audi was *his*. It felt too good to be true.

But the man smiling at him from the passenger seat reminded him it *was* true. Josh couldn't stop smiling.

"How do I use the GPS?" Josh stared at the small screen and James laughed.

"I'll be your GPS for now. We'll learn that later."

"I have a feeling this car has more bells and whistles than I'm used to." Josh laughed too, putting the car in drive and easing off the brake.

"Probably more horsepower too. Don't worry. We'll hit the interstate shortly and you can open her up— within reason of course. No tickets."

"Yes, Daddy." Josh quirked a sassy grin and watched out of the corner of his eye as James all but short circuited.

"Careful, Josh," he warned. Josh just chuckled. He knew exactly how he'd thank the man—and exactly how to rile him up in the meantime.

* * * *

The ride was enjoyable and the car exceptional. Josh was on cloud nine as they arrived at the Barnwell's. He shouldn't have been surprised by the large, beautiful home in a gated community—nothing obscene in size or style, but beautiful all the same. Winifred and George greeted them in the driveway, followed by three wild children Josh hadn't seen since Jamaica. Apparently they hadn't forgotten him as they barreled past their grandparents and into him, wrapping their arms and legs around him in excitement as they yelled his name with glee. He beamed as he greeted them first, James and his parents watching on in delight.

"Oh, honey, the kids adore him," he heard Winifred remark, "just like your sister said."

"They do. They had a blast with him in Jamaica. He's also quite fond of them as well," James stated with a loving smile. George clapped his hand on his son's shoulder.

"You picked a good one, James," his father grinned. "Any kids in your future, baby?" Winifred asked her son. Josh threw James a look but had to school the smile off his own face.

"Mom-m," James drew out the word as children, even grown children do and George hushed her.

"I'm just saying. You know I'm always ready for more grandbabies." She defended herself with a giddy grin. James shook his head.

"We're not even engaged," James pressed her before cutting off the conversation as Becca emerged from the front door and wrapped her brother in a hug.

Once the kids had settled, Josh stepped up to greet James' parents. He was nervous. Meeting a significant other's parents was never easy but knowing that most of their relationship had been fabricated added to his anxiety. Winifred enveloped him in a hug that he accepted with joy, however, and that did help.

"Oh Josh, it's so wonderful to meet you finally!" She squeezed like a mother would before pulling away to let him shake George's hand.

"Pleasure to meet you, sir," George shook his hand firmly as Josh spoke. His smile was kind and he looked like a much older version of James. Josh could tell where James got his looks from. Both his parents were attractive with kind features.

"We're happy to finally meet you, Josh," George greeted. Becca stepped up once their hands separated, and her hug was tight and genuine.

"Hi, Josh," she said into his shoulder. "I'm really happy you're here," she added as she pulled away, and something about the look in her eyes, gentle and kind but *knowing* told him that she might be privy to more than he thought. He flushed a little but smiled wide.

"I'm really happy to be here," he told her before the kids were at his hands and legs again, all going on about showing him their Christmas presents and the pool out back. Laughing, he let himself be tugged away, figuring that if the kids liked him this much then maybe it would be a good sign to James' parents. Everyone laughed and followed along, George and James getting the bags and chatting about the latest local news as Winifred ushered Becca back into the kitchen to help make Josh a pie. Winifred was a supreme homemaker, and the minute Josh tasted her baked treats, he'd most likely want to stay forever.

* * * *

Once the kids were placated and the house quieted down for the first time since their arrival, James took Josh on a tour of the house and showed him to the room they'd be sharing. It was a lavish guest room that had all the touches that said *home*, but it was obvious James hadn't grown up in this room. James went on to explain how he'd helped his parents find this house after his fifth resort had opened. George had been on the cusp of retiring and Winifred had been in love with this particular home. Now that he had the funds to do so, he told Josh that he'd wanted to give back to his parents so he had. Josh found James' love of giving forever endearing, as he was and had just been on the receiving end of that, which was leading him quickly to his next thought as James finished his story and was busy opening his suitcase, going on about dinner and cigars—and Josh couldn't care less in that moment as he approached his boyfriend with one single idea in mind.

"I was also thinking that maybe tomorrow we could go for a drive down to Islamorada." James' words caught as Josh came up behind him, letting his hands roam over his hips. The belt would have to go, he decided, as he slipped his hands to the buckle. "Josh," James chuckled, though he made no attempt to stop him, "what are you doing?"

"I'm about to show you my gratitude," Josh explained as he pulled the end of the belt through the buckle and began his work on the snap and zipper of the slacks James wore. He kissed along the back of James' neck—slow, lingering kisses. He was in no rush and hoped they had at least thirty minutes.

"Oh, you are?" James' words broke with a moan as Josh slid a very confident, very skilled hand into the briefs James wore and cupped his significant length. He squeezed and kneaded lazily, dragging his lips across James' skin up to his ear.

"Mmm-hmm," he hummed. "It's been a few weeks and I think I'm ready to get my mouth and hands on you again." He'd be lying if he said he didn't feel a little vulnerable in light of all that had happened, but he knew now how James felt. It was very clear, all gifts aside. They had grown so much closer. Josh even found himself on the edge of saying those three little words much quicker than he'd anticipated. He'd thought he could keep that under wraps for a little while longer—and he was determined to try. But it was becoming more difficult.

"Josh, you don't have to—" Josh pulled James around so they were eye to eye, ignoring his groan at the loss of contact. He put a finger to James' lips to shush him

"Shh-h. I *want* to. Please. Let me, *Daddy*?" Josh was pleading and he knew James wouldn't be able to resist that—and he was right.

James' eyes all but rolled back in his head and his mouth fell open. "Yes, go on, baby. Have whatever you want," he encouraged Josh. James pushed the suitcase out of the way and sat down on the bed, running his hands through Josh's hair. He'd have to fix it later, but they both knew James would use it to ground himself when Josh swallowed around him.

"I knew you wanted it," Josh mused as he tugged at the fabric and got the slacks and briefs down and off James' legs. He tossed the fabric aside and wasted no time in nuzzling against the base of James' now-swollen cock, inhaling him and reacquainting himself with his now-boyfriend. He kissed along the curve of the length and watched James, who watched him in return. Their gaze felt charged, erotic, and Josh felt a whole new *urge* within him. This was the first time he'd touched James without money between them. This was out of pure and true want and affection. His stomach twisted and emotions threatened to bubble to the surface. He pushed them down and let himself focus on what he knew—pleasing James. He'd been fantasizing about it for weeks and now he could finally do it...the *right* way.

James' sharp moans were as quiet as they could possibly be, but he wasn't very good at being silent. Josh chuckled a little and mumbled a few times, "You've got to be quiet," as he stroked James slowly.

The man was doing his best, Josh knew. The door was locked, so even if a stray moan made its way out, no one could interrupt them.

The first lick sent a shudder through them both. Josh undid his own belt as he toyed with James. Self-pleasure was no longer something he had to ask for. The thought was thrilling. He pulled himself out and James whispered, "fuck yes," as he wrapped his right hand around himself. Blessed with the ability to use his left hand well, he slipped it under James' balls and rubbed the soft skin there, a secret spot he knew James loved. The man's groan was strained, and Josh rewarded him by slipping his mouth over his cock and down to the base, snuggling the tip deep within his throat. He relaxed into it, groaning around the taste and winning a sharp tug at his hair. He swallowed around him a few times before sliding back just slightly to find a slow, easy rhythm. Every few shallow thrusts, he'd deep-throat James. It was exciting, knowing that James was falling apart at his hands, because he knew how to please him — and knowing there was an emotional bond between them now. This orgasm he was about to give them both would be the first of *many* with this attachment and sentiment between them. The thought only made him work harder, stroking himself tighter, quicker, and using his mouth harder and faster on James.

James' orgasm surprised him. It was sudden, without a warning. He all but curled around Josh as he came, gasping for air down Josh's throat. The shock of it, the sudden climax and the way James shook silently against him sent Josh over the edge as well, spilling on his hand and the hardwood floor. His own moans were muffled by James' softening cock as he drank him for all he was worth. When he finally pulled off, he had to rest his head against James' thigh to catch his breath, his messy hand falling away from his own now-oversensitive length.

"This is not the right moment for this," James began quietly, encouraging Josh to look up at him, caressing his cheekbone. "But I can't keep it in any longer." His eyes were so tender that Josh wondered if he was about to cry. His heart stilled in his chest. "I love you." Though the words were hardly audible, only meant for Josh's ears, it was as though he'd shouted them from the rooftop. Josh's heart erupted into frantic beats.

"I love you too," he whispered back. James had skirted around a confession of this sort on the street that night but hearing the three words merged together like this… Josh's throat tightened. "I have for…a long time."

"Me too." James smiled tenderly and closed the distance between their lips. The kiss was closed-lip and intimate. Josh hardly realized he was crying until James was wiping his tears. Nothing about their relationship was conventional, so why should their moment of truth be, Josh realized. He was certain that they both meant it—and that was what mattered.

The kiss dissolved into giggles when Josh raised his sticky hand to embrace James and quickly realized that it wasn't the best move. Foreheads together, they laughed through the moment and the joy, holding this just for themselves. Josh *felt* in love. He'd never felt anything like it. This was real. *They* were real. There was no one else for him but this man right here. James was his *forever*.

* * * *

"Mr. Roberts, I mean Josh, Mr. Barnwell is on line two for you."

Tommy Harrison, Josh's new personal assistant, squeaked from the doorway to Josh's brand-new New York office. Maria had hired him to help Josh focus on his art while Tommy helped make travel arrangements and ran errands, as well as anything Josh needed. It had been a bumpy four-week acclimation, but now they were on the same page and Josh had learned to delegate…mostly. He still felt a little silly, doing what he loved and getting paid for it as well as having a personal assistant. He was trying to settle in to the busy schedule.

Which was why James was probably calling. They'd spent the rest of the Christmas holiday with his parents until after New Year's, when they'd returned to the city. They had been apart since mid-January, set to meet up the first week of March in France. Josh had never seen Paris, and of course James had a hotel there. They'd missed Valentine's Day, thanks to an unforeseen issue with permits on James' most recent project in New Zealand. But Josh knew that came with the territory. And James had instead sent him, Sarah, Andrew and Nadia to where he had made their reservations. They'd had a lovely evening, but Josh had missed James like hell.

They texted all day and talked at night. Time differences didn't matter. They made an effort to talk as much as they could. Josh still lived with his friends, so talking in the middle of the night wasn't their favorite thing, but he did it anyway. He'd rather get hollered at by a tired Nat and live off Starbucks than not hear James' voice. He was in love — and he could talk about it. It was a dream.

"Thanks, Tommy." He grinned at the young man, pleased at the news and at the fact that Tommy was learning to talk to him without using his last name. It made him feel old.

Once his office door was shut, he set his pencil down and picked up his phone, clicking the flashing line. "Hello, Mr. Barnwell," he greeted with a grin, leaning back in his comfortable chair.

"Will you *please* tell him to stop calling me that?" James whined at the other end. Josh laughed.

"Listen... I just got him to call me Josh yesterday. One thing at a time. He's learning," Josh defended him. "How's New Zealand?"

"Hot. Sunny. Beautiful. But I'm ready to come home." Josh heard waves in the background and could imagine James standing barefoot on the beach in his expensive suit.

"Sounds like torture," he teased. "It's snowing here and cold as the arctic. You're not missing anything."

"Except you," James easily replied. Josh flushed despite the distance.

"I miss you too. A lot. My bed is cold. My toes are cold."

"Your toes are always fucking cold"—James laughed—"then my calves are always cold when you try to use them to warm up your icicle toes."

Josh barked a laugh. "I bet your calves are roasting out there in their summer without my icy toes."

They shared laughter for a moment before they settled into easy chat, catching up. James asked about the office and Sarah like a good boyfriend, and Josh asked about the crisis James had diverted and told him his latest projects. He whined a little about his office situation. He hadn't found the right easel yet, and the one from his apartment had broken the previous week. James called him finicky, but it was affectionately true. Josh couldn't deny it.

"Tommy has your flight scheduled, right? Paris is calling us. I need a few days off, especially with you."

"He has," Josh confirmed. "I arrive at two o'clock in the afternoon. My ride is set up to take me to the hotel. All is good, Jamie, unless I get snowed in. Which, as of now, that week is freezing but clear." The weather was still pulled up on his computer so he consulted it again. Sunny but in the twenties all week. Josh shivered.

"You'd better not get snowed in. There are wine and pastries calling our names."

"Is that all?"

"I mean, I can think of a few other things…"

They hadn't had real sex yet, not since their original arrangement. They'd messed around, touches, some oral and other sexier things, but Josh had been holding out. James never pushed either. He was a true gentleman. But Josh was feeling like maybe he was ready, maybe they'd taken enough time. Nearly three months was good, right? He'd asked Nadia and she'd asked when he'd last gone three months without sex. He couldn't remember. He took that as a good sign as well. He'd turned over a heck of a lot of new leaves lately. It felt good. Really good. Amazing, even.

But maybe it was time. He'd been missing it. James had to be too. He'd travel prepared and see how it went. He wanted organic.

He shook his head. He was such a fucking romantic.

"Oh shit." James interrupted in a less-than-pleased tone, "This new general manager is gonna make me entirely gray before I even get to Paris. I've gotta get going," he grumbled.

"Our kids will make fun of you if you're gray before they're even toddlers." Josh laughed before realizing what he'd said. *Wow, that fantasy thought sure wasn't supposed to make its way into the world like that.*

James recovered quickly, to Josh's surprise, "Kids, huh?" He sounded amused. "You got something you wanna tell me?" he teased. Josh flushed hard.

"We both know that ain't physically possible, Barnwell. And even if it was, it takes sex to make a kid, and we haven't done that either, though I haven't stopped thinking about it." He said the last part quietly and spoke quick, knowing James had to go. "But yeah. You know…kids. Just ignore that." Josh laughed. "I'll see you in Paris, without kids. But I'll talk to you tonight, right?"

James' chuckling at his rambles warmed his chest. "Yeah. I'll call you tonight when I get back to the room. I love you. Be safe getting home in that snow, okay? Text me."

"I will. I love you. Get some sun for me."

"Bye, Josh."

"Bye, Jamie."

The call ended and left Josh feeling a little foolish and a lot in love. *God, kids.* He mentally slapped himself. *Keep a lid on your future wants, Roberts,* he chided himself. The last thing he wanted was to rush this and scare James away. And those words seemed like the best way to do it.

* * * *

As much as Josh preferred traveling during the day, the overnight flight Tommy had booked him hadn't been so bad. It was nonstop, at least, and he arrived at the airport in Paris at noon. He'd slept quite a bit of it—thanks to two stiff drinks before flight, a first-class seat and a good audiobook—and didn't feel as awful as he might have suspected as he stepped into the airport with his carry-on, the sun shining through the big windows. It was a little warmer than New York, it seemed. He'd take it.

A driver was waiting for him to escort him to the hotel. Since they'd agreed this was a vacation trip, no assistants would be with them, and there was no work to be done unless it was absolutely necessary—just the two of them for three days. While Josh loved his work, and he *really* did, he missed his boyfriend and their time together. This would be a nice break from the past several weeks. And it would be a few more weeks until they were back together for a week in San Diego in April. Josh was also very excited for that trip.

The ride was exciting, and any fatigue Josh felt left him immediately. The streets were out of a movie. He felt like he'd stepped into a role—which, truth be told, was how he'd been feeling since he'd met James. Surreal was the best way to describe it. The city was gorgeous—and so was the hotel, he realized.

Arrival and check in were smooth. He was expected and the concierge took care of him personally. Since it was James' hotel, the trip would be catered to them specifically, his staff showing off their best sides. Josh turned down the offered champagne for bottled water, because he knew that if he started drinking now, he'd be asleep by five o'clock Parisian time. That was not quite the start to this vacation that he was looking for.

Belle—Josh was delighted with her name, if he were honest—personally saw him to their room. He wondered if he should be used to these moments by now, but he wasn't. When he opened the door of the luxury terrace suite to an exquisite view of the Eiffel Tower directly outside their terrace doors, he was floored yet again. While Belle explained about the suite and the spa, Josh actually pinched the inside of his bicep as he followed her around. *This is real life. How on Earth...?*

"Mr. Barnwell left this note for you," she said at last, as she stood by the door and allowed the bellman to put his suitcase inside the room. "If you need anything at all, I am here for you. Raphael comes on duty this evening and can assist you as well. We're happy to have you, Mr. Roberts. Please let us know if we can assist in any way." She handed the envelope to Josh before excusing herself. Josh tipped them both generously before shutting the door behind them. He wanted to take pictures before he touched anything, and he wanted to toss himself onto the king-size bed he saw upstairs and sleep for a week. He wouldn't—he was too wired—but it was just that inviting. And he was glad a bottle of Dom Perignon was chilling on the terrace, because he now realized he wanted that drink. This was worth an afternoon cocktail celebration.

Realizing James hadn't replied to his *I've arrived in Paris and I feel like I'm in a movie* text, Josh tore gently into the letter, savoring the beautiful black and gold envelope.

Josh,
You have a massage scheduled at two p.m. The spa will welcome you before that if you want to wind down and relax first. I recommend the soaking tubs and the sauna, if I may.
When you return from your two-hour hot stone massage, you'll find a suit waiting for you. Shoes, cufflinks, everything

you need will be ready. My tailor had your measurements from Jamaica. This is one of a kind, just for you, my love.

I'll meet you in the downstairs bar at five-thirty. Order a drink and wait. I promise tonight won't disappoint you.

All my love,

JB

Josh's cheeks heated and excitement ran in his veins. Once again, the man he loved had gone above and beyond to spoil him. There was no arguing, Josh had long-since discovered. Not that he wanted to, but sometimes every gesture felt like too much.

He knew why James was doing all this for him. He knew it now came with the territory, with who the man was. And knowing it was real made it even more incredible and insane. This wasn't some elaborate ruse to sell a fake relationship. Josh's boyfriend had actually bought him an Audi *and* put him up in a hotel suite with an idyllic view of the Eiffel Tower. He pinched himself hard again and swore when it hurt.

Wow.

He really was the luckiest guy in the world.

* * * *

The taste of the whiskey was bitter and yet welcome against his lips. Josh stood against the fancy bar dressed to the nines in his new suit. He felt like a prince — which seemed silly to think, but it was true. He was relaxed from his massage and comfortable in his own skin. He was excited for whatever this night would bring.

He hadn't heard from James all day, but he wasn't worried. His worrying days were over, he was sure of it. They had a connection. The last few months had shown him who James really was. Josh had known he loved him before, but now they were in the best place they'd ever been in.

A hand to his lower back surprised him, and he couldn't quell his excitement as he turned to see James there behind him. He was, however, taken aback by the lack of beard, replaced by a very small amount of scruff, as though it had only been a few days since he'd shaved instead of months, like always. His hair was shorter and styled a little differently. It was shocking.

His eyes widened as he took in the man behind him like they were just meeting for the first time. James' grin told him he didn't mind the thorough once-over.

"Hey, baby," he greeted, rubbing where his hand still lay on Josh's back. Josh opened and closed his mouth twice before he managed to get out a small greeting. James laughed a little. "How's your day been?" he asked casually.

"Holy shit," Josh muttered, looking away to catch his breath. James was too handsome anyway, but the change…went straight to Josh's groin.

James laughed again and let Josh take a minute to gather himself as he stepped up to the bar and ordered a drink. From there, Josh could inspect his profile. The gray was still peppered throughout his dark hair, specifically at the temples and throughout his scruff. He was tan, the sun in New Zealand obviously having treated him well. He was bright. He looked happy.

The bartender slipped James a glass of red wine and Josh raised an eyebrow at *that*, too. "What? It's like you've never seen me drink wine before," James teased.

Josh huffed a laugh. "You show up here with a haircut and a quarter of the beard you had before and order a glass of red wine when we're *not* eating. Yes, I am pretty sure we haven't *met* before. I'm Josh Roberts," he said as he stuck his hand out playfully, "and you are?"

"The man who's so in love with you that his whole world has been changed," he replied easily, sweetly, as he shook Josh's hand. It rocked him to his core.

They shared a moment, standing there with their hands together like they had in fact just met, before James closed the distance between them and kissed Josh as though he'd have died without it. Josh lost himself almost immediately in James' lips. *Home.*

The kiss only lasted a few moments before James pulled away to bring out his wallet and place a few bills on the bar. "Come on, Mr. Roberts," he said, taking his wine and extending his arm for Josh. "We have a whole night ahead of us."

Dinner was extravagant, to say the least. The restaurant was incredible. While Josh knew James would spare no expense, per usual, something about tonight felt different. Whether it was the way he ordered a *very* expensive bottle of champagne — *'We're celebrating our reunion,'* he'd said when Josh had questioned it — or the way he'd ordered the whole flight of desserts when Josh couldn't choose just one — *'We'll just try a bite of them all'* — James was treating Josh to one of the best nights of his life. Though Josh would also have been just as happy to have ordered pizza and sat by the fire in James' brownstone, just being with James made everything better — made everything amazing.

And it was as though they hadn't been apart one day. Josh hadn't realized how comfortable he'd felt with James until now. And he was finally settling into his new role, his new life. Their relationship was as healthy and strong as ever. James always made sure to check in on Josh, to call or text, despite being busy. And Josh did the same. It never interfered with their work. Somehow it always just worked together.

They were still learning about each other, but that was the fun part—one of the fun parts, anyway. Now that Josh had James back with him, he was anxious to explore another fun part he'd been holding off on for some time now.

The night was chilly, leaving Josh glad James had suggested on a car to take them back to the hotel instead of walking. They sat in the back with their hands linked together as they chatted about the evening.

Josh kept feeling like he was about to wake up from this dream. He couldn't shake the feeling that this wasn't real, and he was still escorting back in New York, just dreaming of the day he might make a living as an artist. The night at the Whitney, the night he'd met James, the hot days in Jamaica, the beautiful views in Italy... They'd all been part of an elaborate dream he'd wake up from any minute.

But it wasn't a dream. He was living this incredible life. He was grateful for his opportunities every day— and for James. *God, am I grateful for James.*

They slipped into the hotel hand in hand and headed for the elevators with quick hellos to the staff. Josh was still enamored with James' new look and let him know once more by pulling him close in the elevator and kissing his lips long and slow, savoring it. "I've been dying to do that since the bar," he confessed, their lips hardly parting. James grinned.

"You could have," he replied.

"I know, but patience is a virtue and I wanted to take my time." Josh kept him close as the elevator came to rest on their floor. "You're so handsome," he whispered as the doors opened. James blushed in the beautiful way that made Josh want to ravish him right then and there.

"You sure you like the cut?" James asked for the millionth time that night. Josh took him by the hand again and pulled him out into the hallway, smiling.

"Yes! And I'll show you just how much when we're in our room," Josh teased as they headed for the door.

The door shut behind James and left him feeling a bit vulnerable and highly excited. He didn't know how far they'd go tonight—he had no expectations and no pressures—but something about the air around Josh felt different. Everything felt different...more concrete. Filled with questions, James felt the weight of things to come. *All good things*, he told himself—or at least he hoped. He could be wrong. Maybe it was too soon, but he knew what he intended to do. He couldn't predict Josh's response, but he could try. He'd never wanted to before. But now he couldn't stop himself from getting there.

James stood by the door watching as Josh stripped off his tie and laid it over the plush couch. "You look incredible in your suit," he said. It was Josh's turn to grin and blush.

"So you told me over dinner *and* dessert." Josh chuckled. "Thank you, again, for having it made for me. Thank you for this room—for you, for everything," Josh replied genuinely as he crossed the space back to James. He took his hands, squeezing them.

James knew he could be *a lot*. He was a lot for himself some days. But Josh took it all in stride and basked in it in the most grateful, loving, sweet and gracious ways. *Maybe we really are made for each other*, he considered, as Josh closed the small distance between them and kissed him once more. His brain finally quieted then, at least momentarily, as he let his mouth and hands take the lead, finding Josh's hips as he kissed him back and let himself get lost in it.

The kiss grew heated almost immediately as they slid their hands over parts of each other they hadn't touched in months. James had to give Josh credit. The emotional bonding had been worth every second, and he was glad they'd acted on the suggestion and he'd let Josh lead. It made these little touches, Josh's fingers gliding over his chest, around his hips, over his ass, light fire in his veins and lick pleasure straight up his spine. Every inch of him was aroused in seconds, leaving him desperate for the man at his lips. He was trembling but hungry, grasping for Josh in every way he could get him. It was when he found Josh's cheek with a shaky hand that they separated.

"Are you sure?" James asked breathlessly, a little presumptuous as he assumed where the night was going. Josh's grin was beautiful and filthy, all at the same time, and it reminded James of years prior, when he hadn't known the wonderful man behind that delicious exterior. He'd only known that confident smile that had taken him to places he'd never known.

"Completely," Josh replied without question. "I want you…all of you. If you'll have me." The last statement was a little less confident, a little more vulnerable. And James loved him all the more for it.

"You're all I want, forever," was his reply without hesitation as he pulled Josh to him and kissed him.

Josh lost himself to James for a moment before he remembered what he wanted and how he wanted tonight to happen. Not that he'd planned it, per se, but fantasizing was something he didn't really stop himself from doing. And he'd been thinking about this night for months — the reunion after so much time physically apart.

It had been years since he'd gone this long without this kind of physical contact, so the first time James grazed the hardness that lay beneath his very expensive trousers, he shivered hard. He let the breath out against James' lips before letting his mouth slide down over the man's throat. He scraped his teeth along the sensitive flesh he'd memorized, not forgetting a few special spots. James' stuttering breath made him smile. *I've still got it.*

He thought that as he started backing them up until he bumped roughly into one of the large sitting chairs, almost losing his balance. He rocked and James caught him by the elbows. They broke down in laughter as Josh muttered a harsh *oww, fuck* over hitting the back of his bare heel against the sharp wooden leg, his shoes long gone with his tie. "I'm a little rusty at this, I think," he confessed as his cheeks burned. James shook his head, his eyes bright as he held his boyfriend upright still.

"You and me both, pal." Josh took comfort in that as he separated them and pulled them away from the potential hazards of French furniture. "Would it help you to know I'm nervous?" James offered as they now stood on the soft carpet in the middle of the large open floor. Josh huffed one of those little laughs James loved so much.

"That also makes two of us," Josh admitted as he pulled James close once more. "I'll find my old groove, I promise." James didn't falter, simply reaching up to ruffle his perfectly styled blond hair a bit.

"Don't worry about the old one," James told him sweetly. "Find a new one." And he kissed Josh again. This kiss felt a little more comfortable and a little less trying, and it was only moments before Josh was settled back into his role, dominating James through the kiss.

It seemed—at least for the moment—that maybe they'd work out their nervous jitters. Josh helped James slip out of his clothing, one piece at a time, with no regard for the cost of material. The suit coat landed in a heap on the floor, followed by a tie and a vest. Josh only pulled away from bruising James' lips to unbutton James' shirt like he was opening a very anticipated present.

Button by button, he worked his nimble fingers down James' torso. What Josh found underneath was tanned skin and chiseled muscles. James had always been fit, there was no question about that, but something had changed. His muscles were more defined. Josh's mouth watered at the view and James watched with visible pride as Josh lowered his mouth to the left side of his chest and kissed right over James' heart.

"Fuck," Josh rasped. "You've been killing yourself in the gym, haven't you?" He dragged his tongue down the indents of James' stomach as he dropped to his knees. James keened and moaned, probably sensitive from months of not being touched like that mixed with anticipation.

"What else am I supposed to do?" His laugh was strangled. "I can only jerk off so many times a day thinking of you before my dick is raw," he sassed. Josh stopped his assault on James' now-exposed hipbone and glanced up with wild eyes.

"Well, we certainly can't have that, can we?" Josh bit lightly on the bone, which made James curl around him in pleasure. "I hope you haven't hurt yourself," he added before slipping his hand into James' briefs and pulling them down with one hand as he pulled his hard cock free with the other. James hissed at the touch, and just the sight of Josh holding his length was almost enough to make him come undone. *Almost. Dreams do come true*, he thought to himself with a laugh.

Josh glanced up at him as he stroked the flesh with a practiced hand, watching how it moved with every tweak of his wrist. It was erotic and almost felt like an out-of-body experience for James as Josh touched him with such great pleasure. It only took a handful of strokes before James was reaching out and stopping him, his chest rising and falling rapidly as he swallowed hard. "S-stop," he managed. "I'll never make anything if you keep going." Josh kissed the hand that covered his but pushed it away.

"That's the idea, baby. Don't you know I know you well enough to know what you need? Lemme take the edge off," he asked as he began stroking him once more. James shuddered and babbled a few incoherent words before he couldn't speak any more. A handful of strokes later and James was coming hard and shaking as his eyes rolled back in his head and he let out a moan like a man touch-starved far beyond the few months he had been.

When James finally opened his eyes and managed to look down at his handsome boyfriend, the sight he saw was enough to make his knees weak and his cock pulse within the hand that still held it. "Fucking hell. Look at you. Such a beautiful mess," he spoke as he gazed down at Josh's face, streaked with lines of his cum. He swiped some of the mess off Josh's cheek with his thumb and placed it against those plump lips. Josh licked it hungrily. James groaned deep in his throat. "Let's get you cleaned up." But Josh stopped him, resting a steady hand on his still-clothed thigh.

"I'll clean myself up, baby. *You* go lie down, and I'll come back in just a few minutes," he urged James as he stood up. Josh was still in his suit, with a pearly mess on his perfect cheeks. James was dying in the best way possible. He nodded without argument.

"Yes, baby boy," he responded sweetly. Josh's grin turned devilish.

"Good, Daddy."

James made himself comfortable on the bed, shedding the rest of his clothes before sliding onto the cream-colored comforter, among the dozen pillows that adorned the king size bed. He felt relaxed, comfortable, boneless even. Except he knew that whenever Josh stepped out of that bathroom again, he'd be ready to go with no end in sight.

The moon and the lights from the Eiffel Tower were shining in through the huge, satin-curtain-covered windows. The room was lit only by that and a small floor lamp. It all cast a very romantic glow over the room. James thought briefly about getting up and digging through the bag he'd had delivered for the particular item he'd had specially made for Josh, but that thought was dashed when the bathroom door opened and a freshly showered Josh emerged. But instead of one of the white fluffy hotel towels around his waist, he wore a small pair of black lace boxers that looked especially pleasing on his fit frame. James salivated and his eyes widened as Josh crossed the room to him, looking almost shy as he approached, his half-hard cock on display within the confines of the lace.

His skin was flushed from a hot shower, his hair slicked back and wet. For a moment all James could do was stare. And it was hard, considering there was so much to stare at. His eyes were on overload, trying to drink all of it in as Josh climbed onto the foot of the bed and headed toward him on his hands and knees.

"You like it, Daddy?" he asked, breathy and sweet as he drug kisses up James' already-heated skin. His mouth was hot and his lips felt like feathers on his skin. James shivered again.

"*Fuck*, baby, so, so handsome." He put his hands on Josh's shoulders and stroked the soft skin he found there. "I've missed you," he told Josh tenderly.

"I've missed you more," Josh replied. *Too bad Josh can't compete with the amount of missing I've been doing*, James thought.

"No way," he replied, surging up to kiss Josh hungrily. Josh slid his body up onto James', resting his hips between James' and rubbing together in a way that was both natural and needed.

James pulled Josh away by his thick blond hair, so that he could kiss at Josh's neck. Josh rutted his hips against James' in such a seductive and erotic way that James was sure he'd lose his mind again long before Josh was even inside him. Josh had a natural way of rolling his hips so deliciously that it drove him mad.

James groaned into Josh's flesh as Josh fucked him. It was heavenly — except he wanted more, so much more.

Josh took James' right hand and slid it between them. James let out a moan as he cupped Josh's length tightly through the lace. Josh's sounds were raspy and strangled, but beautiful, nonetheless. Knowing he'd caused them made James proud. He groped at Josh, rubbing him through the fabric until Josh was bucking and rolling his hips desperately. *But no, no, not like this*, James thought as he moved away, and Josh let out a glorious whine of distress.

"Daddy, please…" Josh whimpered. James grinned and pulled back from his neck, the skin now peppered with bruises and red welts.

"You gonna fuck me, baby boy?" James asked, sliding his hands down to Josh's hips, forcing them into his own. Josh pressed up on his palms and drove himself into James, rhythmically thrusting their cocks together, the friction of the fabric causing a delicious drag.

"Oh fuck, yes — so hard, and just like this, so I can see your face," Josh told him through gritted teeth. James' forehead was already beading with sweat, anticipation and desire causing his body temperature to rise rapidly. Josh was flushed and hot to the touch, his freckles visible in the moonlight. The man was an Adonis. James was overwhelmed with attraction. It was almost too much.

"Come on. Do it. Take me. Fuck me. Make me *yours*." He pressed Josh into him, groping his ass and kneading the flesh. When he focused again, James had spread his legs wide and bent his knees. The glint of silver caught Josh's eyes. They widened and he groaned.

"You fuckin' prepped for me?" Josh asked in surprise. He ran his fingers over the rounded end of the silver plug and James chuckled.

"I'm impatient. And I thought you'd be proud."

Josh laughed and nodded, driving back down for a slow kiss before pulling away once more. "Oh, I am. Looks so fucking good on you. You've been wearing it all night?" he inquired. James nodded.

"Mmm-hmm. Desperate for you and hoping we'd have this moment," he replied. Josh pulled at the end and made James hiss then moan low as the muscle stretched around the bulbous end. It was bigger than Josh had expected, and he could tell James had worked himself open to get it in. It made his balls grow tight and his cock throb. James had done it to get ready for him. It was unbelievably sexy — and to think he'd been walking around like this all night, sitting across from him at a fancy dinner with this inside him…

He thrust it back in and pulled it out a few times, loosening him up farther and enjoying the way James squirmed and fisted the sheets, clearly reveling in the play. His hips rolled and he panted as the plug penetrated him over and over. Josh watched his cock bounce and drool against his abs. It was glorious.

But Josh could only take so much, and he knew James could only go for so long. Even though he'd come just a little while ago to take that edge off, it had still been so, so long. He didn't want to lose him so quickly.

Pulling the plug out and discarding it on the side table to be cleaned up later, he grabbed the bottle once again and lathered himself and James up generously.

James was a handsome mess, his fit, tan body on display — and just for him.

Josh kneeled between James' thighs and James couldn't help but drink in the view. Wide shoulders tapering down to an unrealistically small waist, strong arms, abs for days... Josh was as photoshopped as they came. But he was real. And he was James'...all James'.

"Come 'ere, Josh," he whispered, reaching for the love of his life. Josh came more than willingly, as if there were a magnet pulling him in, and James once more lost himself in a searing kiss as Josh maneuvered himself into position between his legs.

The first thrust took his breath away. It was slow, just the tip initially, slick and hot and thick. James panted at the intrusion, and it obviously took every ounce of Josh's control not to push any farther. As they took ragged breaths, forehead to forehead, Josh slid deep and slowly until no space was left between them and they were finally, finally joined as one.

"I love you, Jamie," Josh whispered sweetly against James' cheek as he started to move. James told him how good it felt with his gasps but managed a low, "I love you too" in reply amid them.

While it wasn't their very first time together, it was the first time they'd been together as true *lovers*, as partners, as boyfriends, the emotions real and raw and spoken between them. James hadn't thought this existed in real life — and he'd played the denial card for far too long. At this moment he had no idea why. *This* was far better than any fantasy, any fake dating sham. He wouldn't give this up for the world, he knew now.

Josh started to really move, and James couldn't help but close his eyes. Their kisses became sloppy as they writhed together, James' heels digging into the bed as he met Josh thrust for thrust.

Josh pushed one thigh up, hooking it through his elbow to spread James wider and to change the position. James cried out in pleasure, throwing his head back into the pillows as the new shift had Josh rubbing right where he needed him with every thrust. Josh doubled his pace, losing himself in the clear joy of watching James teeter on the edge of falling apart.

"So fucking beautiful," he muttered through the exertion. "Look at you, Daddy, taking my cock so well." Josh groaned and thrust deeper, slamming his hips into James' ass over and over as he drove them both toward the edge. Shifting his weight back to his heels and moving upright, Josh thrust forward roughly, snapping his hips as he took James' cock in hand.

James cried out again and squirmed, words beyond him now except the incoherent mumbles that were meant to be like Josh's name and the word *please*. James felt himself on the edge, every muscle tightening as he gazed at the man he loved, holding himself back just for Josh's command... It was alluring and completely exquisite. Josh's hips faltered and James whined low.

"Need...Josh, I need..." he ground out brokenly. Covered in sweat, still grabbing at the sheets of the now messy bed, Josh jerked James to his thrusts hard and tightly, begging him to come now.

"Go on, Daddy. Let go for me. Make a mess while I come inside you..."

James' cry was loud and unabashed and almost animalistic as he arched his back and came. He made a mess on his chest and abs as Josh jerked him through it before his own climax caught him. Strangled noises left Josh as he closed his eyes and bowed his head as he came deep within James. It was renewing and powerful and James seemingly lost himself in the emotions as Josh panted through his high, holding onto him for dear life.

When Josh finally opened his eyes, James was gazing up at him lovingly. They were both breathing a bit slower. "Wow, I missed that." Josh was the first to say it, unashamed. James laughed.

"I fucking love you," he grinned, pulling Josh down by the back of his neck into a sweet kiss.

James took a moment while Josh was distracted with cleaning up and the view from the balcony to fetch the small thing from his luggage that he'd been stowing for a few weeks. He couldn't hold on to it anymore. If he didn't give it to Josh now, it would probably burn a hole in the bottom of the little bag he'd been carrying it around in.

He set down his champagne as he approached Josh, music from somewhere below carrying up to their room. Josh was leaning casually against the railing and sipping from his almost-empty glass of champagne. He was a picture against the Eiffel Tower and the stars. James wished he could go back for his phone for a picture, but he had to do this while he could.

"Ya know, Jamie, maybe we should lie to Maria and play hooky for a few more days. I could get used to this view, and after dinner tonight — and *after* — I don't think I'm ready to part with you, so —" Josh stopped talking as he turned around and saw James on one knee before him on the balcony. It clearly caught him far off guard, as James had hoped. "James? What are you — ?"

"Josh, listen to me," James started quietly, trying to muster the courage and read Josh's wide-eyed look as one of good surprise and not bad... "Ever since

December, since truly getting to know you and love you for all that you are and all that you have brought into my life, I can't imagine ever being without you. Maybe in miles, but never in heart. And if you say yes and marry me, I promise to do everything in my power to make you happy and —" His words were muffled by Josh's lips. Josh was on his knees in front of James before he could finish his speech, arms wrapped around his shoulders as he kissed him like the world might end a moment later.

"Yes, Jamie, yes! I'll marry you," Josh said with a voice full of emotion as he kissed James over and over.

"You didn't let me finish," James whined playfully, smiling through his own tears as he kissed Josh back.

"Okay, okay." Josh leaned back and stumbled to stand up, sniffling as he wiped his tears. "Okay, go ahead, finish and let's hope I don't change my answer." He grinned through the tears that continued to threaten to fall.

James rolled his own watery eyes, and this time held the beautiful black platinum and titanium ring up for Josh to see. "I don't remember where I was, but, Josh, will you marry me?" He started out chuckling then slowly grew somber as he finished. Josh's reaction was no less giddy as he all but threw himself once again on James, making him laugh out loud through more tears.

"God, yes, James! I'll marry you!" Josh embraced James tightly. When he leaned back, tears streamed down his cheeks and he kissed him hard. James kissed him back before leaning away, only to find Josh's left hand for the ring. "I can't believe you got me a ring," Josh said, awed as he stared at it. James beamed.

"How could I not? You're mine. I wanted you to feel like it," he told Josh. Josh's smile mirrored his own.

"I already feel like yours."
"And now you will be. Forever."

Want to see more like this?
Here's a taster for you to enjoy!

Companion Required
Brian Lancaster

Excerpt

Kennedy
London, England, August 2016

Two triple-shot espressos down and Kennedy Grey massaged his fingers into his temples. Dull throbbing had begun to resemble a migraine. Not because of the coffee—his lifeblood most days—but because the previous candidate had tried his patience to the limit. *'Is the food safe to eat? Isn't Singapore in China? Aren't gays banned in China? And will there be any fringe benefits?'* Questions about food safety he could accept, especially if a candidate had allergies. He could even appreciate them not being familiar with the geography of the travel destination. For that very reason, he had brought along a one-page map of Asia highlighting Singapore. But asking if there would be any fringe benefits had tipped him over the edge. The advert had been straightforward enough on the subject of remuneration.

Not for the first time that afternoon, Kennedy considered throwing in the towel and abandoning the whole precious idea. Maybe this was the year he made a change. After all, the signs of madness were everywhere, what with a game show host being chosen as the official Republican candidate to run for the US presidency and the people of Britain filing for divorce from Europe.

As a penniless young man straight out of university, he would have trampled heads for a heaven-sent dream of a job like this. On the laptop, he scrolled down to the UK Gay Society billboard and reread the contents of the advert.

Gay Holiday Companion Required

Based in or around London. Must have full ten-year passport with at least seven months remaining and be freely available to travel overseas for the whole month of September 2016. Candidate should ideally be between 21 and 25, non-smoking, social drinker, drug free, and must be able to pull off the role of dutiful boyfriend in front of male sponsor's close-knit circle of friends. Acting experience a distinct advantage. Any ethnicity considered.

Successful candidate will receive an all-expenses-paid holiday to Southeast Asia, starting with round-trip flights from London Heathrow to Singapore's Changi Airport, a three-night stay in Singapore, followed by a 14-night gay cruise to Hong Kong. After a two-night stay in Hong Kong, the holiday will culminate in a flight to Bali, Indonesia and eight nights staying at the sponsor's private luxury villa.

Candidate will receive a guaranteed five thousand pounds in cash for services rendered, and a discretionary bonus, should the candidate's performance exceed expectations.

If you are interested, please respond to gayvaccom@mooddle.com with a recent photo (headshots only, thank you) and CV, to arrange a mutually agreeable time for an interview.

So what if the advert bordered on politically incorrect? Marketing staff at UKGS had assured him that he had breached no advertising codes or legal regulations. Besides, the 'exceed expectations' line had only been tacked on this year, a suggestion from his best friend, Steph — a safe enough addendum, since for the past three years no one ever had.

Moreover, the advertised list of requirements told only half a story. He peered up and scanned the coffee shop. Even a couple of the young men sitting at various tables could have made the grade. In his head, Kennedy had an unspoken list of other requirements, undocumentable, such as the companion being a toned, blond twink, pretty as a royal wedding, but with a relatively low IQ. They should be no more than five feet six, and definitely shorter than his five-ten. Most importantly, they needed to be totally and utterly compliant to Kennedy's whims and wishes. And finally, once they had been paid off and returned to dear old mother England, he never wanted to see or hear from them again.

Since his split with Patrick, his partner of nine years, he'd made a point of continuing to join his friends' annual sojourn to different parts of the globe — his one break each year from the office and the boardroom — but now with a beautiful young acquaintance. Yes, perhaps bringing along a twink companion smacked of vanity, or desperation even, especially for someone in his early forties whose dark hair had begun to display grey streaks at the temples. But the simple truth was that while Kennedy found meeting and conversing with people for business purposes effortless, he found socialising awkward, especially on his own, and had always relied on Patrick to be the catalyst when meeting friends, old and new. Hence, for the past four years, he had paid for a companion to join him.

Palm Springs gay festivals, Hawaiian island hopping, gay tour of Barcelona and Sitges, cruising around the Greek islands with a week in Mykonos.

Pure culture? Maybe not. But a welcome respite from a punishing work life.

Ollie, his first post-Patrick choice, had turned out to be perfect. Previously an intern at Kennedy's corporate security company, the blond Adonis had flirted shamelessly with Kennedy and all other male staff, whether straight or gay. And even though Kennedy had been flattered and tempted, he had never succumbed. After the placement had ended, however, he'd made a point of keeping in touch. Once Patrick had decided to walk, Ollie had been his natural choice as lab rat companion. Perfect, as things had turned out, because Ollie had recently lost his job, so Kennedy had sweetened the deal by offering a sum of money to accompany him. Which was how the arrangement had first begun.

That first year the holiday had gone so well, Kennedy had not only stayed in touch but had invited Ollie along for a second helping. A huge mistake, as things transpired, because Ollie had incorrectly translated the gesture to mean that not only were they equals, but that they were going steady. And Kennedy no longer did 'steady' with anyone.

If his friends suspected anything, they said nothing. Only Steph knew the truth. And he made a point of telling any candidate the arrangement would be strictly nonsexual, unless they wanted more — which was how the idea of the playing card had come into being. But more than anything, he wanted a companion, not an escort. If the rationalisation might have meant anything to any of them, he would have cited Forster's novel *A Room With A View* and the chaperone arrangement between the two main female characters. But after he'd mentioned the reference to Ollie, and had then been lectured about that *'old James Bond movie they keep showing on Netflix'*, he'd stopped bothering to explain altogether.

For the first time since Patrick had walked out, he had been in two minds whether to ditch the charade, to simply bite the bullet and turn up alone. Only five friends had signed up for this year's sojourn—after last year's debacle—and one of those was Leonard Day. Kennedy not only had feelings for him but respected his business acumen. Maybe this year he would finally make his feelings known. If only Leonard didn't come with baggage of his own.

But Kennedy accompanying a plaything had become something of a tradition, a joke among his friends, and he wouldn't want to let them down.

"S'cuse me. You Kennedy Grey?"

Kennedy peered up from his thoughts to find an extremely blond, extremely buff young man standing over him. Steroid buff, Steph would have labelled him.

"I am, yes. And who might you be?"

"Who might I what?"

"Who… What is your name?"

"Francis."

Kennedy glanced down at his notes. Francis Slade, twenty-five years old, three o'clock appointment. Ten minutes ahead of schedule. One point in his favour. Kennedy swore by punctuality.

"Ah yes, Francis. Please sit down. So do you prefer Francis, Frank or Frankie?"

"Francis."

"Great. You've read the advert?"

"Yep."

"Good. So let me go into a bit more detail, give you a few minutes to relax. Then I'll ask you a few questions and finally let you ask any questions you may have. I've got other candidates to see, but I'll let you know whether you've been successful or not by Friday. How does that sound?"

"S'all okay."

Taking the response as his cue, Kennedy went into further detail about the holiday, explaining that in Singapore they would be staying in Kennedy's parents' house. However, the person would be introduced as a friend and would have their own bedroom. Whenever he delved into specifics—especially the rawer aspects—he always studied the candidate's face carefully to see if any of the information caused a reaction. Francis' flat face appeared incapable of showing any kind of emotion.

Whenever Kennedy got onto the subject of the cruise and his friends, he found himself becoming defensive. Yes, they could be a bitchy bunch, and a couple of companions had found them bordering on rude, but they were his long-time friends.

Bali, at the end of the holiday, was not only the cherry on the cake, but the icing, marzipan and ornate decoration. If the companion managed to survive until then, they would be able to enjoy the delights of that magical Indonesian island. By then Kennedy would usually be ready to get back to work, so would spend most of the last week either on his laptop, mobile phone, or writing up proposals.

"So far, so good?"

"Yep," said Francis, yawning and stretching his hands above his head. When his tee pulled tight, Kennedy spotted the outline of nipple rings beneath the material. Tick. Another point in the boy's favour.

"How tall are you?"

"Five-seven."

"Nice," said Kennedy, reaching next to his laptop for the supplementary document. "So here's a list of other requirements. You'll need to take a medical examination before you travel."

"Why?"

"A precaution. To make sure you're in good shape, physically."

"I'm negative, if that's what you're asking."

"That's not..." Kennedy huffed out a sigh. "Look, the year before last, my travel companion came down with acute appendicitis three days into the trip. And due to severe rupturing—which was touch and go for a while—he had to spend six days in a private hospital in Florida after which, quite naturally, he wanted to fly straight home to be with his family. If he had taken a medical examination before the trip, it's likely the appendicitis would have been diagnosed early, avoiding his suffering and my equally ruptured bank account."

"Ain't got an appendix. Got it removed when I was eleven."

"That's not the point—" Kennedy ran a hand through his hair. "I need to make sure the person accompanying me is fit and healthy in all respects. And that condition is non-negotiable. So if it's a problem for you, then you need to let me know right away."

Francis stared down at the paper for so long that for a moment Kennedy thought he'd changed his mind.

"You'll pay?"

"Sorry?"

"For the medical?"

"Of course."

"'S'okay, then."

"Great. Any other questions for me?"

"How old are you?"

"Forty-two."

Francis grinned then. At least, that was what it appeared to be to Kennedy. Either that or the lad had wind.

"You like 'em young, then?"

Kennedy had to stop himself from answering that more than anything, he liked them compliant. And most younger guys tended to be less free-willed, more willing to please, mainly because they needed the money.

"Is that a problem?"

"Nope. I'm into Daddies."

Oh, heck, thought Kennedy, *Steph is going to have a field day if Francis becomes this year's chosen one.*

"So I've got your number. I'll be in touch Friday."

When Francis stood, whether purposely or not, he yawned again and stretched his arms above his head so that the bottom of his tee rode up slightly to reveal a ripped stomach and a dark-blond trail of curly hair running down and disappearing beneath the waistband.

Kennedy almost handed him the job right there and then.

PUBLISHING

Sign up for our newsletter and find out about all our romance book releases, eBook sales and promotions, sneak peeks and FREE romance books!

About the Author

Evelyn has been writing since middle school, constantly getting lost in creating a whole other world (usually loosely based on a fandom of some kind) and falling in love with those characters. An avid reader, she never leaves home without a well-worn book and a notepad for thoughts. She writes almost entirely on her phone, because it's small and easy to pull out at a moment's notice, when the idea for a scene hits. As the wife of a busy husband and as the mother of a young daughter, two big dogs, and a horse, there's not always designated writing time. Writing is her passion and whenever she finds a window of free time, that's what she's doing!

Evelyn loves to hear from readers. You can find her contact information, website details and author profile page at https://www.pride-publishing.com